D1416859

CHAOS THEORY

Recent Titles by Graham Masterton available from Severn House

The Sissy Sawyer Series

TOUCHY AND FEELY

The Jim Rook Series

ROOK
THE TERROR
TOOTH AND CLAW
SNOWMAN
SWIMMER
DARKROOM

Anthologies

FACES OF FEAR
FEELINGS OF FEAR
FORTNIGHT OF FEAR
FLIGHTS OF FEAR

Novels

CHAOS THEORY
DESCENDANT
DOORKEEPERS
EDGEWISE
GENIUS
HIDDEN WORLD
HOLY TERROR
MANITOU BLOOD
UNSPEAKABLE

CHAOS THEORY

Graham Masterton

This first world edition published in Great Britain 2007 by
SEVERN HOUSE PUBLISHERS LTD of
9–15 High Street, Sutton, Surrey SM1 1DF.
This first world edition published in the USA 2007 by
SEVERN HOUSE PUBLISHERS INC of
595 Madison Avenue, New York, N.Y. 10022.

British Library Cataloguing in Publication Data

Masterton, Graham
    Chaos theory
    1. Stunt performers - Fiction 2. Cuneiform inscriptions -
    Fiction 3. Suspense fiction
    I. Title
    823.9'14[F]

ISBN-13: 978-0-7278-6536-6   (cased)
ISBN-13: 978-1-84751-023-5   (trade paper)

All Severn House titles are printed on acid-free paper.

Typeset by Palimpsest Book Production Ltd.,
Grangemouth, Stirlingshire, Scotland.
Printed and bound in Great Britain by
MPG Books Ltd., Bodmin, Cornwall.

'Small changes in initial conditions produce large changes in the long-term outcome.'

Edward Lorenz

'Lo! thy dread empire, Chaos! is restored!'

Alexander Pope

One

The late-afternoon sun was already nibbling at the summit of the Rock and Richard Bullman's temper was starting to fray.

'We're going again!' his sharp British voice crackled in Noah's ear. 'And this time make sure that you don't catch up with him so bloody soon! I want to see much more of that carving across his wake! More spray! More of that bouncing up and down! More bloody *drama*, for Christ's sake!'

Noah gave him a wave of acknowledgement and brought the Yamaha jet ski around in a wide, lazy circle. Sitting behind him, Silja leaned forward and said, 'What is it? He wants another take?'

'He wants more bloody drama.'

'What?' she said, in her stilted Finnish accent. 'I thought it was bloody action he was wanting, not bloody *drama*! Maybe we should do this in bloody Shakespearean costume! Oh, well . . . *mita vittua.*'

They returned to their first position, close to a fluorescent orange buoy that was anchored thirty-five yards off the beach. Noah throttled back the four-cylinder engine to a low, sulky burbling, with occasional blips. Then he took a pack of Marlboro out of his shirt pocket, lit two of them, and passed one back to Silja.

'You ever work with Vittorio Gallinari?' he asked her.

'Gallinari? No. But I was told that he is *very* finickety.'

'Finickety? Gallinari made me throw myself out of a semi seventeen times over, in one afternoon. Didn't like the way I rolled along the blacktop. "Why you flap-a you arms and you legs so much? You look like turkey!"'

Silja laughed. This was only their second week shooting in Gibraltar but Noah had already decided that he liked her. What was even more important, he trusted her, too. She was 5' 11" tall, broad-shouldered and long-legged, although the long black wig she was wearing to double for Rayleigh Martin didn't really suit her watery Scandinavian complexion. She was very feminine, but she was as strong as most men he had ever worked with, and her 'air-sense' was almost miraculous. And she liked off-colour jokes.

Noah would have been the first to admit that he was too old and battered for her. He had celebrated his thirty-eighth birthday last Tuesday, while Silja was only twenty-four. At least he was taller than she was – a rangy, loose-limbed man with an iron-grey buzz cut and iron-grey eyes and a weathered, angular face. He didn't have to wear a wig for this part: he was stunting for Lee Kellogg, who was just as grey as he was.

He leaned forward on the jet ski's handlebars and relaxed. It was late afternoon, but the temperature was still in the high seventies, and the sea was purple. Behind them, the Rock was growing increasingly dark, a massive fang of prehistoric lime-stone over four hundred metres high. Five or six seagulls bobbed on the swell close beside them, as if they had accepted the jet ski as a surrogate parent.

Off to their right, two hundred yards along the greyish sands of the Eastern Beach, a long black Fountain powerboat was moored to the end of the jetty. Three mechanics were working on it, and now and again its engines would start up, then help-lessly cough like two old smokers having an argument, and fall silent again. This was the express cruiser in which the evil genius Karl Mordant was supposed to be trying to escape from secret agent Jack Brand and his feisty assistant Morning Glory.

'More bloody *drama*,' Silja repeated, contemptuously, tossing her cigarette butt into the sea. 'To jet-ski or not to jet-ski, that is the bloody question!'

'Maybe you could stand up two or three seconds earlier,' Noah suggested. 'You could spread out your arms, too, like a bareback rider. *That* would be dramatic.'

'Oh, sure. Especially if I fell top-over-bottom into the ocean.'

'I could gun the engine a bit more, just as you get up on to your feet. Bring the nose up, too, so that you can steady yourself against my back.'

'OK. If you want to try it, I'm game. The worst thing I could do is splat into the side of the powerboat at eighty kilometres an hour. Eat out your heart, Wile E. Coyote.'

They waited with the supreme patience of people who spend most of their working lives waiting. They smoked another cigarette. Every now and then, a plane would take off from Gibraltar's single landing strip, only two hundred yards to their left, and rise up, sparkling, into the late-afternoon sky. Jack Brand and his feisty assistant Morning Glory were supposed to have pursued Karl Mordant by dropping out of the rear doors of a twin-engined transport plane, just as it lifted off over the ocean, riding astride their jet ski as if it were a flying horse.

Noah hadn't bothered to protest that – in reality – the water was so shallow that both of them would have been killed, or at least broken most of their bones. He was a stuntman, not a script editor.

The powerboat's engines had been silent for a long time now and Richard Bullman eventually stalked to the end of the jetty to find out what was wrong. Noah clearly heard the word 'bloody' at least twenty-five times.

'I don't know why he doesn't call it a day,' said Silja.

'Forecast says hazy cloud tomorrow. Besides, we have to be in Agadir by Friday afternoon.'

Suddenly, the powerboat's engines bellowed into life. Richard Bullman stalked back along the jetty and climbed back into his crane. In his pink T-shirt and his flappy white shorts, he looked like a very cross toddler.

'*Marker!*' he shouted. 'And – *action!*'

The two actors playing Karl Mordant and his bodyguard Drillbit came sprinting along the jetty, pursued by plain-clothes police. The police were firing their pistols, but Drillbit turned around and sprayed them with an Uzi. Three of them staggered and cartwheeled into the water.

Mordant and Drillbit clambered into the powerboat and cut the mooring lines. With a masculine scream, the powerboat leaped away from the jetty and headed out to sea, immediately followed by two more powerboats, both carrying camera crews.

Noah revved up the jet ski and waited for his signal. When it came, he let out the throttle and the jet ski surged forward, its hull bumping and blurting on the water. It felt as though they were speeding along a cobbled street on a motorcycle with no tyres.

They quickly caught up with the powerboat's wake – two deep furrows of white foam. This time, Noah slewed the jet ski violently from side to side, criss-crossing from one furrow to the other, so that they were hurled up into the air and slapped back down again. His spine was jolted again and again, and as they came closer to the stern of the powerboat, the water was churning so ferociously that the jet ski almost nosedived under the surface.

Through the spray, he could see Karl Mordant gripping the rail around the sun deck, scowling and gesticulating at them, and Drillbit pointing his machine pistol at them, two-handed. A cameraman with a hand-held Arriflex was dodging between them.

The jet ski and the powerboat were making too much noise for Noah to be able to hear the gunfire, but he could see snatches of smoke being carried away by the wind. He ducked his head from side to side as if he were trying to avoid bullets.

Drillbit had to reload, and this was Noah's signal to push the jet ski right up to the powerboat's stern. He twisted the throttle as far as it would go, and the jet ski surged forward, its nose rearing up like Jaws.

Silja climbed to her feet, holding on to Noah's shoulders until she found her balance. He could feel her knees against his back, and he could see by her shadow that she was spreading her arms wide, so he gunned the jet ski again. It collided with the powerboat just as Silja sprang up on to his shoulders and performed a forward somersault in mid-air.

She landed exactly where she was supposed to land, in the middle of the sun deck, but Noah had given her far too much momentum. She helter-skeltered across the powerboat, colliding with the cameraman. Both of them rolled over the portside railing and splashed into the sea.

'*Cut!*' screamed Richard Bullman, right in Noah's ear. 'Cut-cut-cut-bloody-cut! What the bloody hell was that all about?'

The powerboat's engines died, and Noah circled around it to help Silja and the cameraman out of the sea. Silja was doing a slow backstroke and laughing, but the cameraman was frantically doggy-paddling around in circles. 'My camera! Dropped my camera!'

Silja climbed up on to the jet ski, and reached down to take the cameraman's hand. But he kept on thrashing around, peering into the water for any sign of his Arriflex. The sea was shallow here, and very clear, but the Arriflex was grey and white, and wouldn't have been easy to see.

'Noah, what's going on?' asked Richard Bullman.

'Sorry, Richard. I kind of misjudged my speed.'

'You're not bloody joking. Get back to your first position and we'll see if we can try it one more time, before we lose the light altogether.'

'We have a slight problem here, Richard. Mac's dropped the Arri.'

'Shit. Is it damaged?'

'I'm not sure. He's dropped it into the ocean.'

There was a lengthy pause. Noah imagined that Richard Bullman was probably finding it difficult to speak. The sun was already half-eclipsed by the Rock, and it was obvious that they weren't going to be able to shoot this scene again – not today, and not tomorrow, if the weather forecast was accurate. They might even have to come back again, after they had finished filming in Morocco.

The next voice that Noah heard was Kevin Langan's. Kevin was the production manager. He sounded dry and unemotional, as if he were reading out a list of technical specifications, but then he always spoke like that, even when he was furious.

'Noah . . . you'll find a marker buoy on board the cruiser. Underneath the seats on the sun deck, third locker on the starboard side. Take it out and mark your position.'

'OK, then what?'

'Tomorrow morning, first light, you put on your scuba gear and you go down and you find that camera for us.'

'It ain't going to be easy, Kevin. There's a whole lot of weed down there.'

'I don't care, Noah. You're going to find it. If you *don't* find it, I shall be quite unhappy.'

Noah knew what that meant. Several cameramen and technicians who had made Kevin Langan 'quite unhappy' hadn't worked again for years.

'I'm hearing you, Kevin. Over and out.'

Two

They were out on the Alboran Sea at first light the next morning, in a small diving-launch which smelled strongly of sardines and diesel oil. As predicted, the cloud was high and hazy, and there was scarcely any wind.

Noah had a hangover like a head-on car crash. Last night the crew had all gone to La Bayuca for a long and noisy dinner, and he had drunk two bottles of Rioja too many, which meant a total of four.

Silja said, 'You don't have to do this, if you're not up to it. I can do it.'

Noah blew out cigarette smoke and shook his head. 'No. It was my fault, so I have to do it. Kevin will never let me forget it, otherwise.'

The boat's owner nudged up to the marker buoy and cut the engine. 'You ready, mate?'

'Ready as I'll ever be.'

He stood up. He was wearing bright green shorts with palm trees and parrots on them, which he had bought last year in Honolulu, when he was filming *Hurricane Force*. His body was stringy and muscular and tanned to a light oak colour, with scars and welts all across his chest and a Seabees tattoo on his upper arm – a cartoon bee in a Navy cap, flying through the air with a power drill and a collection of wrenches.

He checked his regulator, fitted his mask over his face, and then tipped himself backward into the sea.

Even though it was only mid-September, the water was surprisingly cold. Summer had been a long time coming this year, and the Mediterranean had never warmed up to its usual temperature. Noah twisted around and gave a strong kick which took him vertically downward.

He swam through a glittering school of rainbow sardines. The ocean here was less than eighteen metres deep, and he could see the bottom clearly. Most of it was covered with seaweed, which undulated like pale green hair. This was the mutant seaweed *caulerpa taxifolia* – originally bred for aquaria in Monaco – but which had now choked up thousands of acres of the Mediterranean seabed.

He saw something shining through the weeds, and swam towards it. It was one of dozens of empty wine bottles, which must have been thrown overboard from somebody's party, as well as countless broken dinner plates. Greeks, probably, having a crockery-smashing session. But no sign of Mac's Arriflex.

Using the marker-buoy anchor as his central point, Noah swam around in wider and wider circles. He would have enjoyed this, if his head hadn't been hammering so hard. He had learned to dive when he was in the Gulf, with the Seabees, and he had become one of their best underwater fitters. His specialty used to be wet underwater welding – repairing the plates of bomb-damaged boats without having to tow them into dry dock.

Ahead of him lay a weed-filled depression, almost seventy metres wide. Noah swam over the edge of it, and there, amongst a tangle of nets and lines, he glimpsed the crescent-shaped gleam of a camera lens. He reached down, found the camera's handle, and hefted it up. He hoped to God that Mac's footage was still intact. The Arriflex and its accessories were worth upwards of $70,000, but the images on the film inside were worth a hundred times that.

He half-swam, half-jumped his way back towards the marker-buoy anchor, as if he were walking on the moon. Up above him he could see the hull of the fishing boat and the diamond-shaped patterns of the waves.

He crossed over a wide stretch of bare sand where divers had obviously been clearing away the *caulerpa taxifolia* with suction pumps. It was a losing battle: as fast as the divers sucked it up, the weed grew back again, far more rapidly than any native variety.

Noah found himself bounding in slow motion through a wide scattering of assorted debris – bits and pieces of wreckage and jetsam that must have been sucked out of the sand along with the weed, but which had sunk back down to the seabed.

He saw the aluminium armrest of an old-fashioned aircraft

seat. Beside it lay the empty frame of a suitcase, with a handle and even a luggage tag, but no sides. There was a man's lace-up shoe, once black probably, but now greyish-green. An enamel mug, rusted in half; an umbrella; a tangle of fishing-nets; and a whole variety of blocks and tackles that looked as if they had been used for hauling up sails.

He had almost reached the weed again when he saw a binocular case half-buried in the sand. It was canvas, bleached white by the sea, but there was a chance that the binoculars inside might have survived. Noah had lost an expensive pair of Nikon Premier binoculars when he was filming two months ago in Montreal, and he hadn't had the chance to replace them yet. He swam over and picked the case up.

It didn't seem heavy enough to contain binoculars, but when he gave it a shake he could hear something rattling inside it – something that weighed six or seven ounces at least. He tried to open it, but the catch was far too corroded, so he looped its straps around his belt.

He carried the Arri back towards the marker-buoy line. He tied the handle securely and then gave the line three sharp tugs downward, to indicate that he had found the camera and that the boatman could haul it up. Some inquisitive wrasse came swimming past him, but quickly scattered when he kicked his way up towards the surface.

Silja leaned over the side and helped to pull him out of the water. 'Well done. Now you can buy me breakfast. I think full English, with fried bread and black pudding, too.'

'You have to be joking. All I want is a large Bloody Mary – Stolichnaya, with extra Tabasco and Worcestershire sauce.'

They took a taxi back to the O'Callaghan's Elliot Hotel on Governor's Parade, where the whole crew and cast of *Dead Reckoning* were staying, and went up to the Rooftop Restaurant for breakfast. Through the panoramic windows they could see the Straits of Gibraltar, Southern Spain and Morocco, although the hazy sky made the view appear strangely ghostly.

'You amaze me,' said Noah, as he watched Silja cutting up a fat British-style sausage.

'I have a very efficient metabolism,' she said, smiling at him. Without her dark Rayleigh Martin wig, she didn't look so anaemic. Her own hair was so blonde that it was almost white, and cut into a feathery, elf-like style. She had high cheek-bones and blue eyes that were pale like a winter's sky. But Noah still found her physical strength to be the most attract-ive thing about her . . . the thought that he probably couldn't beat her in unarmed combat.

Richard Bullman came over to their table, wearing a dishev-elled green linen suit, John-the-Baptist sandals and yellow socks. He had a pouchy, sallow face like Deputy Dawg. His wiry black hair was uncombed and he looked as if he hadn't shaved for three days.

'Just thought you'd like to know that Kevin's had the Arri checked over. The bloody electronics are toast but the footage looks OK, no bloody thanks to you.'

'Will we have to shoot that scene over?' Noah asked him.

Richard Bullman wobbled his jowls. 'No, thank God. I almost hate to say it, but I looked through the rushes last night and they're bloody terrific. Not exactly what I had in mind, but the way Silja goes hurtling across that bloody deck – human bloody cannonballs aren't in it.'

'That's a bloody relief.'

'For you it is.'

He caught sight of Jean Bottaro, one of the movie's producers, sitting on the other side of the restaurant, and raised his arm to her. 'Jean. I must have a word with bloody Jean . . .'

Once he had gone, Noah lifted the binocular case on to the table. He picked up a butter knife and started to chisel at the catch.

Silja said, 'You don't seriously think there are any bin-oculars in there?'

He shook the case hard. 'No. But there's *something*.'

A waiter stood close by, frowning disapprovingly as Noah scraped black fragments of rust on to the tablecloth. Eventually, he managed to force the tip of the knife in between the catch and the canvas, and pry the lid open. First he took out a red-and-gold tobacco box, spotted with corrosion, and then he shook out a large black medallion, about seven centimetres in diameter and half a centimetre thick, attached to a heavy black chain.

He picked up the medallion and examined it closely. On one side it was engraved with an arrangement of parallel lines that looked like primitive drawings of arrows. On the other, he could make out a crescent moon shape, an arrangement of raised circles, and the letters P R C H A L.

'What is it?' asked Silja. She took out her rimless half-glasses and peered at it across the table.

'I don't have any idea. It looks pretty old though, doesn't it?'

'What is P R C H A L? Maybe initials for something . . .'

'Who knows? Let's see what's inside this box.'

The box was enamelled, with a picture of a scarlet devil on the lid, smoking a long-stemmed pipe. It was embossed with the words *Tabak Cert.*

Noah slowly forced it open. Inside there was a small quantity of coarse black tobacco and six or seven pieces of blotchy-looking newsprint, carefully torn into rectangles.

'Looks like somebody was running low on cigarette papers,' he commented. He picked up one of the pieces of newsprint and tried to read it. 'Can't understand a word. What do you think it is? Hungarian, something like that?'

Silja took the piece of paper and said, 'Czech. See here, this word "*nemocnice*", that means "hospital". I tore my Achilles' tendon once when I was filming in Prague, and they took me to the "*nemocnice*".'

'So maybe P R C H A L means something in Czech. Maybe it's not initials at all. Hey, maybe it's the Czech for "prickle". Well, hey, it *sounds* like it, doesn't it – "*prchal*"?'

Silja looked at him over her half-glasses, unamused. She passed over another piece of newsprint and pointed to the edge of it. 'Here, look, there's a date here. 30 June 1943. This is more than sixty-five years old.'

'So somebody lost this case during World War Two. Could have dropped it off a boat, I guess. Or maybe it came from a plane crash. There were all kinds of bits of aircraft wreckage down there, and it was pretty much in line with the end of the landing strip.'

Silja poured herself another cup of black coffee. 'Well, I don't think we'll ever find out, will we? Whoever used to own this box, he died before he could enjoy his last cigarette.'

Noah took out two Marlboros, and lit them both. 'My daddy always used to warn me that smoking kills.'

Three

A deola Davis woke up and stared at the alarm clock beside the bed. 5.57 a.m. Shit. She wouldn't have time for her morning workout. She would hardly have enough time to take a shower.

She heaved Rick's arm off her and sat up. 'I'm late,' she said. 'I have my first meeting at six forty-five.'

Rick was still sleeping. He mumbled, *'Don't* . . . you really don't want to do that, dude . . .'

Adeola flung back the bedcover and bounced out of bed. 'You said you'd wake me. You *promised* you'd wake me. Jesus Christ, it's your *job* to wake me.'

Rick opened one eye and looked up at her, confused. 'What's the matter, baby? What's happening?'

'I need to be sitting across a table from the Ethiopians in forty-seven minutes, that's what's happening. I need to look fresh, and perfectly groomed, and I need to have my head together. I need to be utterly composed.'

She crossed the room, scooping up her blue silk bathrobe as she went, and opened the bathroom door. 'I do not need to look puffy-eyed and dishevelled and exhausted, nor do I need to smell as if I've been having all-night sex with my head of security.'

Rick propped himself up on one elbow. 'But you *have* been having all-night sex with your head of security.'

Adeola went into the blue-tiled bathroom and looked at herself in the mirror over the washbasin. God almighty, she looked like one of those juju masks they sold in the backstreet markets in Lagos. Her short hair was all frizzy, her eyelids were swollen, and her lips were pouting. She climbed into the glass shower cubicle and turned on the shiny designer faucet.

'Coffee?' asked Rick, coming into the bathroom naked. He was stocky and muscular, with a black crucifix of hair on his chest. He had a handsome, heart-shaped face with some disturbing femininity in it, like a young Tony Curtis or a Ray Liotta.

'Cranberry juice, that's all.'

He opened the door of the shower cubicle and stood watching her as she soaped herself. He had a slight tic in his right eye, the result of a gunshot wound inflicted in Kuwait, so that he looked as if he were winking at her. 'Are you sure that's all? Cranberry juice? I mean . . . forty-seven minutes, that's just about long enough . . .'

She turned to him. 'There's a time for everything, Mr Kavanagh. A time to live and a time to die. A time to be a lover and a time to be a fighter. And a time to get the hell out of the bathroom and put some pants on.'

'You're a goddess, you know that? Look at you.'

Adeola had a long, exotic face with feline eyes and a very strong jawline. This morning she might have thought that she looked like a juju mask, but she looked exactly like her mother, whose extraordinary appearance had made the UN African Affairs Director fall in love with her thirty-three years ago during the course of a single dinner party in Abuja, and marry her within three months. A year later, Adeola had been born. Her name meant 'loved by all'.

Her father was white, so Adeola's skin was paler than her mother's, but she had her mother's full breasts, and her hips flared out in just the same way, although her legs were much longer, like her father's.

When she was growing up, Adeola had been repeatedly asked if she had considered a career in modelling, or acting, but she was too intense for that, too serious, too political. She wanted to do some good in the world. That was why she had eventually joined DOVE, which was now the most influential privately-financed aid agency in the world.

'Your juice, m'lady,' said Rick, as she came out of the bathroom, her hair wrapped up in a towel turban. He was already dressed in a white linen shirt and sand-coloured chinos. He had strapped on his shoulder holster but his black SIG-Sauer P225 semi-automatic pistol was lying on the table next to the bowl of papayas and oranges.

'Did you talk to Captain Madoowbe about security?' Adeola asked him, picking up her juice.

'I did, but he's more excited by firepower than he is by good intelligence. Personally I don't give a flying fig how many rocket-propelled grenade launchers he and his goons are toting around. If somebody's sneaked in and placed a bomb under the conference table, it's goodnight Vienna.'

'Or goodbye Dubai, in this case,' said Adeola. She went to the window and looked out. Her suite was on the forty-eighth floor of the Emirates Towers Hotel, with a view of the royal stable buildings and the desert beyond, which was a bright pink colour this morning – almost the same colour as her cranberry juice. She could never look at the desert without having the strangest of feelings. It was like seeing her own death, waiting for her.

She went through to the bedroom and opened the closet. Most of the clothes that she had brought to Dubai were very plain and sober. Today she took out a pale lemon suit she had bought on her last trip to New York. It was a little too Hilary Clinton for her taste, but the men with whom she had to negotiate in Africa and the Middle East expected women to be modest and respectable. Even talking to a woman on equal terms made them tetchy.

'We're taking all three SUVs,' called Rick, as Adeola sat in front of the dressing table, struggling to pin up her hair. 'You'll be in the third one, for a change. We'll drive straight up to the entrance of the Taj Hotel, Jimmy and Miko will get out and make sure that the scenery looks tight before they give you the signal. Then and only then will you disembark.

'If anything looks at all screwy, your vehicle will back up at high speed, execute a one-eighty, and head south-east on Al Rigga Road, foot to the floor.'

Adeola had the tip of her tongue between her teeth as she fastened an Igbo buckle into her hair.

'You hearing this?' said Rick.

'I'm hearing it. I'm just having so much trouble with my freaking hair. What did I *do* last night?'

'You mean you can't remember?'

Jimmy, Miko, Charles and Nesta were all waiting for them down in the hotel lobby. They were all discreetly dressed, just like Rick, in white shirts, navy-blue sport coats and chinos, except for Nesta, who was wearing a blue blouse and a knee-length black linen skirt. They could have been mistaken for travel-company staff, rather than bodyguards.

Charles checked his huge stainless-steel watch. 'We're three minutes ahead of schedule,' he said. 'Do you want to wait or do you want to go now?'

'We'll wait,' said Rick. 'Safer to stay here than hang around at the Taj. Miko – any radio chatter?'

'Nothing that related to us.'

'OK . . . I haven't received any cautions from Al Ameen, either. All the same, this is a highly sensitive conference, polit-ically speaking, so I'd like us all to be extra watchful.'

'I went out first thing this morning and checked out the rooftop opposite the Taj,' said Jimmy. 'There's no possible access, and in any case you'd never get a clear shot from there.'

'How about the apartments?'

'All occupied – and again, you'd never get a clear shot. Too many trees, and the SUVs would be blocking your line of fire.'

'OK, happy with that. Any other thoughts, before we roll?'

'You're confident about Captain Madoowbe's people?' asked Nesta.

'No. But then I'm never too happy about African state secu-rity, no matter which country I'm in. You can be halfway through a job, and they have a military coup back home, and all of a sudden your smiley chum is your fanatical machete-swinging enemy. There's a couple of guys on Captain Madoowbe's team who did some pretty dubious things in Mogadishu, so let's keep our eyes on them, too.'

They left the air-conditioned chill of the lobby and stepped out into the hotel portico. Although it was still early, the temperature had already climbed to thirty degrees and the heat hit them like an oven door opening. On the far side of the portico, three shiny black Ford Explorers were parked nose-to-tail by the curb, watched over by the sixth member of Adeola's security team, Reuben Brock. It was difficult to mistake Reuben for a travel executive. In spite of his dark blue yachting blazer and his well-pressed chinos, and the way that his hands were discreetly clasped over his genitals, he had the bull-headed look of a minotaur, with no neck what-soever, and a top-heavy torso that had earned him the nick-name Rube the Cube.

He came across to join the rest of the team as they escorted

Adeola to the rear Explorer. 'Everything OK?' he asked in his gravelly Pittsburgh accent. 'Are we ready to roll?'

'Ready to roll.'

As they were opening up the Explorer's doors, a young Arab in a loose-fitting black coat and baggy pants came hurrying towards them from the street, his sandals slapping on the asphalt. He called out, *'Assalam alekum! Keyf haleck?'*

Adeola turned. The young man looked innocent enough. He couldn't have been older than seventeen or eighteen, with a maroon knitted hat and the first dark wisps of an immature moustache. When he saw Adeola, he raised his hand and said, 'Miss Adeola Davis! *Sabah al-khayr!* Good morning to you!'

Rick immediately seized Adeola by the hips and hoisted her into the back of the Explorer. 'Get down! Flat across the seat!'

Reuben crossed the portico and intercepted the young Arab before he could get within twenty yards of Adeola's Explorer.

'Back off, kid. You can't come over here.'

'Assif, I'm sorry. I recognize Miss Adeola Davis.'

'Sorry, kid. You didn't recognize nobody.'

'Please – I am a great admirer of Miss Adeola Davis. She is my heroine, working so hard in the Middle East for peace. All I want is autograph.'

The young Arab reached into his inside pocket. Reuben immediately heaved out his Colt automatic and said, 'Hold it, kid! Don't even think about it!'

But the young Arab folded back his coat to show that he had nothing in his inside pocket except for a spiral-bound notebook. 'All I want is autograph.'

'Sorry, kid, you made a mistake. Wrong person. Now beat it.'

Two of the uniformed doormen had come over now, and started shouting at the young man in Arabic, ordering him to go away. One of them kicked at him, although he missed, and almost fell over. Eventually, the young man raised both hands in mock-surrender. 'OK, OK. *Mafi mushkila.* I go.'

He turned around and walked away, with his sandals still slapping.

Rick opened the Explorer's door just as Reuben came back. 'False alarm. Some autograph hunter, that's all. Let's get out of here before we run late. Wouldn't want to keep His Excellency Ato Ketona Aklilu waiting, would we?'

They climbed into the three SUVs, and pulled out of the Emirates Towers Hotel with their tyres squealing on the baking-hot asphalt.

Four

Captain Madoowbe and his security team were waiting for them outside the Taj Palace Hotel. There were eight of them altogether, all wearing flappy brown suits and mirrored sunglasses, except for Captain Madoowbe himself, who was dressed in an olive-green military uniform, beautifully tailored and pressed, complete with medals and ribbons and insignia.

'The whole of the surrounding environment is totally secure,' he announced, as Rick and Reuben escorted Adeola up the hotel steps.

Rick took off his sunglasses and looked around with his eyes narrowed. 'Pleased to hear it.'

Captain Madoowbe was short, with a large head and intensely black skin. His eyes were hooded and he had decorative patterns of scars on his cheeks. It may have been his strong accent, but Adeola always thought that he sounded incredibly arrogant. She had never seen any reliable evidence, but it was rumoured that Captain Madoowbe had been involved in the notorious torture and killing of several Oromo people in the Jarso district of Wollaga, several years ago, including a pregnant woman and her unborn child.

'OK,' said Rick. 'If we can give the conference room a quick once-over . . .'

'That has already been done to my complete satisfaction,' said Captain Madoowbe.

'All the same.'

'That has already been done to my *complete* satisfaction,' Captain Madoowbe repeated. He made no move to stand aside.

Rick lowered his head a little. Then he looked back up again and said, 'You have your foreign minister to protect,

Captain, and I'm sure you do that to the best of your ability. But Ms Davis is my responsibility, and I have to insist on vetting the conference room for any security problems that may specifically affect her.'

'I do not care for your implication.'

Adeola put in, 'Mr Kavanagh isn't implying anything, Captain. But either he and his colleagues are permitted to vet the conference room or there *is* no conference, and I'd like to see how you explain *that* to His Excellency. You have ten seconds. That's it. We're leaving.'

'But that was not ten seconds!'

'You're right. It wasn't. I changed my mind. Just like you're going to change yours.'

The meeting with the Ethiopian Foreign Minister lasted for four and a half hours. In common with most of the meetings that Adeola had attended in Africa and the Middle East, it was dreamlike and prolix.

They sat in a cool white room with a high ceiling and white muslin drapes drawn across the windows, so that all Adeola could see of the city outside was the occasional sparkle from a car window.

A long low table was laid out with various Ethiopian snacks which had been prepared by His Excellency's own chef – bowls of *dabo kolo*, little balls of crunchy fried bread; plates of the warm raw meat called *kitfo*; and several different vegetarian dishes, like *misir wat*, which was made of lentils, and *fosolia* string beans.

There was coffee, and Ethiopian herbal tea, but no alcohol. Adeola drank only Ambo, the fizzy Ethiopian mineral water. She found it far too salty and metallic, but she wanted to show respect for her host.

Ato Ketona Aklilu was a small, languid man, with an obsessively neat beard and bulging eyes and an aquiline nose. He was immaculately dressed in a white silk shirt and a pale beige tailor-made suit. A large gold Rolex hung loosely on his wrist. He spoke perfect but rather pedantic English with a cut-glass British accent. He had been educated at Harrow, after all.

'What you have to realize, my dear lady, is that since 1991 Ethiopia's foreign policy has been to reduce our dependency on Western aid. Aid is always appreciated, especially in years of drought and famine. But the problem with aid is that it always comes with political provisos, does it not?'

'Well, you're right,' said Adeola. 'And I can tell you that DOVE has authorized me to offer you a substantial amount of new aid, particularly medical supplies and foodstuffs – well over and above this year's agreed quota from USAID. But I'm not looking to attach any strings to it – not in the way you're talking about. I want to work *with* you – not dictate to you. All I'm asking from you is that you seriously consider what I have to say.'

One of the foreign minister's servants passed Adeola a plate of *injera*, the flat bread with which most Ethiopian foods are eaten. She tore off a piece with her right hand and used it to dip into the *misir wat*. She wasn't going to touch the *kitfo*. It might be highly popular in Ethiopia, but her friend Ruth had tried some and spent nine agonizing days on the toilet.

'We are rebuilding our political standing in the world, that is the point,' said the foreign minister. 'We have poverty, we have backwardness, we have illiteracy. These shortcomings we freely admit. But they are all the result of centuries of foreign oppression and continuing aggression from our neighbours.'

Adeola said, 'I understand that, Your Excellency, but you will never be fully respected by the international community while you go on committing acts of repression and ethnic cleansing against your own people.'

The foreign minister frowned, as if he had never heard such an accusation before. 'Repression? Ethnic cleansing? I don't know who has been supplying you with such misinformation. We have strict law enforcement, of course. In a nation as disparate as ours, this is necessary. Sometimes – because of drought – we have to move whole populations from one location to another, for their own humanitarian benefit. But no *repression!* No *ethnic cleansing!* My goodness!'

But Adeola persisted. 'In particular, Your Excellency, I'm looking for some guarantees for the Anuak people in Gambella.'

'Guarantees? What guarantees would you need to look for? The Anuak are very rebellious. *Very* awkward, *very* ungrateful. But they are always treated fairly, in spite of this.'

'With respect, sir, the Anuak have always been a peaceful

people. They're farmers, not insurgents. But my office is still regularly receiving reports of some terrible acts of violence by government forces. Women being beaten and raped, men being punished for doing nothing more than talking to each other in the street.'

'No, dear lady. Of course I have heard some of these false reports myself. But I can assure you that they are all lies and exaggerations spread by those who seek to besmirch the good reputation of the Ethiopian People's Revolutionary Democratic Front.'

And so the hours went by, with Adeola repeatedly asking for the Ethiopian government to stop treating their African minorities so harshly, and Ato Kenota Aklilu repeatedly denying that they ever had, or would. 'Let me say this – compared with the appalling suffering of many peoples in Africa, the Anuak, for instance, are living in clover.'

'Oh, really? So why have they been thrown off their farms? Why did government forces shoot nearly five hundred of them?'

'I can arrange for you to visit Gambella yourself within a few weeks. There you can see for yourself that I am telling you the truth.'

'OK. I'll take you up on that offer. I'd be delighted for you to prove me wrong.'

Like most meetings, this one appeared to end inconclusively. There were *salaams* and handshakes and smiles, except from Captain Madoowbe, who stood in a corner, his eyes glittering with resentment. But nothing seemed to have been agreed, or guaranteed, and no commitments seemed to have been made on either side.

All the same, Adeola was smiling as Rick and Reuben escorted her down in the express elevator to the hotel lobby.

Rick said, 'You look pretty damned pleased with yourself.'

'Of course. I got him to blink, and that was all I was looking for.'

'He blinked?' asked Reuben.

'Oh, yes. He invited me to visit Gambella to see how wonderfully well the Anuaks are being treated. He wouldn't have done that if he hadn't wanted that extra aid so badly. But let's face it – this year's drought has been the worst for seventeen years, and I think he would rather stop persecuting the Anuaks

for a while than lose five and a half million dollars worth of
food.'

'Seems like everything has a price, doesn't it?' said Rick.
'Even human decency.'

They crossed the shiny marble lobby. A crowd of reporters
and TV cameramen were waiting for Adeola outside. They
were supposed to be held back behind a velvet rope, but as
she stepped out on to the hotel steps they pushed forward with
their microphones held out.

'Ms Davis! Have you managed to reach any kind of agreement with the Ethiopian government?'

'Ms Davis! Did they give way on any human rights
issues?'

'Ms Davis!'

Adeola paused for a moment. 'I'll have a full statement for
you at six this evening, when I hold my media conference at
the Emirates Towers. Right now, I can tell you that His
Excellency and I had a very constructive discussion in which
a number of important issues were raised, including humanitarian aid and human rights.'

'How about the Anuaks? Did you discuss the situation in
Gambella?'

'Yes, we did. And His Excellency has kindly invited me to
visit Gambella to see the conditions there for myself.'

That will skewer the bastard, she thought. Now I've announced
it publicly, he won't be able to withdraw the invitation without
looking as if he has something to hide.

Rick took her elbow. 'Come on, time to haul ass. We're too
exposed out here.'

The three black Explorers nosed their way towards the front
steps. Rick was staying close to Adeola and looking around
anxiously. The media people were milling about everywhere,
as well as a recently-arrived party of French tourists, and Rick
was never happy when there were too many people for him
to keep his eye on. The Explorers' doors opened and Charles
climbed out of the rear vehicle and beckoned Rick to hurry
up and bring Adeola down the steps.

At that moment Adeola heard the slap-slap-slapping of
sandals. The young Arab who had approached them outside
the Emirates Towers Hotel was hurrying up the steps towards

them. He was smiling, just like before, and he called out, 'Ms Davis! *Assalam alekum!*'

'Your fan, the autograph hunter,' said Rick. 'Persistent little pest, isn't he?'

'Hey, buddy,' said Reuben, holding out his hand to prevent the young Arab from coming any further up the steps, 'I told you before, didn't I? That's as far as you go.'

'Oh come on, Reuben,' Adeola called out to him. 'He only wants an autograph.'

'All I ask for is autograph!' the young Arab repeated.

'Well, OK,' said Reuben, and stepped aside so that the young Arab could climb the steps towards them.

But it was then that Rick said, 'Holy Christ, his coat's buttoned up – and where's his hat?'

Adeola said, 'What?' But it was then that she realized that the young Arab's black coat was fastened, and he looked much bulkier than he had before. Not only that, he had replaced his knitted hat with a black scarf, tied tight around his temples.

'*Rube!*' yelled Rick, and tugged out his semi-automatic.

Reuben came storming up the steps and threw himself at the young Arab in a massive football tackle. The two of them started to topple sideways, but they hadn't fallen even halfway to the ground before there was an explosion so loud Adeola couldn't even hear it.

The young Arab's head sprang from his shoulders as if somebody had kicked it, and hurtled high up into the air. Adeola was knocked backward, and as she fell she saw a blizzard of body parts flying over her, followed by a warm, wet spray against her face. She felt Rick snatching at her sleeve, but she still hit the steps awkwardly, and tumbled down six or seven of them before she ended up beside one of the Explorer's rear wheels.

The hotel's front doors shattered and plate glass burst out everywhere. The press caught the worst of it, and a female reporter screamed as a scimitar-shaped piece of glass sliced off her left cheek and part of her chin. A cameraman raised his hand to protect his face, only to have it hacked off like a knuckle of lamb. One of the hotel's doormen was thrown face-forward, as if he were diving, and was impaled through the chest by the brass stanchion that held up the velvet rope.

The explosion lasted only a fraction of a second, but it

seemed to Adeola to go on for ever. Blood came running down the hotel steps, and the air was filled with pungent brown smoke and whirling paper and tatters of clothing.

She tried to sit up. Rick was right beside her, with a pattern of scratches on his face. 'Are you OK?' he asked her.

She could hardly hear him. 'I think so.'

'Keep low. There could well be another one. We have to get you out of here.'

He stood up. Immediately after the bomb had gone off, there had been an eerie silence, broken only by the tinkling of falling glass. But now a woman started to scream, wildly and hysterically, and a man started to shout out for help, and suddenly there was a cacophony of voices, like a choir from hell – begging, pleading, moaning, whimpering, crying out in pain.

Rick opened up the Explorer's door and helped Adeola into the front passenger seat. As he did so, she saw a jumble of images. People staggering aimlessly up and down the hotel steps, their hair sticking up like clowns', smothered in blood. Bits of luggage and bits of bodies scattered everywhere.

As Rick climbed in beside her and started the engine, she looked out of the window and saw Reuben lying face down on the steps. His eyes were open and he seemed to be grinning at her. It was only when Rick backed the Explorer up that she saw that both of his arms and both of his legs were nothing but bloody stumps, and that he was grinning at nothing at all.

They pulled out of the forecourt and sped south-east on Al Rigga Road. Fire trucks and ambulances and police cars were already heading towards the Taj Hotel, their lights flashing and their sirens blaring.

'Nesta?' said Adeola. 'Charles, Miko, Jimmy – did you see any of them?'

Rick checked his rear-view mirror. 'They're OK. They're right behind us.'

'Oh, God. Reuben!'

'Rube saved us. Rube the Cube. If he hadn't jumped on that bastard—'

'Who do you think did it?'

Rick looked at her. 'Who do I think *did* it? Who have you

managed to upset in your three and a half years as diplomatic representative for DOVE? The Somalis? The Eritreans? The Palestinians? The Israelis? The Sudanese? The Chinese? The Taiwanese? You've upset just about everybody on the entire goddamned planet!'

'Well, I'm going to find out who did it,' vowed Adeola. Her voice was shaking. 'I'm going to find out who did it and I'm going to make them pay.'

Rick said, 'Come on, you're in shock.'

'No, I'm not. I'm going to get my revenge for this.'

'Hey, don't forget, blessed are the peacemakers.'

Adeola stared at him defiantly. 'In that case, this is where I stop being blessed.'

Five

Noah was in the kitchen stirring a pot of gazpacho when his cellphone played the Dead March from *Saul*. As usual, his blue-fronted Amazon parrot joined in.

'*Marilyn*,' he snapped, 'will you for once in your life shut your goddamned beak?'

'Noah? It's Silja.'

'Oh, I'm sorry, Silja. I was remonstrating with my parrot. Hey – I thought you were in Britain?'

'I was supposed to be, for the new James Bond picture, but there have been so many delays. I came back Friday for my sister's wedding.'

'I never knew you had a sister. Older or younger?'

'Older.'

'Shoot – you should have introduced me. But if she just got married – well, it sounds like it's too late now.'

He picked up a small handful of chopped green chillies and scattered them into the gazpacho. 'Are you around at all? You want to come to my place for dinner? I'm having a few friends around this evening and you're more than welcome.'

'Sure, that would be great. I want to see you in any case. I have something interesting to show you.'

'Around seven, how's that?'

He set the round oak table that stood on his terrace. He tried to remember how Jenna used to lay out all the cutlery, and the side plates, and how she folded the napkins. He even found a clear-crystal vase and made a decorative arrangement of purple orchids, placing it in the centre, between the candles.

Jenna had been one of the few civilizing influences in his life, and even after eighteen months he still missed her. But the stuntman and the jewellery designer? You couldn't even make a situation comedy about it, let alone try to live it out for real.

He went back into the kitchen and peered into the oven to make sure that his Moroccan chicken wasn't burning, and then opened a very cold bottle of Pinot Grigio.

'Here's to civilizing influences,' he said, raising his glass.

'Screw you,' croaked Marilyn.

He stood by the railing, looking out over Laurel Canyon. Beside him, his flag hung limp and motionless on its flag-pole. His neighbour, Cy Winterman, was having drinks by the pool. He could hear Cy's baying laughter and the screaming of his children as they threw each other into the water.

Far below, Los Angeles was covered by gilded haze, like a city seen in a dream.

Noah spent only a few weeks of each year at home in California. When he did, though, he always became reflective, and started to question what he was doing with his life, and who he really was. He was standing in for actors who were pretending to be people who didn't even exist. How was that for questioning your identity?

He heard a car pull up in front of the house. The doorbell chimed and it was Silja. She was wearing a white diaphanous dress with big yellow poppies printed on it, and wedge-heeled sandals that were laced all the way up her calves. She kissed him directly on the lips. Her perfume smelled like summer flowers.

'Am I the first?'

'Yes, but that's OK. It'll give us a chance to talk. Mo Speller's coming round tonight and he never lets anybody else get a word in edgewise.'

'Nice place,' said Silja, walking through to the living room. It was still decorated according to Jenna's tastes – with pale lemon walls and white-upholstered couches, and white ceramic jugs and figurines.

'I've been here nearly eight years now. Bought it from Jimmy Volante when he retired. You know, the guy who used to do Happy Pappy on children's TV. Or probably you don't know. Way before your time.'

Silja went out on to the veranda. The setting sun shone through her dress, and Noah couldn't help noticing that she was wearing nothing underneath but a white lace thong. He coughed and said, 'How about a glass of wine?'

'Why not? I have two days free before I have to fly back to London. God, I hate that Pinewood Studios. It's like a prison camp. And it never stopped raining.'

'So what's this interesting something that you wanted to show me?'

'I tried to call you, but I can never work out the time difference. Is it nine hours behind or nine hours ahead? Anyhow, when I found out that I was coming back here, I brought it with me.'

She opened her small white purse and took out a folded page torn from a magazine. She spread it out on the table and said, 'This was in the *Telegraph* magazine last Saturday. It was an article about suicide bombers. I was only reading it because I was bored and there was nothing else to read.'

The headline said, *Destination: Heaven.* There were several pictures of Middle Eastern suicide bombers, posing in front of political banners. To Noah, they all looked pretty much the same, their heads tied with scarves, some of them trying to look intimidating, some of them grinning as if they were posing for holiday photographs, but all of them painfully young.

'What am I looking for?' he asked.

'This one,' said Silja, and pointed to the largest photograph. It showed a young man in glasses with a wispy moustache. Unlike the others, he was standing in front of a plain background, with no Arabic messages written on it. He was wearing a black shirt, open at the front, revealing a chain and a circular medallion.

The caption underneath the photograph read, *Abdul al-Hamiz, 21, who blew himself up in front of the Taj Hotel,*

Dubai, in an abortive attempt on the life of Adeola Davis, the diplomatic representative of DOVE.

'And?' said Noah.

'Look closer. Look at his medallion.'

Noah picked up the page and held it at an angle, so that the evening sunlight fell across it. The young man's medallion was decorated with a criss-cross pattern of arrows. It looked exactly the same as the medallion that he had retrieved from the bottom of the Mediterranean.

'Now, is that strange or is that not strange?' asked Silja.

'Well, maybe. Here—' Noah went into the living room and opened the top drawer of his white oak desk. The medallion was lying there, together with the *Tabac Cert* box and all kinds of other junk that he had picked up on movie sets – a chrome-plated whistle; six or seven cigarette lighters; several pairs of spectacles with no lenses in them; an Iron Cross; and a large magnifying glass (from a Sherlock Holmes picture, with Michael Caine).

He laid the medallion on top of the photograph and examined both of them closely.

'You're right. They're identical. Eleven – twelve – thirteen – fourteen arrows each. But come on, do you really think that means anything? This is probably a very common pattern in the Middle East. You know, like the Celtic cross in Ireland, or the swastika in India.'

'I don't think so. I have travelled all over, and I have never seen it before. When I saw this picture, I thought to myself, What is the chance that I would come to England and pick up this magazine and see this medallion?'

'Pretty remote, I guess. But that's coincidences for you. Most of the time coincidences are – well, they're very coincidental.'

'No – I don't think this *is* a coincidence. This young man blew himself up less than a month ago. The medallion you found is more than sixty years old. I think this is destiny, trying to explain something to me. Fate.'

Noah didn't know what to say. Wherever he went, he always carried a lucky wooden clothespin with a face painted on it, which his father had made for him when he was a boy. Whenever he spilled salt, he always threw a pinch of it over his left shoulder. But otherwise he wasn't really superstitious. He performed highly hazardous stunts for a living, and he knew that survival wasn't a question of luck: it was a question of timing, judgment, and meticulous preparation.

'We should show this to somebody who knows about these things,' said Silja. 'Didn't you tell me that your ex-girlfriend was a jeweller? Maybe she could tell us.'

'Well, yes, she probably could. But whether she *would* – that's a different story altogether. Let's just say that she and I didn't exactly separate on the friendliest of terms. Crockery was involved. Lots of crockery. And a fish tank.'

'Then maybe a museum?'

'I don't know. I can always *try* talking to Jenna. It's been nearly two years now. Maybe she's cooled off by now.'

The doorbell chimed again. Noah went to open it, and there was Mo Speller, with his third wife, Trina. Mo was wearing a loud purple-spotted shirt and carrying a bottle of wine in each hand. Trina was dressed in a bright yellow dress with a huge bow at the back. She came teetering into the hallway on absurdly high stilettos.

'I'm thinking of buying a pair of those shoes myself,' said Mo. 'I'm sick of all of my wives being two feet taller than me.'

'How are you, Mo?'

'I'm good, I'm good. I'm working too hard, but there you are. It takes a river of blood and an ocean of sweat to write a funny TV show, not to mention a mountain of Chinese take-out.'

'Mo, Trina, this is Silja Fonselius. She and I worked together on *Dead Reckoning*.'

'*Dead Reckoning*? That was Richard Bullman, wasn't it? What a *putz* – excusing my French.'

'Couldn't agree with you more, but the money was good. How about a drink?'

'Just a soda for me, thanks. I had a physical last month and my liver was hiding behind my pancreas and waving a white flag.'

'I'll have a white wine spritzer, if that's OK,' said Trina, batting her eyelashes.

'Easy on the white wine,' said Mo. 'I don't want you falling off those shoes. There could be innocent people passing underneath.'

They took their drinks out on to the veranda. 'Ah, this

wonderful city of ours,' said Mo. 'Don't you think the smog looks ravishing at this time of the day?'

Noah said, 'Silja came over to show me this article. It's all about suicide bombers in the Middle East.'

Mo looked serious. 'One of my cousins was killed that way. In a bar, in Haifa, about fifteen years ago. Well, I didn't know him. But what a way to go. They're devils, those people. Devils. May they all be reincarnated as camel shit.'

Silja leaned forward to show him the photograph. 'I noticed the medallion around this one man's neck,' Silja explained. 'You see it is just the same as *this* medallion, which Noah discovered on the bottom of the ocean off Gibraltar. Look. Identical. But Noah's medallion dates from way back in 1943.'

Mo took off his thick-lensed spectacles and scrutinized the photograph and the medallion from less than two inches away.

'Yes, you're right. That's interesting, isn't it? I mean, I don't know *why* it's interesting, but it's interesting. It's interesting like the number of chickens you can squeeze into a Ford Edsel is interesting.'

'How many exactly *is* that?' asked Trina. 'Chickens, I mean.'

Mo put his spectacles back on and stared at her. 'I was talking hypothetically, my angel.' He looked back at Noah and rolled his eyes up for God to grant him patience. 'But I'll tell you what else is interesting, if you didn't know this already. What do you think these marks are – the ones that look like pointy arrows?'

'I don't have a clue,' Noah admitted.

'Well, I'm going to impress you now. It's some kind of ancient writing. My dope of a son came home from college a couple of weeks ago and he was wearing this purple T-shirt, and it had marks on it just like these.'

'Really?'

'Almost exactly the same. He's taking a course at the UCLA Centre for Jewish Studies, and apparently this was how the Babylonians used to write when the Hebrews were in exile in Babylon. Pointy arrows, scratched into clay tablets. It was a great system. If the scribes wanted to keep what they'd written, they'd bake the tablets in the oven. If they didn't, they rolled them out and turned them into exile souvenir ashtrays.'

'So the marks on these medallions – they probably mean something?'

'I can't be sure, but my son's college professor could probably tell you. The writing on my son's T-shirt, it's a three-thousand-year-old riddle. Something like – when you walk into this house, you're blind, but when you walk out of it, you can see. What kind of a house is it?'

'Not a bar, that's for sure,' put in Trina. 'That would be the other way around. You know, you can see pretty good when you walk *into* it—'

'Thank you, my lovely,' Mo interrupted her. 'We all get the point.'

Silja said, 'Why don't you take this photograph and have your son take it to college? Look – I can use a candle to make a rubbing of this medallion, so that his professor can compare the two of them.'

'Why not?' said Mo. 'My dope of a son might even get some course credits for it.'

Six

Two days later Noah drove up the coast to San Luis Obispo to see Jenna. He had persuaded himself that he only wanted to satisfy his curiosity about the P R C H A L medallion, but at the same time it had given him a legitimate excuse to call on her.

Jenna lived in a white single-storey house on North Tassajara, not far from Cal Poly, with orange trees in the backyard, and a view of the mountains. Noah pulled his black Ford Super Duty truck into the curb a few houses away, and smoked a cigarette before he climbed out. Now that he was here, he was surprised that he felt so apprehensive. What if she was just as attractive as ever? What if she wasn't alone? Jesus – what if she were married?

He walked up the curved concrete path in front of the house and rang the doorbell. Across the street, an old woman in a saggy blue dress stood in her living-room window and stared at him. Noah winked and nodded at her but the old woman didn't acknowledge him.

There was no answer to the doorbell, so Noah walked around the side of the house to the small design studio that Jenna had built on the end of her garage. The door was open and there she was, sitting at her workbench, soldering an elaborate silver brooch.

She had grown her hair. When she and Noah had been together, she had always had it cut into a short, severe bob. Now it reached all the way down her back, shiny and brown. She was wearing a pale blue embroidered blouse and jeans.

He knocked loose-wristed on the open door. She didn't look up at first, because she was concentrating on her soldering. 'Just a second – soon as I've done this. You can leave it on the bench if it doesn't need to be signed for.'

Noah waited until she'd finished. She put down her soldering iron and turned around. 'My *God*,' she said. 'Noah – the return of the living dead!'

'How are you doing, Jenna?' He smiled. He glanced around the studio walls, which were cluttered with sketches and photographs of bracelets and earrings and brooches. 'Looks like you're keeping yourself busy.'

'Busy? It's crazy. I'm freelancing for B. Anthony and Company – engagement rings, mostly. Things have been really, really great.'

'I'm happy for you. You're very talented. You deserve it.'

'How about you?'

'Oh, the usual. Falling off buildings, jumping through hoops, setting fire to myself.'

'You look good. Thinner. A little more grey.'

'Well, time takes its toll.'

She switched off her soldering iron. 'Are you here for a reason? Don't tell me you just happened to be passing along North Tassajara and you just decided to drop in.'

'No, I came to see you to ask your opinion about something.' He took the P R C H A L medallion out of his pocket and held it up. 'I found this on the seabed off Gibraltar. I was wondering if you knew what it was. I showed it to Mo Speller and he said it had some kind of ancient writing on it. Babylonian, that's what he thought.'

Jenna took the medallion and laid it on the workbench in

front of her. She put on a pair of magnifying eyeglasses and examined it carefully, both sides.

'*Mo Speller* knew what this was?' she asked, incredulous.

'Yes – I was surprised, too. But his son is studying ancient Jewish history at UCLA. Mo recognized the characters from some T-shirt the kid was wearing.'

Jenna frowned. 'Well, I'm not a linguist, or an archaeologist, but I think he could be right. The one thing I can tell you for sure is that this is a very old piece of jewellery.'

Noah watched as she turned the medallion this way and that. He wasn't sure that he liked her hair so long. It made her look younger and freer, and maybe that was why. She was just as alluring, though, with those large brown eyes and that heart-shaped face that had always reminded him of a fairy from a children's picture book.

'What's it made of?' he asked her.

'It's black because it's so tarnished, but I'm pretty confident it's solid silver.'

'And when you say "very old" . . . ?'

'I couldn't be sure,' said Jenna, taking off her glasses. 'But a couple of years ago some Israeli archaeologists found a collection of Babylonian jewellery in a cave near the Dead Sea. Like – historically – it was a really important find, because it proved beyond any question that the Jewish aristocracy had been taken into exile in Babylon by King Nebuchadnezzar and then sent home again forty-eight years later by Cyrus the Persian. You know – 'by the rivers of Babylon, where we sat and wept, when we remembered Zion . . .'

'I know. Boney M, wasn't it?'

Jenna smiled. 'The archaeologists found a silver mirror, and a make-up kit, and a pendant that was very much like this one. You see this crescent-shaped moon? That's absolutely typical of Babylonian designs, and these small circles are supposed to be pomegranates. The Babylonians made some amazing jewellery. They knew how to weld, how to mix alloys, they even knew how to enamel. If this is genuine, it could be more than two and a half thousand years old.'

'Jesus! That's a serious antique.'

Jenna handed the medallion back to him. 'Like I say, I can't be absolutely certain. You'll have to have it properly tested. But it could be worth a heck of a lot of money. I can give you the names of a couple of jewellers in LA who specialize in antiquities.'

'What about the letters on the back, P R C H A L?'

'I don't know – but they were engraved much more recently, in modern times. Do you know what they stand for?'

Noah shook his head. 'I looked up P R C H A L on the Internet and all I found was an eminent professor of applied physics from the University of Someplace Unpronounceable in Eastern Europe.'

Jenna stood up and swept back her hair with both hands. 'Is that all you wanted me to look at?'

'Of course not. I wanted you to admire my suntan.'

'Would you like a glass of wine? I have some of that Stag's Leap Chardonnay you always used to drink.'

'Sure, yes, if you're offering.'

They sat on a beech-wood bench in the backyard under one of the orange trees. It was almost noon now, and the mountains rippled in the rising heat.

'You – uh – *seeing* anyone?' asked Noah. Jenna was wearing mirrored sunglasses now and all he could see in her eyes were two curved images of himself.

'Casually, yes. He's a lawyer.'

'A lawyer? I can't imagine you dating a lawyer.'

'Why not? He's a very smart lawyer. He's also a very handsome lawyer and a very wealthy lawyer. How about you?'

'I met this three-hundred-pound belly dancer in Morocco – but, no – there's nobody special. Not at the moment. After you and me, I guess I'm kind of wary about commitment.'

Jenna smiled. 'You'll find somebody some day – somebody who doesn't mind your unpredictable moods and your pesky little habits and the illogical nonsense you talk when you're drunk.'

'Hey – I don't drink these days. Not so much, anyhow. And when did I ever talk illogical nonsense? And moody? I never thought I was *moody*. And what's so pesky about wanting somebody to squeeze the toothpaste tube at the end instead of the middle?'

'There you go again, and you've only had half a glass of Chardonnay!'

Noah stayed for nearly an hour. He still enjoyed Jenna's

company, and he was still captivated by the way she looked, but he knew there was no point in trying to rekindle their affair. He would never change, and neither would she. In spite of her fairy-book face, she had always been stubborn and wilful and she always spoke her mind. Their relationship had been one long argument, punctuated by long nights of sweaty grappling in bed.

As Noah left, Jenna took off her sunglasses and said, 'Let me know what you find out about that medallion.'

'Sure.' He kissed her on both cheeks, but then she kissed him directly on the lips.

'Don't get any ideas,' she said. 'That was for old times' sake.'

He turned his truck around and gave her a wave and a blast on his horn. As he drove away, he glimpsed her in his rear-view mirror, standing by the curb. She lifted her arm once, although she couldn't have known whether he was watching her or not. He had been aware that he would have mixed feelings about her when he met her again, but he had never realized how conflicting those feelings would be, or how strong.

Just because they were so obviously bad for each other didn't mean that he didn't still want her.

He had almost reached the end of the street when he saw a silver Buick sedan draw up outside Jenna's house and park. He slowed down and pulled over. Maybe this was the lawyer. It would be interesting to see what he looked like, and how old he was. Noah had always been self-conscious about his age, compared to Jenna's. When they had been together, he had lost count of the times that he had been gushingly greeted with 'How *wonderful* to meet you! You must be Jenna's father!' He had always tried to convince himself that it was his prematurely grey hair that aged him so much.

He saw Jenna lean over and talk to the passenger. Then he saw the driver get out and walk around the car: a heavily-built black man in a pale grey suit. The passenger got out, too, a blond-haired man with sunglasses. It looked as if they were taking hold of Jenna's arms and leading her back into the house.

Noah twisted around in his seat. What the hell was all that about? He hadn't been able to see too clearly, but the way the two men had hurried Jenna through her front door had given him the distinct impression that she had been *forced* inside, against her will.

He backed his Super Duty up the street, very fast, and slewed it around 180 degrees in front of Jenna's house. He jumped down from the driver's seat and ran up her path. The door was closed, and when he tried the handle, he found that it was locked. But he hammered on it with his fist and shouted out, 'Jenna! It's Noah. Is everything OK? *Jenna!*'

He hammered again, but there was no answer, so he decided to try around the back. Just as he turned away from the front door, however, another silver sedan came speeding up the road and slid to a halt right behind his truck. Two more men climbed out, both wearing dark glasses and light grey suits. One of them was tall and bulky, and walked with a muscle-bound waddle, like a wrestler. His face was flat and round, maybe Hawaiian, and his hair was knotted at the back of his neck in a tiny pigtail. The other man was short and slight and spidery, with an unusually small head.

'Who are you?' Noah demanded. 'What's going on here?'

'Who has the medallion?' asked the spidery man. 'Did you give it to your girlfriend, or do you still have it?'

'What? What the hell are you talking about? What medallion?'

'Come on, Mr Flynn. You know darned well what medallion.'

'Who the hell are you? Are you cops or what? Where's your ID?'

The spidery man came up to him and took off his dark glasses. He had a bony, complicated nose and glittery eyes that were too close together, as if there had scarcely been enough space on his face to crowd in all of his features. He smelled strongly of mentholated chest rub.

'The medallion doesn't belong to you, Mr Flynn. I need you to give it to me.'

The Hawaiian-looking man came closer, and stood with his legs apart, interlacing his fingers and flexing them backward and forward. He was such a typecast heavy that Noah couldn't help shaking his head in derision.

'Something's funny?' asked the spidery man.

'On the contrary. Something's very serious. You're obviously not cops. So – if you don't get off my girlfriend's property right now, you and Kwongo here are going to be in very serious trouble.'

'I don't think you understand the position you're in, Mr Flynn.'

'Oh – I understand all right. I understand that I've had more than enough of you for one lifetime, and I'm less-than-politely requesting that you leave. You, and those two guys indoors. I'm guessing by the matching sedans and the matching suits that you all belong to the same scout troupe?'

The front door suddenly opened and the black man appeared. 'She says she don't have it.'

'Do you believe her?'

'Oh, sure,' said the black man. 'I believe her.'

Noah immediately stalked over to him and seized him by the lapels. 'What are you doing to her? Have you touched her?'

He forced the man backwards and banged his head against the side of the door before losing his balance and lurching sideways. But the spidery man snapped, 'Mr Flynn! Hold it, Mr Flynn!'

Noah let the black man drop on to one knee, and turned around. The Hawaiian-looking man was holding open one side of his coat to reveal that he was pointing an automatic at him.

'John here *will* shoot you if you cause us any trouble, Mr Flynn.'

Noah didn't say anything, but cautiously raised his hands. He had a deep respect for firearms, especially when they were pointing in *his* direction.

'Let's go inside, shall we?' said the spidery man. 'Kind of public, out here on the street.' Across the road, the old woman in the blue saggy dress was standing at her window, watching them. 'You first, Mr Flynn.'

Noah walked through the narrow hallway that led to the back of the house, and the three men in grey suits followed him. The Shaker-style kitchen was filled with sunshine, and a vase of sunflowers stood on the window ledge.

Jenna was sitting tied to one of the wheel-back chairs, next to the butcher-block table. Arranged on the table in order of size were six or seven knives – carving knives, vegetable knives and boning knives.

'Noah?' she said, in a high, frightened voice. 'Noah – what's going on? They said they wanted your medallion. They said they'd kill me if I didn't give it to them!'

Seven

Noah turned to the spidery man and demanded, 'What the hell is this? Who are you people?'

'You really don't need to know that,' said the spidery man. 'You already know far more than is healthy for you, believe me.'

'I don't know nothing about anything! This is crazy!'

The spidery man held out his hand. 'The medallion, Mr Flynn.'

Noah lifted the P R C H A L medallion out of his shirt pocket and held it out. The spidery man snatched it, gave it a quick sideways glance, and dropped it into his own pocket.

'You see? That wasn't very difficult, was it? There was no need for anybody to be unpleasant.'

'So – you've got what you came for,' said Noah. 'You can go now.'

The spidery man carefully ran his fingers through his black, slicked-back hair, as if he were searching for phrenological bumps to predict his immediate future.

'Problem is, Mr Flynn, that you and your young lady here both know the significance of this medallion.'

'What significance? I just told you! I don't know what the hell it is or what's written on it or what P R C H A L means or nothing!'

'You know much more than you think you know. And that is why I have to make sure that this all finishes here. Today. Now.'

The spidery man clicked his fingers, and the black man and the Hawaiian approached Noah from either side and seized his arms. Noah tried to struggle, but the Hawaiian pushed the muzzle of his automatic hard against his right cheekbone.

The spidery man came close to Noah, reeking of menthol.

'You want it sooner, Mr Flynn, or later? The choice is entirely yours.'

'What's this really all about?' Noah panted. 'If you're going to kill us, I think we deserve to know why.'

The spidery man gave a snort of disbelief. 'You don't seriously think that I'm going to stand here for ten minutes and give you a detailed explanation of why you have to die? What do you think this is, *Murder, She Wrote?*'

'At least tell me how you found out that I had the medallion, and how you tracked me down.'

'No.'

Now the blond-haired man stepped forward. He was the only one who kept his dark glasses on. He was slim, and obviously fit, and he walked rather like a dancer, with an uncanny gliding motion. He went up to the butcher's block table and examined the knives. Eventually he picked up a poultry knife with a thin, ten-inch blade. He ran the edge of it along the ball of his thumb. A bead of bright red blood appeared, and he sucked it.

Noah struggled even harder to wrench himself free, but his captors were both powerful men and the Hawaiian jammed the gun muzzle even harder into his face. 'You want it now? You want to say *aloha 'oe* even before you find out what happens to your girlfriend?'

'Up your *okole*,' Noah grunted. He was bursting with fear and adrenaline but also a blazing sense of injustice. Why were he and Jenna going to be killed, just because he had showed her that medallion? It may have been stolen from someone who was prepared to kill to get it back, but it had been lying on the seabed for over sixty years, so it was obvious that Noah himself hadn't stolen it. And even if it had some political or criminal significance, Noah certainly had no idea what it was.

'I can tell you just one thing,' said the spidery man. 'Everything in life is connected to everything else, and you, you poor idiot – you found out how. Or *will* find out, if I allow you to live.'

'Noah – please – don't let them hurt me!' Jenna begged. 'Noah – I'm pregnant!'

'*What?*'

'I'm three months' pregnant. David – I'm having his baby!' Noah turned to the spidery man in fury. 'Do you hear that?

She's pregnant! You can't kill a pregnant woman! You'd be killing her child as well!'

'I'm sorry. Maybe you should have thought of that before.'

'I didn't *know* that before! I didn't know nothing before! I still don't know nothing! I don't understand what any of this means and I don't understand why you want to kill us! I mean, what significance can that medallion possibly have, that you have to kill people before they find out what it is? *What?*'

The spidery man leaned closer – so close that Noah could feel his breath against his cheek. 'Chaos,' he whispered. 'Chaos and old Night.'

Noah swallowed hard. He felt as if he had a large knot of gristle in his throat, and his eyes were filling with tears of frustration.

'I don't know what you mean,' he said, hoarsely. 'I simply don't understand why. Please – don't hurt her. Don't kill her baby. I love her.'

The spidery man stayed very close, his face only inches away. He smiled, and then he said, 'Love is no excuse for mercy, Mr Flynn.'

'You're going to regret this, you son of a bitch!'

'No, I'm not. Go on, Henry. We don't have all day.'

The blond-haired man walked around behind Jenna's chair.

'*No!*' Noah roared, but without any hesitation the blond-haired man reached around and drew the poultry knife across Jenna's throat. Jenna stared at Noah in horror and disbelief as the front of her blouse was suddenly drenched in bright, wet blood.

Noah twisted and kicked, but he was professional enough to realize that struggling wasn't going to do him any good. He had also witnessed enough serious injuries to know that Jenna's wound was fatal, and that even if these men allowed him to try, there wasn't a hope in hell that he could save her life.

More than that, he knew that nothing was going to stop them from cutting *his* throat, too.

Jenna's head dropped forward on to her chest. She was wheezing and choking as she gasped for breath. A large pink bubble of blood swelled from the side of her neck and then burst.

'See?' said the spidery man, with obvious satisfaction. 'Pretty painless way to go, as ways to go go.'

Noah said nothing, but squeezed his eyes tight shut for a moment and filled his lungs with air. He expanded his chest and braced his arm muscles, like a bodybuilder.

The blond-haired man pulled a dishcloth off the rail and wiped the poultry knife. Then, with a grin, he came gliding around the kitchen table, holding the knife up high as if he were a matador, about to give the *coup de grâce* to a helpless bull.

'I wish I could say I was sorry about this,' said the spidery man, with a sniff. 'But, you know – needs must.'

As the blond-haired man approached him, Noah exhaled and relaxed his muscles and dropped to the floor as if his legs had given way. He fell out of his captors' grasp as if he had vanished altogether, leaving nothing but his empty polo shirt and jeans.

He knew what a risk he was taking. The Hawaiian could shoot him on the spot. But in a sleepy neighbourhood like North Tassajara, he was gambling that they were reluctant to attract attention with gunfire.

He tilted himself forward and then sprang to his feet. Without any hesitation, he vaulted over the kitchen table and charged straight for the French doors that gave out on to the backyard. Shielding his face with his upraised elbows, he threw himself through the left-hand door. Glazing bars splintered, glass shattered, and then he was tumbling across the red-brick patio in a classic stuntman's roll.

He heard the spidery man shouting, 'Stop him, Makaha, you moron!' But there was no shot. He picked himself up and sprinted around the side of the house, past Jenna's studio, across the front yard and into the street. As he was climbing into his truck, the Hawaiian and the black man came bursting out of the front door.

Noah started up the Super Duty with a deep whistling roar from its 6.8-litre engine, and pulled away from the curb with an operatic scream from its tyres. But instead of heading back towards the coast, he deliberately drove uphill. If he could lose these bastards anywhere, he could lose them on the curves and chicanes of the Santa Lucia Mountains.

He glanced in his rear-view mirror. The Hawaiian and the black man were already climbing into their sedan, and the spidery man and the blond man were running towards the other car.

After a mile, the neat suburban houses disappeared, and the ground began to rise steeply. The road became narrower, with rocks and scrub on either side, and then bristlecone fir trees and ponderosa pines. Noah swerved around one curve after another, keeping his foot flat on the accelerator, and allowing the Super Duty's natural understeer to hold it on the road. The sun flickered through the trees like an old-fashioned movie projector.

As he climbed higher, Noah glimpsed the ocean off to his left, intensely blue. The last time he had driven up here, Jenna had been with him. He had pulled off the road and they had sat and talked about their future together – or, rather, their mutual realization that they didn't have a future together.

He saw a flash of silver in his rear-view mirror. The Hawaiian and the black man were gaining on him. When he took a right-hand curve, their silver sedan disappeared behind the trees, but when he took a left-hand curve, he could see that they were less than a hundred yards behind him. The Hawaiian may have looked like a B-picture heavy, but he was obviously a skilful driver.

The mountains grew steeper, and as they did so the curves became tighter. Noah struggled with the steering wheel as the Super Duty threatened to lose its grip on the road, and now its tyres were almost constantly howling. He saw the silver sedan go into a wide, drifting skid around one curve, but the Hawaiian managed to keep it on the road with a snake-like twitch of its tail.

They sped around a long, left-hand curve. As they did so, Noah heard a shot, and then another. Missed, both of them. But then a bullet hit the back of his cab, with a loud metallic bang. A few seconds later, just before the road curved to the right, his rear window shattered.

Damn it, these guys were good. It was one thing to drive in a movie car chase, in which every twist and slide had been meticulously choreographed beforehand, and every bullet-strike was nothing but an electronically-detonated squib, but these guys had no idea where he was taking them, yet they were quickly catching up with him, and they were hitting him, too.

He was only a half-mile away from the place where he had turned off the road to talk to Jenna – a very steep, down-sloping parking area on the right-hand side of the road, with a view through the trees toward Morro Bay, coming after a long right-hand, curve.

Noah managed to keep well ahead of the silver sedan as his Super Duty screamed around the curve. Now and then he caught sight of their gleaming front grille, but he didn't give them the opportunity to take another clear shot.

He flashed past the sign that warned 'Dangerous Curve', and put his foot down even harder. He could see that the silver sedan was accelerating too, but he needed to be out of sight when he reached the next bend. He didn't want them to see his brake lights.

He was screaming around the curve at fifty-five now – sixty – sixty-five – and the Super Duty was swaying and rolling like a boat in a heavy sea. Two or three miles an hour faster and it would lose its grip on the road altogether, and go tumbling over and over into the trees. Noah could feel its tyre treads clawing to keep their hold on the blacktop, and how close they were to breaking away: he had rolled two trucks for the movie *Race With The Devil*, and he could almost hear the rubber screaming to him in panic.

The turning was suddenly up ahead of him. He saw the gap in the trees, the slope that led down to the parking area. He stood on his brakes and the Super Duty's tyres gripped the road so hard that they smoked. Even so, he was still going too fast as he hurtled and bounced down the hill, and he had to spin the steering wheel so that the Super Duty slithered sideways. There was a low retaining wall at the bottom of the parking area, made of pine logs, and he collided with it broadside.

But his plan had worked. As he sat there, winded and bruised, there was a bang like a cannon going off. The silver sedan came flying over the parking area, its engine screaming, and crashed into the trees below. There was another bang, but much deeper this time, and a ball of orange flame rolled up into the sky.

Noah jumped down from his truck and balanced on top of the retaining wall. He could see that the silver sedan was wedged on its side between two tall pines, and that it was blazing fiercely. Nobody could have survived that.

He waited a little longer, to see if the second sedan would appear. One minute went past . . . two. All he could hear was birds twittering and the odd buckling sound of overheated metal. At last he climbed back into his truck and drove cautiously back up to the highway. The road was deserted. No cars, no emergency services, nothing. If the spidery man and the blond man had been following close behind, they had probably decided that discretion was the better part of being cold-blooded killers, and carried on going.

Noah drove slowly back down to North Tassajara. Three police cars and an ambulance were already clustered around Jenna's house, their red lights flashing. Presumably the old lady across the road had called them. Noah parked and walked up to the police line.

'Help you?' demanded a freckled young police officer.

'I shouldn't think so,' said Noah. 'Not unless you know how to bring dead people back to life.'

Eight

I t was 9.07 that evening before Detective Willis came in to say, 'It's OK, Mr Flynn. You can leave now. And your ride's arrived.'

'Hallelujah! Are you sure you don't want to ask me the same questions all over again? That's all you've been doing since you brought me here.'

'I'm sorry, sir. When it comes to homicide, we have to be thorough.'

Noah stood up wearily. 'You'll keep me in touch with any progress, won't you? Especially if you find out who those two dead guys are.'

Detective Willis gave him a non-committal blink. 'We'll call you if we need to ask you any more questions, sir. Or if we need you to make any IDs.'

'You catch those other two sons of bitches, that's all I'm asking for. The blond one in particular. I want to be sitting there watching when they give him the needle.'

'We'll be doing our best, sir, believe me.'

Noah looked at him. Detective Willis was a short, pot-bellied man with a stringy comb-over and two double chins. He looked like Martin Balsam's less successful brother. He had been interviewing Noah continuously since three that afternoon, joined from time to time by two other detectives from the San Luis Obispo Police Department and two officers from the California Highway Patrol.

Noah had told Detective Willis everything that had happened, six or seven times, in painstaking detail. How the blond-haired man had cut Jenna's throat. The high-speed chase through the mountains. But in all of that he hadn't mentioned the medallion. His visit to Jenna had been totally spontaneous, he had explained, simply to see how she was getting along.

He didn't exactly understand *why* he hadn't mentioned the medallion. After all, it could have helped Detective Willis to establish motive, and to identify their assailants. But his natural reticence told him that it was more prudent if he kept it to himself, at least for now.

First of all, he felt that he needed to find out what the medallion really was, and why those men had wanted it so badly. How had they known that he had it in his possession? He had told almost nobody about it, except for Silja and Mo and his friend Bob Fairman, a set designer for *Dead Reckoning*.

How had they known that he was taking the medallion to show Jenna? And why had they thought it necessary to kill them both? He had no idea what the medallion signified, if it signified anything at all. Jenna had told him that it was very old, probably Babylonian, but he still didn't know where it had originally come from, or what any of the markings on it meant. Up until today, he hadn't been particularly interested in finding out.

He knew from the photograph that Silja had shown him that there was a second medallion in existence, but that was all. Maybe that was the key to it. Maybe P R C H A L was the key to it. If he found out what P R C H A L meant, or who P R C H A L was, everything would click into place. Or maybe not.

'I'll call you tomorrow, Mr Flynn, when the Highway Patrol have finished with your vehicle,' Detective Willis said, interrupting Noah's ruminations.

'OK.'

'I know this hasn't been easy, sir, and we're very sorry for your loss, but if you do think of anything else, you will call me, won't you? I'd really like to find out why those jokers attacked you.'

'Just didn't like our faces, I guess.'

'That's possible. Your common or garden variety sadism. But, usually, when somebody's attacked the way you were, it's for one of two reasons. Either it's revenge for some insult or betrayal, real or imagined—'

He hesitated, took out his handkerchief, and wiped his nose.

'Yes?' Noah prompted. 'What's the second reason?'

'The second reason is to keep the victims permanently quiet, because they know something the perpetrators don't want anybody else to know, ever.'

There was a lengthy, uncomfortable silence. At last Noah said, 'Well, Detective, wish I could have helped you more. But like I told you, I didn't know any of those men from Adam, and I certainly don't know why they should have wanted us dead. For whatever reason.'

Detective Willis said nothing, but nodded, as if he only half-believed him.

Silja was waiting by the front desk, in a green silk sweater and tight blue jeans. When Noah came out, she hurried over to him and put her arms around him.

'Oh, Noah. I'm so sorry! What a terrible shock!'

'Thanks. I don't think it's really sunk in yet.'

'Do the police know who it was who attacked you?'

Noah shook his head. 'I gave them a full description, but no. They're not on any wanted lists, either. But listen, let's get out of here. I need to talk to you.'

'What do you want to do? Do you want to go home? You can stay with me if you don't feel like being alone.'

'Let's just drive.'

Silja's red Mercedes convertible was parked outside on Walnut Street. Detective Willis followed them out and stood on the steps of the police station with his arms folded, watching them as they climbed into the car. It was a warm, windy night, and a newspaper helter-skeltered along the gutter.

'That's one suspicious cop,' said Noah.

'He's suspicious of *you*? What did *you* do?'

They pulled away from the curb and headed south, back towards Los Angeles. Silja said, 'It was on the news, on the TV, what happened. It was dreadful. I can't understand why those men should have wanted to kill you.'

Noah turned around. They were out of San Luis Obispo now, heading south towards Pismo Beach, but he wanted to make sure that nobody was following them.

'They wanted the medallion,' he said. 'In fact, they took it from me.'

'The medallion? You mean your medallion from Gibraltar? Why did they want that?'

'I don't know. But they seemed to think that I knew. That was why they cut Jenna's throat and that was why they were going to do the same to me.'

'I don't understand.'

'Me neither. But I'm going to find out, even if it kills me.'

Silja glanced at him. 'Don't say that. It's terrible enough that Jenna should be dead.'

'That's why I have to find out who they are, and why they wanted the medallion so badly.'

'Don't you think you should stay away from people like that? As far as possible?'

Noah patted his pockets for his cigarettes. 'Maybe the medallion is like a clue to something, like sunken treasure. Maybe it's some kind of religious talisman. Maybe they think they can use it to raise the devil, or identify the true Christ.'

'Or maybe your imagination runs away with you like a mad person.'

'Do you have a cigarette? Thanks. I don't know, Silja, I can't just sit on my hands and wait for the police to find out who killed Jenna. I'm grieving too much. I'm *hurt*. I'm too fucking angry.'

'Maybe Mo's son has found out something about it. He was going to show that newspaper photograph to his college professor, yes? And that rubbing I made, with the candle.'

'Yes – that's a thought. Mind you, knowing Leon, he's probably lost both of them.'

Noah tried calling Mo on his cellphone, but all he heard was his answerphone message: '*You have reached the poverty-wracked home of Moses Speller. If you are an ex-wife with a*

*query about alimony, your call will be answered in strict rota-
tion. If you are a representative of the IRS, or if you are trying
to sell me a year's supply of geriatric incontinence pads,
please hang up now.'*
'Not picking up,' Noah said. 'He usually hits the sack early.
I'll call him tomorrow.'

They drove towards Los Angeles in silence. As they waited
to turn left on to Sunset, Silja turned to Noah and took hold
of his hand. 'It doesn't matter if you wish to cry,' she said.
    Noah wiped his tears with his fingers. 'Goddamned bug in
my eye, that's all.'

Silja drove him back to his house, and parked outside, underneath the purple jacaranda tree.
    'Come in,' he told her. 'Have a drink. I don't like to drink
on my own.'
    'If I have a drink, I cannot drive.'
    'Then stay.'
    They went inside the house. It smelled of cedar wood and
the Arabica coffee that he had filtered that morning, before
he had driven to San Luis Obispo to see Jenna. He switched
on two or three table lamps but he didn't close the drapes.
He wanted to see the glitter of Los Angeles spread out below.
It was like a complicated puzzle, made out of millions of
coloured lights.
    'Wine?' he asked.
    'Yes, white, please. I wonder if you're still on the TV news.'
    'If I am, I don't want to see it.'
    Silja sat down on one of the white leather couches and
kicked off her wedge-heeled sandals. 'Did you have the chance
to show the medallion to Jenna? You don't mind my asking
this?'
    Noah came in from the kitchen with two bowl-like glasses
of Pinot Grigio, very cold. 'Of course not, no. She said it was
made out of silver and it probably came from ancient Babylon,
because of the writing on it. It could have been over two and
a half thousand years old.'
    'That's amazing! And that's also very strange, don't you
think? If it is so old, it must be very rare. Yet here was this
young suicide bomber wearing one almost the same.'

Noah sat down next to her, lit two cigarettes and passed her one. 'You know something, I was going to give up smoking after this pack. Too damned dangerous.'

'These men are much more dangerous. If they wanted today to kill you, because of this thing you are supposed to know, who says they will not try again to kill you? I think you should stay someplace else for a while. Someplace where they can't find you.'

'What's the point of that? I have script meetings all next week. Don't tell me they won't be able to follow me home from the studios, no matter where I go.'

'Then cancel your meetings.'

'I can't afford to. Besides, I'm damned if I'm going to let them intimidate me. I'm staying here, no matter what.'

They stayed up until two thirty in the morning, talking and drinking. At first, Noah thought he was going to be too upset to sleep, but suddenly he was overtaken by a dark wave of exhaustion, both physical and emotional. He let his head drop back on to the sofa cushion.

'What's wrong?' asked Silja.

'I'm totally bushed. I have to go to bed.'

'OK. That's OK. Some sleep will do you good. Do you want me to stay?'

'It's your choice. Do you have to make an early start tomorrow?'

'I'm supposed to be meeting my sister. We were planning to go to Rodeo Drive and spend her husband's money. But I can always make it another day.'

Noah stood up. 'I'll find you some clean towels.'

'No – I can take care of myself. You just go to bed. You look terrible.'

'Thanks for the compliment.'

She put her arms around him and held him close. 'Get some rest. What happened to you today, you're going to need all of your strength to get over it.'

'Thanks, Silja. You don't know how much I appreciate this.'

He went through to his bedroom, stripped off his polo shirt and tossed it on to the chair. Then he sat down on the end of his bed and unfastened his jeans. Like the rest of the house, the bedroom hadn't changed since Jenna had redecorated it. The walls were a cool eau-de-Nil colour, and the cotton drapes over the head of the bed were cream with pale green lilies on them. On the walls hung splashy silk-screen prints of tulip fields by the Dutch artist Jan Cremer.

Noah crawled under the sheet and drew it over his head, to close out the world. It takes the average person seven minutes to fall asleep. It took Noah less than two.

Almost immediately, he began to dream. He was walking along a corridor with a stone-flagged floor. There were windows on either side, covered with pierced wooden screens. Through the screens he could see that it was hot and sunny outside, and that scores of people in black robes were silently gathered under large black sunshades.

'Chaos,' said a disembodied voice. 'Chaos, and old Night.'

He began to feel uneasy. Something was wrong. He started to walk along the corridor more quickly, the soles of his shoes scuffing on the floor.

Jenna. Somebody was threatening Jenna . . .

He reached a door and tried the handle. It was locked. *Jenna.* He rattled the handle hard but it still wouldn't open.

He hurried to the next door. That, too, was locked. *Jenna where are you? Jenna!*

He heard a click. The first door had swung open, all by itself. He stared at it, afraid to go back, afraid of what he might see. But he went, very slowly, as if the air in the corridor were as thick as warm glue.

He reached the open doorway and looked inside. The room was crowded with dozens of different chairs: some modern, some antique; some Oriental, some Western.

'You see,' said the disembodied voice, 'all of these chairs are empty now. And why?'

He turned towards the window. Jenna was standing there, with her back to him, looking through the pierced screen. She was wearing a black robe like the people outside.

Jenna!

He started to move towards her, but as he did so she slowly turned around. At least her body turned around, but her head had been completely severed, and it tilted sideways and fell. He could see her face staring at him as it dropped to the floor.

Her lips were moving as if she were trying to call out to him – trying to tell him something important.

Her head hit the floor with a spattering of bright red blood, and rolled underneath one of the chairs.

Jenna!

He felt long cool arms entwined around him, and he heard a woman saying, 'Hush. Hush, Noah. It's only a dream.'

He opened his eyes. His eyelashes were wet, as if he had been crying. He turned his head and saw that Silja was lying close beside him.

'Silja?'

'Hush,' she said, stroking his forehead. 'You were shouting in your sleep. I only came in to calm you down.'

He didn't say anything, but allowed Silja to shush him and stroke him. She was naked apart from a tiny pair of white panties. She was so pale that her skin was almost luminous in the darkness. Her shoulders were wide and angular, but her breasts were small and rounded, with a visible tracery of blue veins, and nipples that were tinged with only the faintest of pinks.

'You were dreaming of Jenna?' she asked him, touching his eyelids with her fingertips.

He nodded. 'I can't understand why those men thought they had to kill us. Neither of us knew anything about their goddamned medallion.'

'Maybe you're wrong. Maybe you *do* know, but you just can't see it. Maybe it has something to do with that suicide bomber. You should talk to the woman he tried to kill – what was her name? Why did they want her dead?'

'Adeola Davis. She's famous. She's some kind of freelance peace ambassador – flies around the world trying to persuade the Palestinians not to blow up the Israelis and the Israelis not to shell the Syrians and the Syrians not to invade Iraq. And so on.'

'You should try to get in touch with her. Maybe she knows what you know.'

'OK, I'll try, right after I've talked to Mo.'

Silja stayed in his bed for the rest of the night but he didn't try to sleep any more. He was afraid to. He sat in his armchair by the window watching her. She stirred only occasionally, and once she whispered something in Finnish.

He thought she looked beautiful. Everything about her was striking and appealing. Her narrow hips, her long toes, the hollows above her collarbone. At another time, he thought, under different circumstances, they could have become lovers, if only for a few weeks. But he knew that he couldn't have made love to Silja without seeing Jenna, and that poultry knife sliding across her throat, and that sudden rush of bright red blood.

Nine

'You had a lucky escape, then?' asked Denis O'Connell, as he passed Adeola a cup of coffee.

'It wasn't luck. My bodyguard took the force of the blast, and he died.'

'Grim business, this sectarian violence. As if we haven't seen enough of it here. As my old father used to say – religion, I don't believe in it.'

'I'm not so sure this was religious. I don't honestly know why that young man wanted to kill me. One of the inspectors from Al Ameen said he was half-Albanian and half-Greek, and that he had flown to Dubai from Athens. For the express purpose of assassinating me, it seems.'

'Well, I suppose you never know with these Middle Eastern characters,' said Denis O'Connell. 'They have some very curious politics, I'd say. At least in Ireland we know where we stand. Whatever it is, we couldn't care two monkeys about it.'

Adeola was meeting with Denis O'Connell on the last leg of her trip back to the United States. They were sitting in the gloomy, high-ceilinged lounge of the Parknasilla Hotel in County Kerry. Outside the window the sky was grey and overcast, and palm trees rustled in a strong, damp wind.

Denis O'Connell was a short, thickset man with curly black

hair. His eyes were bulging and bright blue, and he had a bulbous nose that looked as if God had been left with a little too much nose-putty but blobbed it on regardless. He wore the tan pants from an expensive Italian summer suit, and a blue striped shirt by Charvet, the same French tailor who used to make shirts for the late Taoiseach Charlie Haughey. He was drinking a Beaune that retailed at €345 a bottle.

Adeola said, 'What about Paraguay? You obviously care quite a few monkeys for what's been going on there.'

'I was in Ascensíon only the once, two years ago.'

'And you said your devotions in the Cathedral Blas San de Dia.'

'Yes, I did. And what a wonderful building that is. Very inspiring. I only wish my dear old mother had still been alive to see it.'

Adeola looked across the lounge. In the far corner, Rick and Nesta were sitting, with a tray of coffee between them, staring out of the window like a married couple who could no longer think of anything to say to each other. Adeola knew that close behind her, where the archway led through to the bar, Miko was stationed, and that Jimmy and Charles were keeping watch outside. This might be a highly respectable hotel on the south-west coast of Ireland, but her security arrangements here at Parknasilla had to be as tight as they were in Prague or Panama City.

Adeola said, 'I wonder what your mother thought of the company you were keeping when you said your prayers that morning. Five Muslims. Strange place to meet with Muslims, the largest Roman Catholic cathedral in Paraguay . . .'

Denis O'Connell gave her a sly smile. 'They were my hosts. They were doing nothing more than showing me the sights, so they were. And very gracious they were too.'

'You wouldn't have been discussing a possible trip to Paraguay by Michael Doody and Vincent O'Donovan to train the Jihadi in the making of explosive devices?'

'Adeola, I'm shocked that you should even think such a thing! The idea of it! And who told you?'

Adeola didn't look amused. She was wearing a black trouser suit today and a grey silk shirt, with no jewellery apart from a three-stranded pearl necklace. She knew what a clown Denis O'Connell could be, and she had wanted to appear as grave as possible. There was nothing funny about Muslim terrorists using the mountains of Paraguay as a hideout and a training camp. Operatives from Al-Qaeda were there, as well as Hezbollah, and Hamas, and Islamic Jihad. German intelligence had called the area 'a ticking time bomb'.

'Denis,' said Adeola, 'I know that I'm not going to change your political affiliations, nor am I trying to. But I'm asking you not to pour more gasoline on to the fire.'

Denis O'Connell lifted his glass and swirled his wine around. 'I'm not a man of violence, Adeola. But sometimes in this cockeyed world of ours, things can only be changed by standing up to those who oppress us.'

'DOVE is prepared to make you a deal, Denis.'

'A deal, is it? What manner of deal? Will they pay for the Israelis to pull out of Gaza, or the Yanks to pull out of Iraq? Will they give cash to the British government to surrender at last the occupied territories of Northern Ireland?'

'No. But we will pay you twice what the Jihadis are paying you, and we will guarantee that Doody and O'Donovan are immune from prosecution. Just order them home, and nothing will be said.'

'And what makes you think that I have the influence to do such a thing, even if I wanted to?'

'If you haven't, why did you agree to come here and talk to me?'

Denis O'Connell sipped his wine and patted his lips with a clean white handkerchief. 'You know that I can never resist a beautiful woman, Adeola.'

'Then don't resist me now. Bring Doody and O'Donovan back from Paraguay, and help to make the world a safer place.'

'My God, Adeola. I wish I had your idealism.'

They parted on the understanding that Denis O'Connell would talk to his friends in Dublin, and get back to Adeola when she returned to New York.

'I'm hopeful that we may be able to do some business,' he told her.

'Well, you know what George Herbert said: "He that lives in hope danceth without music."'

'And you know what W.B. Yeats said: "How can we know the dancer from the dance?"'

He kissed her on both cheeks, and then he winked at her.
As he stepped out of the front entrance of the hotel, Rick
came up beside Adeola and asked, 'Think you made any
progress?'

'I'm not too sure. He's about the least trustworthy man I
ever met.'

Rick checked his wristwatch. 'We'd better think about
hitting the bricks. We have to be at the airport by three.'

'Sure. Did you bring my bags down?'

'They're all in the Range Rover.'

Charles appeared, holding up a large golf umbrella. 'It's
just started to rain again. Are you ready?'

Adeola took his arm and together they hurried across the
hotel driveway, with Rick following close behind. The rain
was drifting in from the west, across the Kenmare estuary, a
silvery-grey expanse of water with misty grey mountains on
its southern side.

As she climbed into the shiny black Range Rover, Adeola
turned and took a last look at the hotel. It was a huge Victorian
building, in the Gothic style, with a tower, and had once been
a favourite holiday haunt of George Bernard Shaw. For the
first time in a long time, she wished that she could stay a few
more days, and stop worrying about terrorism and petty wars
and insurrection. The rain smelled so refreshing, and the
estuary was so silent. There were chairs arranged on the patio
overlooking the water, but all of them were empty.

Jimmy and Miko came out of the hotel and looked up at
the rain. Their grey rented Mercedes was parked a hundred
yards away, under the trees.

'We'll catch up with you, OK?'

Nesta was the last to get into the Range Rover, shaking her
head. 'I just washed my hair this morning, and now look at it!'

She turned to smile at Adeola, but as she did so the window
next to her exploded and the left side of her head blew open,
so that blood and brains were sprayed all over the luggage
stowed in the back.

Rick shouted, '*Down!*' and Charles slammed his foot on
the gas. The Range Rover's tyres slithered on the wet asphalt,
and it catapulted forward into the empty chairs, scattering
them in all directions.

There was a loud slamming noise, and then another, and

another, as three high-powered bullets hit the Range Rover's doors. Charles twisted around in his seat, engaged reverse gear, and hit the gas pedal again. The Range Rover sped backward, past the hotel entrance, and Charles yanked the handbrake so that it slewed around in a semicircle.

Just as he was spinning the steering wheel to turn them towards the hotel exit, however, the windshield shattered. Adeola saw it in slow motion, millions of fragments of glittering glass, tumbling over and over. Charles's jaw was blasted away, and then another bullet hit him in the right ear. The Range Rover ran over the herbaceous border that surrounded the hotel lounge, and then collided with the wall.

Rick yelled, 'Adeola! Open the door! Drop to the ground and roll under the vehicle!'

Adeola tugged at the door handle. As she did so, another shot thumped into the Range Rover's bodywork, with such impact that the vehicle swayed. Although the Range Rover was jammed against the side of the building, Adeola managed to open the door wide enough to force her way out of it, one hand reaching down to the ground first, to support herself, and then her head and her shoulders.

She dropped into the wet herbaceous border, and wriggled herself underneath the Range Rover's running board. She heard yet another shot, and another, and she heard Jimmy shouting, 'Miko? *Miko!*'

'Rick?' she called out. 'Rick – where are you?'

She saw Rick's feet as he jumped down from the Range Rover's front seat and came running around to the back. He crouched down and said, 'Come on – we have to get out of here!' His left cheek was decorated with blood.

'Are you hit?' she asked him.

He touched his cheek with his fingertips. 'No. This is Charlie's. Come on, we have to go. If we stay here, they'll come right over and shoot us at point-blank range.'

'Oh, God!'

'Just keep your wits about you. Stay close behind me. Stay low. And keep running.'

'Rick—'

'Save it. Come on, now. On three.'

She crawled out from under the Range Rover and crouched down next to him. It was raining harder now, but apart from the gurgling of the gutters and the drainpipes, the hotel and the grounds around it were strangely silent. Nobody was shouting. Nobody was coming out to see what had happened. There was no sign of Jimmy or Miko.

She could hear somebody's cellphone warbling but that was all. It sounded like Nesta's.

'OK,' said Rick. '*Three!*'

He took hold of her left arm and dragged her out from behind the Range Rover into the open. Crouching down low, they scurried along the front of the hotel towards the entrance.

'Not inside!' said Rick. 'They'll have somebody waiting for us!'

They hurried past the front door. As they did so, Adeola heard a flat, distinctive crack, and a chunk of stone flew across the driveway in front of her. There was another crack, and a privet hedge shivered, as if it were alive.

Rick pulled her across the tennis courts, their feet splashing in shallow puddles. Then they dived down a flight of wet stone steps, and into a series of ornamental gardens.

'Keep running!' he told her.

The gardens were overgrown with large, dripping trees. Adeola saw sundials and blind cherubs and unicorns with moss on their backs. She stumbled and lost one of her shoes but Rick wouldn't let her stop to pick it up. She hopped for a few paces and then kicked the other one off.

Adeola didn't say anything, didn't ask questions. She knew that it was Rick's job to protect her and her best chance for survival was to do what he told her.

They came running out of the gardens to the water's edge. A plank causeway led along the side of the estuary, towards a cluster of small, dark, densely-wooded islands. They ran along it hand in hand, with Adeola's bare feet slapping on the wet planks. They reached the first of the islands, where there was a small bathing hut and a wooden bench. Rick quickly looked around. 'Bastard! He's coming after us. He's not going to give up, this guy.'

Adeola started to turn her head, too, but Rick wrenched her hand and pulled her past the bathing hut and into the woods. After a few yards, however, he stopped.

'You go that way,' he panted, pointing off to the right. 'Keep on running, fast as you can.'

'Where are you going?'

'I'll be looking after you. I promise.'

'But—'

'Go, Adeola – I won't let you down.' He gave her the briefest kiss on the cheek and then he said, '*Go!*'

She started to run along the narrow, zigzag path that led between the trees. The path was stony and wet and tangled with roots, and Adeola's ankles were lashed by stinging nettles, but she bounded along it like a hunted deer. She could hear herself gasping as she ran, almost as if somebody else were running beside her.

The path climbed steeply, and then descended again. She saw water gleaming through the trees ahead of her, and realized that she had reached the far side of the island. She came out beside a wide tributary of the main Kenmare river, over fifty yards wide. Its surface was circled with raindrops. On the opposite bank there was another island, with more woods.

She looked to her right, and saw that there was a narrow dam connecting the two islands, about a hundred yards upstream.

She was just about to start running again when an unfamiliar voice called out, '*Stop!*'

She turned around. A man in khaki camouflage was walking briskly towards her. He was quite slightly built, with a shaven head and a neat black beard. He had a narrow, hawk-like face and close-set eyes. He was carrying a rifle with a very long barrel and telescopic sights.

'Stop, please,' he said. 'There is no profit in your trying to run any further. I will catch you.'

Adeola stayed where she was, her heat drumming, her chest rising and falling.

'You will kneel, and you will close your eyes,' said the man.

'Oh, you think so?' said Adeola, her voice shaking. 'You've just shot two of my friends, you bastard.'

'You *will* kneel, and you *will* close your eyes,' the man repeated.

'And if I won't?'

'Then I will have to kill you standing up, with your eyes wide open. That is all. But it is better for you if you kneel, and close your eyes.'

'Have you ever heard the expression "fuck you"?'

'You should not die with an obscenity on your lips. You

should die with a prayer for forgiveness for all of your transgressions.'

He came closer, and lifted his rifle. Adeola was surprised to see how young he was. Twenty-four, twenty-five, not much older than that.

'Who are you?' she asked him.

'You do not need to know that. You are going to die anyway.'

'What's your name? At least you can tell me your name.'

'You do not need to know my name.'

From the trees on the other side of the river, two or three crows flapped up, cawing harshly. Adeola thought of what Rick had assured her: *I'll be looking after you. I promise.* She looked back at the young man with the rifle and she said, 'All right, then, I'll kneel and close my eyes, if it makes your job any easier.'

'This is not personal hatred,' said the young man. 'I have no ill-feeling for you as a woman.'

'That's good to know. I'd hate to think you were going to kill me out of petty spite.'

'Please,' he said, gesturing with his rifle.

Adeola slowly knelt on the ground. It was soaking wet, peaty, and slippery with layers of half-decomposed leaves.

'And, please, close your eyes.'

She closed her eyes, but then almost immediately opened them again.

'I want to see your expression when you kill me,' she said.

The young man looked disconcerted. It suddenly occurred to Adeola that he might have shot plenty of people at long distance, but never face to face.

'You should close your eyes,' he insisted.

'No, I'm not going to. When I get to the other side, I want to find your ancestors, and I want to tell them exactly what you looked like, when you murdered an innocent woman.'

'You should close your eyes!' he shouted, and he actually stamped his foot.

He was so agitated that he didn't hear Rick emerging from the bushes – or if he did, he didn't realize what it was. That rustling of leaves, that crackling of roots; that could have been the rain, after all. But Adeola watched in fascination as Rick crept right up behind him, close enough to lay a hand on his shoulder, if he had wanted to.

There was a long moment when time seemed to stand still. Adeola felt that even the raindrops were suspended in mid-air. Only the crows continued to squabble, on the other side of the slow-moving river.

Rick whipped a garrotte around the would-be assassin's neck, so fast that Adeola barely saw him do it, and twisted it, hard. The young man's eyes bulged, and he dropped his rifle and reached up to his throat with both hands. But Rick had twisted the garrotte so fiercely that he wasn't even able to exhale.

The young man kicked, and struggled, and clawed at his neck, but Rick stayed firm, never easing the pressure once. For over thirty seconds there was no sound except for the kicking of the young man's heels amongst the leaves. But then his knees gave way, and his arms dropped to his sides. Rick was able to release the garrotte and let him fall sideways on to the ground. He gave an odd, petulant whine as his last breath was finally allowed to escape from his lungs.

Rick thrust the garrotte into his pocket and came over to help Adeola up.

'My God,' she exclaimed. 'You killed him! I can't believe it. But thank you.'

'Didn't have much of a choice,' said Rick.

'Of course not. Of course you didn't. Look at me, I'm shaking like a leaf.'

Rick took off his coat and hung it over her shoulders. 'Come on, we need to get you out of here. I bet all hell's broken loose, back at the hotel.'

'Nesta, and Charlie . . . It's terrible. I hope Jimmy and Miko are OK.'

Rick bent over the young man's body. 'I wonder who the hell he is, and why he wanted to kill you.'

In the distance, Adeola could hear police sirens. 'We should just leave him here. I can square this with the Gardai, I'm sure.'

But Rick was deftly rifling through the young man's pockets. 'No papers. No passport. No driver's license. No wallet. Three clips of ammunition and four or five hundred euros, but that's all.'

'Come on, Rick. Let's go. I'm really not feeling so good.'

'Hey, you're in shock. It's understandable.'

He pulled open the buttons of the young man's combat

shirt. He reached inside and lifted out a heavy silver medallion.

'Leave him,' said Adeola. 'Let's go.'

But Rick unfastened the medallion's chain and held it up. 'Where have you seen one of these before?'

'What? I don't understand.'

'A medallion like this, with these markings on it. That guy who tried to blow us up in Dubai, he was wearing one.'

'I never saw it.'

'His picture was in *Time* magazine. I showed it to you but maybe you didn't really take it in.'

'Well, I kind of remember, but I don't remember any medallion.'

'Exactly like this. With these arrows on it.' He turned it over. 'Look – there's Roman lettering engraved on it, too. K A Z I M I.'

'Ms Davis!' called out an Irish voice, somewhere in the woods. 'Ms Davis! Armed Gardai!'

'I'm here!' Adeola called back. 'I'm OK!'

Rick stood up. He held up the medallion for a moment, and then stowed it in his pocket.

'You're not going to show that to the Gardai?' asked Adeola.

'You think the Kerry cops have the capability to find out who these people are? I've just lost two people, Adeola, and that's supposing they didn't hit Jimmy and Miko, too. I need to know who we're dealing with here.'

Adeola thought about it, and then she nodded. 'OK. I need to know, too.'

Rick put his arm around her, and helped her make her way back up the path. As she hobbled over the stones and the roots, the sun came out, and shone between the trees, like the sun shining through the window of a great cathedral.

Ten

There was a knock at the door and a short, red-faced man appeared, wearing a crumpled green suit.

'Ms Davis? Detective Garda John Maguire. How are you feeling now?'

'Much better, thanks. Any news of Jimmy and Miko?'

'The Japanese gentleman has just come out of surgery, so they tell me, and they're expecting him to make a full recovery. The other gentleman was hit only once in the thigh, but he lost a powerful amount of blood, so I'm afraid it's a little bit touch-and-go with him. Serious, they said, but stable. Or maybe it was the other way about. Whatever – this is a very fine hospital, and I'm sure they'll pull him through for you.'

He went to the window and peered out, frowning, although there was nothing to see in the gardens of Kenmare Community Hospital but a skinny boy with a wheelbarrow, listlessly hoeing the rose beds.

'Your other friends,' he added, without turning around, 'I'm very sorry for your bereavement.'

'Thank you.'

He came away from the window and sat down close to her. His breath smelled of onions. 'This was a very unpleasant business, altogether.'

'Yes, it was.'

'There's no doubt in my mind that your man was hired to kill you. And if your own fellow hadn't had his wits about him, he would have succeeded.'

'Rick was a special agent for the US Secret Service before he came to work for me,' said Adeola. 'He used to run close protection for Vice-President Gore.'

'Yes, he told me that. He and I, we've already had quite a chat. He was telling me that he didn't like to speculate as to who might have been wanting to kill you. Could have been anybody, so he said. Seems you've been putting up people's backs the whole world over.'

'You could say that. I'm a professional putter-up of backs. I'm just sorry that Nesta and Charlie had to pay the price for it.'

'Is there one person's back that you've put up more than any other?'

Adeola shook her head. 'I think I'm equally disliked by just about every political faction I've ever dealt with – Iranians, Syrians, Israelis, Lebanese. The thing of it is, I bribe them with large charitable donations to stop slaughtering each other. Most of the time, they take the money, and they call a cease-fire. But it doesn't stop them from hating their enemies as much as they always did – and me, too, for paying them to behave like civilized human beings.'

'You've been talking to Denis O'Connell. I wonder what you and he could possibly have had to discuss.'

'It was a private conversation.'

'Amicable, would you say?'

'Mostly.'

'You wouldn't have been putting *his* back up, then?'

'I don't think so. Not enough for him to want me killed, anyhow.'

Detective Garda Maguire sat and smiled at Adeola for a long time, but didn't ask her any more questions about the shooting. Eventually, he said, 'I gather you're booked to fly back to the States tomorrow morning?'

'That's right.'

'Well, you'll keep in touch, won't you? And if any ideas should occur to you, about who was trying to bump you off . . .'

'Believe me, Detective, I've lost three of my bodyguards in less than a week, and they weren't just bodyguards, they were friends, too. Whoever it was, I'm not going to let them get away with it.'

When Detective Garda Maguire had left, Rick came in. He had changed into a clean blue shirt and khaki chinos.

'Are you ready to go?' he asked Adeola. 'I have a Land Cruiser waiting outside, and the cops are going to escort us to Cork.'

'I feel so guilty about leaving Jimmy and Miko.'

'Don't worry, they'll be OK. I just looked in on Jimmy and he's really holding his own. There's nothing more that we can do here, honestly.'

'What about Nesta and Charlie?'

'The coroner's coming, day after tomorrow. The police are going to call me about the funeral arrangements.'

'I need to call their next-of-kin.'

'Wait till we get to Cork. I'm not at all happy about the security around here.'

'You think they'll try again?'

'Sure of it. For some reason, those bastards really want you dead.'

With one white police car ahead of them and one behind, they drove along the undulating road that led out of County Kerry and into County Cork. Over the mountains, the clouds hung down like filthy grey curtains and it looked as if it were going to start raining again.

'This is like a bad dream,' said Adeola.

'You always knew the risks. Why do you think DOVE employed five bodyguards for you?'

'I knew the risks, for sure, but I never realized that anybody was going to be so determined to kill me.'

'I think we may be making some progress with that,' said Rick. 'I took a photograph of the medallion and sent it to my old Secret Service buddy Bill Pringle. Bill's an expert in terrorist splinter groups and assassination squads.'

'Did he have any idea what it was?'

'He wasn't sure. But he thought the Roman letters K A Z I M I were somebody's name rather than an acronym. Apparently Kazimi is a pretty common surname in Iran. The arrows aren't arrows at all. They're a kind of ancient writing which was used in the Middle East about five hundred years BC – cuneiform. He said that it shouldn't be too difficult to translate, and he's going to find out what it means and let me know ASAP.'

'You told him about the other medallion – the one that suicide bomber was wearing, in Dubai?'

'Of course. He's going to download the picture and check it out. But more than that, he has very good contacts with Al

Ameen, and he's going to try to find out if the kid was wearing the medallion when he blew himself up – and, if he was, where it is now. He says it looks as if the arrow-writing is the same on both medallions, but he's interested to see if there's a different name on the other side.'

'But he's never seen any medallions like these before?'

'Never.' Rick checked his rear-view mirror to make sure that the police car was keeping close behind them. 'Mind you – he says that they may not have any political or religious significance at all. Like, how many millions of people walk around wearing a crucifix, and that doesn't even mean that they're Christian, let alone religious fanatics. These medallions could be nothing more than jewellery.'

'You think so? It seems like too much of a coincidence to me.'

'Well, me too. And Bill's the first person to admit that he doesn't know every single splinter group that might be affiliated to Hamas or Al Qaeda or Hezbollah. Some of these terrorist cells, they've been around for decades, assassinating politicians they don't like and setting off bombs, but because they never seek publicity for what they're doing, nobody knows who they are. Some other group takes the credit, but they don't care. They've killed the person they wanted to kill, or done the damage they wanted to do, and for them that's enough.'

Their three-car motorcade wound down through the mountains and into the small market town of Macroom, and then along the flatter roads beside the River Lee. A very fine rain began to fall, sweeping across the river valley like a succession of grey ghosts.

As they approached Cork City, Adeola said, 'I've been trying to think of who might want me dead – I mean who might want me dead to the point that they're prepared to sacrifice the lives of their own people to make sure that they kill me.'

Rick turned to look at her. His eyes were the same grey as the rain. 'And?'

'All I can say is, it must be somebody who hates the idea of the world being at peace.'

They stayed that night at the Ambassador Hotel on Military Hill, overlooking Cork from the north. The Ambassador was a fine, red-brick Victorian building that had once been a British Army hospital, but the Gardai recommended it because access to its main entrance was limited, and Adeola could have a suite at the end of a long corridor, which was easily defensible.

Rick ordered leek-and-potato soup and steaks on room service, although Adeola insisted that she wasn't hungry. They sat at a small round table in Adeola's room, with a thick Irish linen tablecloth, under a painting of the Punchestown racecourse.

'What time do we fly out tomorrow?'

'Ten o'clock, connecting in Edinburgh. We should be back in New York at six forty-five Eastern time.'

'Rick—' she said, reaching across the table and laying her hand on top of his.

'I know,' he interrupted her. 'I didn't expect us to carry on the way that we have been, not after this.'

'I feel very strange. I never felt this way before. I feel so *angry*, like the inside of my brain is boiling.'

'It's called vengefulness. You've seen it enough times, in the people you negotiate with.'

'Seen it, yes. But never *felt* it.'

Rick put down his fork, wiped his mouth and stood up. 'I'm going to logon – see if Bill's come up with anything yet. You should eat some more of that steak. It's going to be a hell of a long flight tomorrow.'

'Rick, I love you, and I need you. Thank you for taking care of me.'

He kissed her. 'Somebody has to.'

Adeola slept badly that night, even though she took sleeping pills, and she kept seeing Nesta's face as the gunman's bullet blew off the side of her head. Rick came in to wake her at 7 a.m., sitting on the side of her bed and gently shaking her shoulder.

'Good morning. It's a grand day, as they say here in Cork. The sun's shining and we're on our way home.'

'Urggghhh . . . I feel like I've been dragged feet-first through a sewer pipe.'

'Nothing that a good strong cup of coffee won't put right. By the way, I've heard some more from Bill Pringle.'

Adeola sat up. She was wearing a red satin scarf tied around her hair, so she looked more like an African princess than ever. 'Could you pass my robe, please? Thanks. What did Bill have to say?'

'He checked on the cuneiform writing on the medallion. According to the most authoritative database he could find, the characters are *emu ki ilani*. That means "to become like the gods".'

'"To become like the gods"?'

'Don't ask me. Bill said it was kind of a philosophical ideal of the Babylonians, back in the days of King Nebuchadnezzar, around six hundred BC.'

'So what does that have to do with somebody trying to kill me in 2008?'

'I don't have any idea. And Bill doesn't know of any terrorist organization called Emu Ki Ilani, or any group that uses that phrase as its watchword.'

Adeola climbed out of bed and went to the dressing table. 'God, I look like shit.'

'No, you don't. You look great, considering what a shock you've had.'

'Can you order me some coffee? And some prune juice, if they have any. If not, grapefruit.'

Rick watched her as she took off her scarf and shook her braids free. 'Bill's going to follow up some more leads today,' he said. 'I've told him that we have to find out who these jokers are, and quick. You can't spend the rest of your life worrying if the person standing next to you is carrying a bomb, or if your head is in somebody's cross hairs.'

Adeola smiled, but she didn't feel like smiling. She had argued and fought against violence all of her life, but this was the first time that violence had ever made her feel truly afraid.

'You will take care of me, won't you?' she said.

Rick stood behind her and laid both hands on her shoulders, looking at her face in the dressing table mirror. 'Anybody who wants to harm you, they'll have to come through me first. I promise you.'

Eleven

Noah usually started the day with nothing more than three cigarettes and two mugs of horseshoe coffee, but this morning Silja had prepared him a bowl of muesli and sliced bananas and dried apricots, and he didn't have the heart to refuse it. He sat out on the terrace and tried to call Mo while he was eating, but all he heard was the same recorded message.

'Maybe he had to go out of town,' Silja suggested.

'Maybe,' said Noah, with his mouth full of oats and nuts. 'But he never mentioned it, and he's not answering his cellphone, either.'

A little after ten thirty, he called Mo's office on Beverly Boulevard. The nasal voice of one of his production assistants said that Mo hadn't yet appeared, but 'you know, Mo is Mo. He comes and he goes.'

After he had finished his breakfast, Noah decided to drive over to Santa Monica to see for himself if Mo was at home. 'He could be sick. Who knows?'

'If he's sick, his wife would answer the phone, wouldn't she?'

'I don't know. I just have this feeling that something isn't right.'

Silja put her arm around his shoulders. 'I know that you have lost your Jenna, but you must not think that all the world has become bad.'

The weather had turned unseasonably hot, and by the time they reached Mo's house on Lincoln Boulevard the temperature was almost up to 115 degrees F. Inside the Super Duty, the air conditioning was set to Nome, Alaska, but outside the sidewalks were rippling with heat.

Mo lived on a corner plot, in a pale blue split-level house that was typical of the development of the 1960s. It looked like the kind of place that Lucille Ball's neighbours might have lived in. There was a sloping lawn in front of the house, most of it burned patchy brown, and a scrubby yew hedge around the veranda.

Mo's thirteen-year-old Cadillac was parked in the driveway, a bronze Fleetwood with sagging suspension.

'Looks like he must be at home,' said Silja, as they pulled up outside.

Noah shook his head. 'He doesn't drive much these days, because of his eyesight. He says he's so long-sighted he has to go next door to read the newspaper.'

They walked up to the front door and Noah rang the bell. There was no answer. He rang it again, but there was still no answer.

'There, you see,' said Silja. 'He must be out of town.'

'His office would have said so. He may not put in regular hours, but he still has to work to a tight production schedule.'

Noah walked along the veranda and tried to peer in through the living-room window, but the dark brown drapes were drawn and all he could see was his own reflection.

'Mo!' he shouted. 'Mo, it's Noah! Are you in there, Mo? Is everything OK?'

'Maybe we should try around the back,' Silja suggested.

They opened the side gate and went into the backyard. There was nobody there, only a sun-faded airbed floating in the middle of the circular pool. Noah looked in through the kitchen window. Three beefsteak tomatoes and a cucumber were arranged on one of the counters, as if somebody was right in the middle of preparing a salad, but the kitchen was deserted.

He tried the window of Mo's den. Mo wasn't there, either, although his desk was strewn with at least a dozen crumpled-up balls of paper, and his computer was still switched on. On the walls were Mo's framed certificates from the Screenwriters' Guild, and several autographed photographs – *'To Mo from Dick Van Dyke'* – *'To Mo, The Only Man Nearly As Funny As Me, Mel Brooks.'*

'We should call the police,' said Silja.

Noah nodded. 'Maybe you're right. This is very weird. Very unlike Mo.'

He walked back to the kitchen and tried the door. It was unlocked. He hesitated, and then opened it a little way and called out, 'Mo? Anybody at home? It's Noah!'

He stepped inside. The kitchen was unnaturally chilly. Not only was the air conditioning on full, but the refrigerator door was wide open. Noah closed it.

'It could be that some thieves broke in, and attacked them,' said Silja. 'That happened to a friend of mine in Venice, right in the middle of the day. They tied her up and made both of her eyes black.'

Noah went through to the den. Mo's brown leather chair was set at an angle, as if he had suddenly pushed it back and stood up. There were more crumpled-up balls of paper on the floor, and also a pair of spectacles. Noah bent down and picked them up.

'It's beginning to look like you're right. Somebody did come in here and attack them.'

It was gloomy in the living room, with the drapes drawn tight. Silja tugged them open, while Noah looked around. There were no signs of a struggle – no chairs knocked over, no cushions on the floor. On the gilt-painted coffee table in the centre of the room there was a neat stack of *Hollywood Reporters* and a box of Caramel Matzoh Crunch.

They looked into the master bedroom. The king-size bed was covered in a pink satin throw with ruffles all around the edges, and two pink-and-white stuffed penguins were propped on the pillows, but again there was no indication of any violence.

'This is like the goddamned *Marie Celeste*,' said Noah.

They went into Leon's bedroom. It was catastrophically messy, but only in the way of any other college student's room, with DVDs and socks and discarded jeans all over the floor, and a wall covered with pin-ups of Britney Spears and Paris Hilton and basketball pennants and photographs of Leon's last trip to Israel.

Then Noah tried the bathroom. He had to push the door hard to open it because the bathmat was rucked up. 'What's the matter?' asked Silja.

As soon as he saw the shower he knew at once that something terrible had happened here. The glass partition was decorated with a palm-tree-shaped pattern of dried blood, and there was a dark shape hunched in the shower tray.

He pushed the door wider. To his left, in the white bathtub itself, lay the pallid body of Mo's wife, Trina. She was naked, with her arms and legs twisted at awkward angles underneath her. Her throat had been cut so deep and wide that she had almost been decapitated, and her neck was hanging open like a huge, leering grin.

The bottom of the bathtub was an inch deep in brown, congealed blood, as dark as molasses.

'Noah?' said Silja. 'What's wrong?'

'Don't come in,' he told her, turning around.

'What?'

'Don't come in. They're here. They're both dead. Somebody's killed them.'

Silja covered her mouth with her hand. 'Oh my God! Oh, Noah.'

Noah carefully crossed the bathroom floor. The small white tiles were covered in bloody handprints and bloody footprints, as if Mo and Trina had been playing a macabre game of Twister while they bled to death.

He opened the shower door. Mo was sitting there, staring at him with his eyes wide open. He was wearing only a grey turtleneck sweater, the front of which was black with blood. He had been emasculated, too. Between his hairy white thighs there was a nothing but a gaping wound, as dark as pigs' liver.

Noah stood and stared at Mo for nearly half a minute, as if he expected him to say something. But then a blowfly landed on Mo's lip, and started to walk across it, rubbing its proboscis together, and all Noah could do was turn around and leave the bathroom and close the door behind him.

Silja was in the kitchen, talking on her cellphone.

'Who are you calling?' he asked her.

'The police. What else?'

'Of course. You're absolutely right, yes. Go ahead. God!'

'Are you all right?'

Noah leaned against the counter. The kitchen seemed to shrink all around him, and Silja sounded as if she were talking to him from another room.

'I'm OK,' he said. 'Just give me a minute.'

'You look terrible.'

He pulled out a high-legged stool and sat down. 'I can't believe this. First Jenna, now Mo and Trina. What the hell is going on here, Silja?'

'Yes,' said Silja, on her cellphone, 'Lincoln Boulevard, Santa Monica – Noah, what number is it?'

'Five forty-eight.'

When she had finished talking to the police, Silja came up to Noah and held him close. 'I'm so sorry. I'm so sorry. How were they killed?'

'The same way as Jenna. Their throats were cut. Mo – they cut him down there, too – castrated him.'

'Oh my God. Do you think it was the same people?'

'I don't know. I don't understand it at all. Who would want to murder an innocent guy like Mo? He wrote *comedy*, for Christ's sake. He wrote jokes.'

They were still waiting for the police when they heard a key turning in the front door.

Noah immediately stood up and reached for the knife that Trina had been using to prepare her salad. He gestured for Silja to stay well back in the alcove beside the refrigerator, and then he crossed the kitchen and stood next to the door.

Without any hesitation, a curly-haired young man in an orange T-shirt walked in, and tossed a canvas bag on to the kitchen floor. Noah wrapped an arm around his neck and held the point of the knife up against his right side. 'You move – you *blink*, even – you're going to be very, very dead.'

The young man froze, with one arm still lifted, as if he were playing statues.

'What are you doing here?' Noah demanded.

'What am I doing here? I *live* here, man!'

Noah hesitated, and then he relaxed his grip. 'Leon?'

'That's right.'

Noah let him go, and lowered the knife. 'Jesus, Leon, I didn't recognize you. Last time I saw you, you were only knee high to a high knee.'

'Mr Flynn! What are you doing here? Where's my dad?'

Leon was a taller, skinnier version of Mo, with a pale face and close-set eyes and a large, curved nose. His upper lip was dark with an incipient moustache. On the front of his T-shirt was a large picture of the Jewish reggae singer Matisyahu.

'Leon, you'd better sit down.'

'Why? Why do I have to sit down? Where's my dad?'

'Leon, something bad has happened.'

Leon stared at Noah in panic. 'What? What's happened? Tell me!'

'Somebody's broken in here. Somebody's broken into your house and your dad and Trina are both dead.'

'*What?* What do you mean dead? Where are they?'

'You don't want to see them, believe me.'

'I want to see them! I want to see my dad! I don't understand any of this! Who broke in? What did they do?'

It took Noah almost five minutes to calm Leon down. By that time the police had arrived, three squad cars and two detectives. Then an ambulance from the coroner's department, and two Humvees from the CSI. A few minutes later, two mobile TV trucks turned up, and several more cars, until the whole block looked like a battle scene.

As the house began to fill up with police officers and crime scene investigators and medical examiners, Noah took Leon out into the backyard, and stayed close to him, with his hand resting on his shoulder.

'I tried to call Dad last night,' said Leon. 'I should have known that something was wrong when he didn't answer.'

'It's not your fault, Leon.'

'Yes, it is. I should have been here. If I hadn't stayed over with my friends in Sherman Oaks—'

'There's no question, Leon. If you had been here, they would have killed you, too.'

'But who could have done it? My dad never hurt anybody in his entire life. Dad was just Dad. He made everybody laugh.'

A tall black detective came out of the house, with his coat slung over one shoulder. He had a grey walrus moustache and his bald head sparkled with perspiration.

'Mr Finn, is it?'

'Flynn. As in, "in like Flynn".'

The detective dragged out a large white handkerchief and patted the back of his neck. 'Hell of a mess, this, Mr Flynn. Any ideas at all who the perpetrators might have been?'

'There was more than one of them, then?'

'That's what the footprints are telling us. And one of the neighbours saw two men approach the house round about three o'clock yesterday afternoon. They were wearing grey suits, the both of them, that's what she said. She thought they were Mormons, or maybe Bible salesmen.'

Noah pulled a face. 'I don't know who they could have been.

Mo was everybody's friend, and it wasn't like he had anything much to steal. A few screenwriting trophies, that's all.'

The detective looked around the yard, and at the faded sunbed that was circling in the swimming pool. 'I hate cases like this. There's a reason they got killed. There's always a reason. But the reason is so goddamned bizarre you can never work out what it is.'

When the detective had gone back inside, Noah said to Leon, 'Listen – you're going to have to call your family. You have an uncle in San Diego, is that right?'

'That's right, Uncle Saul. And two aunts in Pasadena. And all my cousins and all. My granddad died last summer.'

'You'd better come home with us first. Why don't you grab some clothes and a toothbrush and we'll get the hell out of here?'

'OK,' said Leon, and then his eyes suddenly filled up with tears. 'I just wish I could have said goodbye to him properly. You know, instead of arguing.'

'You argued with him?'

'He called me in the morning and gave me a hard time because I hadn't taken that stuff that you wanted my professor to look at. That cuneiform writing, you know?'

'Yes, I know. And that wax rubbing, too.'

'Well, the reason I left them at home was because I was taking a couple of days off college. My friends in Sherman Oaks and me, we were setting up this dating website for single Jewish students. We thought we were going to make a bundle out of it.'

'But your dad didn't know about it?'

'Uh-hunh. He would have totally flipped. He takes all of this Jewish Studies thing real serious. He says Jews should never forget what we are and where we come from. Not ever. If he'd known that I was planning to cut class—'

'But then he found out that you were?'

Leon smeared the tears from his eyes with the back of his arm. 'Yeah. And he said I was disrespectful and all kinds of stuff like that. And I said what does it matter about the ancient frickin' Babylonians but he said that he'd promised to find out for you what the writing meant and a promise is a promise and if I wasn't going to do it then he was going to take the stuff and show it to my professor himself.'

Noah frowned. 'And so far as you know, that's what he did?'

'I guess. I didn't speak to him again. But when Dad says he's going to do something, he always, like, does it.' He hesitated, and sniffed, and then corrected himself, 'Always *did* it.'

Noah ushered Leon back towards the house. The kitchen was crowded with CSI and photographers and police officers, but they all shuffled respectfully out of the way as Noah and Leon came inside.

Noah stood with Leon in his bedroom as Leon packed a few T-shirts and shorts. 'Who's your professor?' he asked. 'The one who your dad was going to show the writing to?'

'Julius Halflight. He kind of specializes in the siege of Jerusalem and Nebuchadnezzar and all that stuff.'

'OK. Maybe I should talk to him.'

Leon was folding up a pale blue T-shirt with cuneiform writing on it.

'Is that the T-shirt with the ancient riddle on it?' Noah asked him.

'That's right. "What building do you enter blind, but when you leave it, you can see?"'

'All right. So what's the answer?'

'A school,' Leon told him.

Twelve

Noah popped another Momint as he walked under the archways of Royce Hall. He had swallowed two large glasses of Jack Daniel's as soon as he had arrived home from Santa Monica, one after the other, and he didn't want Leon's professor to smell it on his breath.

He had been to Royce Hall twice before, but only to shoot campus-based movies. In *Nightmare At UCLA* he had abseiled down one of the two tall red-brick towers and chipped his left ankle. In *The Philosopher's Stone* he had run along the college cloisters with his clothes on fire, and singed off his eyebrows.

Underneath the archways, it was cooler and shadier. He found the door to the Centre for Jewish Studies and walked along the corridor to the secretary's office. Three young students in yarmulkes were standing in one of the window bays, arguing loudly about the relative merits of *Splinter Cells* and *Sid Meier's Pirates*. So much for Jewish studies, Noah thought.

The secretary had sounded like a middle-aged dragon on the phone, but she turned out to be a dark, pretty girl in glasses, with a beauty spot on her right cheek. Her hips were too big for Noah's taste, with a purple sash around them, but Noah thought, What the hell, there must be plenty of men out there who like a woman with a wide undercarriage . . .

'Noah Flynn. I have an appointment with Professor Halflight.'

'That's right. You're so lucky to have caught him. He's flying to Israel first thing tomorrow.'

'Well, I appreciate him taking the time to see me.'

'Can I bring you a soda? It's so *hot* today, isn't it?'

'No thanks.' *But I could murder another Jack Daniel's, straight up, no ice, if you're hiding a bottle in your filing cabinet.*

He waited almost ten minutes while the secretary tapped away at her computer. Outside in the sunlight, he could see students laughing and talking and jostling each other as they crossed the quadrangle. In here, it was cold and hushed and it smelled of stationery, mingled with the secretary's strong, musky perfume.

On the walls of the office hung black-and-white framed photographs of all of the centre's faculty. Noah stood up and examined them. Carol Bakhos, assistant professor of Late Antique Judaism; Saul Friedlander, professor of Holocaust Studies; Lev Hakak, professor of Hebrew Literature . . .

And here he was: Julius Halflight, chair of the department of Middle Eastern Languages and Culture. A broad-faced man, with slicked-back hair and heavy eyebrows, and pitted cheeks. The camera flash seemed to have reflected in his eyeballs, because they looked totally blind and silver – more like ball bearings than eyes.

Noah was still staring at the photograph when the secretary's phone gave a sharp buzz. A thickly-accented voice said, 'Marcia – do you want to show my visitor through to my office?'

The secretary led Noah across the corridor. She knocked on the door of the office opposite, and opened it.

Professor Halflight was standing in the bay window with a small brass watering can, carefully tending to a tall pot plant with spiky white flowers. His photograph had failed to show how big he was. He was nearly 6' 4", with a massive head, and immense shoulders. He was wearing a black long-sleeved shirt, with a long black necktie, and a pendulous belly that hung over his belt.

Noah waited in the middle of the office while Professor Halflight finished his watering. It was a huge room, yet Professor Halflight was so large that Noah felt claustrophobic, as if he were crowded into an elevator with an elephant. The walls were panelled with dark oak and covered with dozens of framed diplomas and certificates, which made Noah feel even more enclosed.

'You know what it is, this plant?' asked Professor Halflight, without even introducing himself.

Noah squinted at it. 'Sorry. Plantology – that's not exactly my strong point.'

'Botany, you mean, don't you? This is an asphodel, one of the earliest recorded plants in history. *Asphodelus ramosus*, also known as the King's Spear. It was mentioned in writings that go as far back as the eighth century BC.'

He turned around, and as he did so he gave a half-lurch, as if he were suffering from a serious hip injury.

'The ancient Greeks believed that the asphodel grew in abundance over the fields of Hades, the meadows of the underworld, and they used to plant it close to tombs, because they believed that the dead would feed off its roots.

'King Nebuchadnezzar himself ate the roots of the asphodel, baked in hot ashes, and drank a spirit made from asphodel roots, too.'

'Gather you're quite an expert on good old King Nebuchadnezzar,' said Noah. 'And Babylon.' He hoped he wasn't making too much of a fool of himself.

Professor Halflight reached across and took hold of a walking stick that was propped against his desk. The walking stick had a silver knob on top of it, almost the size of a man's fist, sculpted into the shape of a Judaic lion. The shaft was carved to look like intertwining snakes.

He came hobbling over to Noah with a complicated gait that took him sideways rather than forwards, and Noah could hear a mechanical creaking in his right leg. Professor Halflight held out his hand and said, 'Mr Flynn, isn't it? A friend of that gentleman who came to see me – on Tuesday afternoon, wasn't it?'

'Moses Speller, that's right.'

'Well – what your friend showed me was very interesting, Mr Flynn. The photograph, and the rubbing. Very interesting indeed, even if they weren't especially valuable. The two medallions were almost certainly Babylonian, from the sixth century BC, with cuneiform inscriptions on them. You know what cuneiform is, I suppose?'

Noah nodded. 'Picture-writing, kind of. Could you translate what they said?'

'Oh, yes. It wasn't particularly difficult. There's always some room for speculation and argument when it comes to cuneiform translation, but I am fairly sure they said "*emu ki ilani*", which means "to emulate the gods".'

'And – uh – that means?'

'To live like the gods, Mr Flynn. To be all-knowing, all-wise, all-just, all-powerful – and most of all, to control the destiny of other men.'

'I'm still not sure I get it.'

'It was how King Nebuchadnezzar wanted to live. Not only to be master of the territory over which he ruled, but to be master of the world beyond it. And how do you think he was going to do that?'

Noah said, 'That wax rubbing – that was taken from a medallion I found in the ocean off Gibraltar, when I was diving.'

'Yes, your friend told me,' said Professor Halflight. His expression was unreadable.

'The thing is, it was stolen from me yesterday. Four guys attacked me and they would have killed me, if I'd given them the chance. The way they were talking, they were really desperate to get their mitts on it, and I was wondering if you might know why.'

Professor Halflight shrugged. 'As far as I know, they meant very little, those medallions. They were forged in their hundreds in Babylon, when the royal palace was completed, and the hanging gardens were finished, and the triple walls were built around the city to protect it from any invader. Perhaps they were forged in their *thousands* – who knows? They were nothing but good-luck charms, that's all. Mementoes.'

Noah said, 'My girlfriend, Jenna, had her throat cut in front of my eyes, Professor. These guys took my medallion and then they killed her. I mean, for Christ's sake, what kind of a good-luck charm is that? It must mean something pretty damned important to somebody.'

He took a breath, and then continued. 'Moses Speller has been murdered, too – and so has his new wife, Trina. I'm wondering if there's any connection.'

'Are you with the police?' asked Professor Halflight. 'I'm flying to Israel early tomorrow morning. I can't afford any trouble with the police.'

'Do I look like I'm with the police? I'm just trying to find out what this is all about. I was hoping you could explain it to me.'

'I wish I could. I'm deeply sorry to hear about your friend. He was very amusing, very animated. He made me laugh.'

'But you can't think of any possible link between the medallion that I found off Gibraltar and the medallion that suicide bomber was wearing? Those guys who took it from me, one of them said that I knew too much, but even if I *do* know too much, I'm damned if I know what it is.'

'Maybe it is more than a coincidence, Mr Flynn, but believe me, I am as mystified by this as you are. All I can do is express my condolences.'

There was nothing more that Noah could say. If one of America's most respected experts on Babylonian antiquity didn't know why his medallion was so critically important, then who else could he turn to?

'Thanks for your time,' he said. 'If you think of anything else, maybe you could call me.'

Professor Halflight took Noah's card but didn't even look down at it. 'Life is full of mysteries, Mr Flynn. Most of them are insoluble, and it is probably better that they stay that way.'

Noah called DOVE headquarters in New York, and asked to speak to Adeola Davis.

'Ms Davis has only just returned from Europe, sir. She won't be back in her office until Monday morning at the earliest. May I ask what you're calling about?'

'I need to ask her about the bombing in Dubai.'

'I don't think she'll be answering any questions about that, sir. But I can put you through to our public relations department.'

'I need to ask her about the medallion the guy was wearing.'

'I'm sorry?'

'The guy who tried to kill her, the suicide bomber, he was wearing a medallion. I need to ask her about it. Maybe she knows if it's a symbol of something, some organization, maybe – some terrorist group.'

'Well, I'll try to mention it to her, sir, but I can't promise that she'll get back to you.'

'Tell her that I've seen another medallion like that. Tell her that a good friend of mine was killed by some people who were trying to steal it.'

'I'm sorry, sir. I can't take messages. I think you'd be better off speaking to our public relations department.'

'Listen, I don't want to speak to your public relations department. All I want you to do is tell Ms Davis that I've seen another medallion the same as that guy was wearing before he tried to blow her up, and that I think there could be some kind of connection.'

The receptionist hung up without answering. Noah tried calling DOVE again, but all the lines were busy.

'No luck?' asked Silja, as he tossed the phone on to the table.

'I don't know. I could try emailing her, couldn't I?'

Silja sat down close beside him and took hold of his hand. 'Maybe Leon's professor was right, and these medallions don't mean anything at all.'

'No, I think they do. In fact, I think he was lying to me. Or not exactly telling me the whole story.'

'Why should he lie?'

'How should I know? But when I think about it, he was so damned nonchalant about the whole thing. "So, Mr Flynn, you found a medallion in the ocean, and purely by chance some suicide bomber in Dubai was wearing the exact same medallion, and for some reason some mysterious guys jump on you and steal it, and kill your girlfriend, and then your best friend happens to make some enquiries about it, and he and his wife get hacked to death, all in the space of a few hours? Oh, dear, I'm so sorry to hear it. Now if you'll excuse me, I have a plane to catch."'

'I guess if you put it that way.'

Noah shook two cigarettes out of the pack and lit both of them. 'How's Leon?' he asked, with his eyes narrowed against the smoke.

Behind him, an unsteady voice said, 'Hey – I'm OK.'

Leon came out on to the balcony. He looked pale, and his eyes were puffy, but he sat down at the table and said, 'I've been listening to what you've been saying.'

'Leon – I'm only speculating. I don't know what the hell's going on, any more than you do.'

'But those medallions – they were the only things that your Jenna and my dad and Trina had in common, weren't they?'

'I guess.'

'So that's what you know, but you don't know that it's important that you know.'

'Excuse me?'

'You know that these medallions have something in common. That's all. They don't want you even to start to make a connection. Which means there must *be* a connection.'

Noah took another long drag on his cigarette. 'Leon – your dad didn't send you to college for nothing, did he?'

At that moment, the phone warbled. Noah picked it up, and said, 'Flynn.'

A very tired and elegant voice said, 'This is Adeola Davis, Mr Flynn. I'm returning your call.'

Thirteen

They met Adeola and Rick at dusk the following day, at Burbank airport. On Rick's insistence he and Adeola had flown from La Guardia in New York to Dallas, changing airlines and flying to Phoenix and then changing again before flying to Los Angeles.

Adeola came out of the arrivals gate wearing huge dark sunglasses and an ankle-length kaftan in pale green silk, so that she looked to Noah like a praying mantis. Rick was holding her elbow, and Noah could immediately tell by his taut, muscular swagger that he was both fit and alert. Behind his purple-lensed Ray-Bans, his eyes constantly flicked from side to side, looking over Adeola's shoulder.

'Appreciate your flying out here, Ms Davis,' said Noah, taking Adeola's Louis Vuitton bag.

'I was coming out here anyhow, in three days' time, for the International Peace Convention. And as I told you on the phone, Mr Flynn, I will do whatever it takes to find out who these people are. I want justice for my friends, as much as you want justice for yours.'

'Justice? Maybe. I was thinking more along the lines of revenge.'

'Well – you managed to account for three of them, didn't you? Have the police managed to identify them yet?'

'If they have, they haven't told me, and there's been nothing more about it in the news.'

'I believe something is happening that is very dangerous,' said Adeola. 'I think that without realizing it we have stirred up a hornets' nest.'

'Where are you going to stay?' asked Noah. 'You're welcome to put up at my place, but I'm not sure how safe it is – especially if they're still after me, too.'

Rick said, 'I've booked a cottage for Adeola and me at the Bel Air, under assumed names, of course. A couple of my old Secret Service buddies live in West Hollywood, and they've agreed to help out with security until the peace convention starts. I'm not taking any more risks than I have to. Not after what happened in Ireland.'

'From what you told me, that was just horrific. But it didn't even get a single mention on the news over here.'

'The Garda managed to keep a lid on it,' said Rick. 'Well, not the shooting itself. They put that down to a disgruntled ex-employee going postal. But they left out the fact that Adeola was involved. She wasn't visiting Ireland officially, and the Irish government didn't want the media to know that she'd been talking to certain people linked to certain unsavoury activities in Paraguay.'

Noah led the way to the curb and opened up the tailgate of his Super Duty. 'I'm real glad you didn't get hurt. There's some people out there who really have your card marked, and that's for sure.'

They climbed into the SUV and Noah headed west on Burbank Boulevard. Traffic was heavy, and they had to keep stopping and starting. This made Rick nervous, and he kept twisting around in his seat, checking the vehicles all around them.

'So, Mr Flynn – these men in grey suits took the medallion that you found in the Mediterranean?' Adeola asked him.

'Hey, you should call me Noah.'

'All right – Noah.' Adeola opened her green silk purse and held up the medallion that the young sniper had been wearing in Ireland. 'Was it anything like this?'

Noah glanced at the medallion and then took it from her. 'Exactly. Exactly the same.' He turned it over. 'Except for the inscription on the back. Mine had the letters P R C H A L on it.'

Rick said, 'My pal Bill Pringle at the Secret Service thinks that K A Z I M I is a name, so I'd guess that P R C H A L is, too. Bill's trying to find out if the suicide bomber in Dubai was wearing his medallion when he blew himself up. We know that *his* name was Abdul al-Hamiz, so if his medallion has H A M I Z on the back of it, I think it's pretty clear that we're dealing with a distinctive and identifiable terror organization.'

'Amazing that nobody's ever heard of them before,' said Noah. 'They must have been around at least since 1943.'

'Well, you're right,' said Rick, 'that's a long time for a terrorist group to be active without giving themselves away. Even Black September have only been around since 1970, and Lashkar-e-Tayyiba wasn't founded till 1989.'

'The question is, what's their agenda?' asked Adeola. 'Why are they so determined to kill me, and why don't they want anybody to know that these medallions are connected?'

They had dinner at Noah's house, out on the terrace. Silja cooked them Finnish pasties, filled with smoked trout, and served with sour cream and chives.

'You have a find there,' said Adeola, as Silja went back into the kitchen to fetch the dill-and-cucumber salad.

'Silja? No. She and me, we work together now and then, that's all. She's a totally amazing stunt artiste. One of the best in the world. She should be in England, working on the next James Bond flick, but they've put it back for a couple of months.'

He looked between the flickering candles at Leon, who was solemnly cutting up his pasty. 'It's OK,' he reassured him. 'It may be Finnish, but it's kosher.'

He had tried to persuade Leon to go to his uncle Saul, or one of his aunts in Pasadena, but Leon had asked if he could stay. 'If you're going to go looking for the people who killed my dad and Trina, I want to help you.'

Leon wanted revenge, just as much as Adeola, and just as much as Noah. All three of them were hurt. All three of them were grieving, and it had created a deep, unspoken bond between them. Just because Leon was young, that didn't make his pain any easier to cope with. Besides, there was a good chance that he could be very helpful. He might have been less enthusiastic about Jewish history than his father, but he'd been studying ancient Babylon for two semesters, and he knew all about cuneiform writing and the empire-building of King Nebuchadnezzar, and so he might be able to discover more about Emu Ki Ilani, and what it really meant.

Adeola said, 'We need to find out as much about these medallions as we can. For instance, the medallion you found in the ocean: let's suppose that it belonged to somebody called Prchal. Who was Prchal? And why was his medallion in his binocular case, at the bottom of the sea? How did it get there?'

'Mr Prchal probably dropped it off his boat,' said Noah. 'That's how I lost *my* last pair of binoculars. In fact, that's how I lost my second-to-last pair of binoculars, and the pair of binoculars before that.'

'But Prchal is a Czech name, isn't it?' said Rick. 'And you say that Prchal had pieces of Czech newspaper in his binocular case, to roll cigarettes. So that would pretty much confirm that he was Czech.'

'I guess so.'

'But what was a Czech doing in a boat off the coast of

Gibraltar in 1943? It was wartime, right, so he wouldn't have been fishing, or sightseeing.'

'You're thinking that he was in a plane that came down.'

'It seems more likely. You said yourself that there was airplane debris on the bottom. And it was in line with the end of the airstrip.'

'Let me use your pc, Mr Flynn,' Leon said. 'I can check it out.'

'OK – but take the rest of your supper with you. And call me "Noah" from now on, OK?'

'Yes, sir – Mr Flynn – *Noah.*'

When Leon had taken his plate inside, Noah said, 'Poor kid. Thank God he didn't see what those bastards did to his dad and his stepmom.'

'We don't know for sure that it was the same people.'

'They cut his stepmom's throat, same as they did to my Jenna. I'm pretty sure it was them.'

'But how did they find out that your friend Mo had been asking questions about the medallions?'

'How did they find out that I had the medallion, and I was taking it to show Jenna? I don't know, maybe we need to talk to the cops about this. Maybe I should have told them in the first place.'

Adeola said, 'No, Noah. Your instinct was right. Let's find out more about these people first. For all we know, they are involved with the police. If there's one thing that I have learned in international diplomacy, it is to believe nobody and trust nobody.'

At that moment, Noah's parrot squawked, '*Bastards. All of them. Bastards.*'

'Pretty salty vocabulary, your parrot,' Adeola remarked. 'She must have belonged to a sea captain.'

'Uh-hunh. Doorman, from the Beverly Wilshire.'

A little after 10 p.m. they were sitting in the living room with a bottle of Pinot Grigio when Rick's friend Bill Pringle called him.

'Rick? How are you, good buddy? Listen, I think I've found something that's going to interest you.'

'Oh yes?'

'I've been talking to an old friend of mine who used to be the curator at the Secret Service Archive on H Street Northwest.

I'm hoping to meet him in the morning so I should have some more information for you tomorrow.'

'So what's he come up with?'

'Sorry, good buddy, maybe I'm being paranoid after all these years, but it only takes a key word, doesn't it, and somebody starts to listen in. Let's just say that – if it's for real – it could be the story of the century. This century *and* the last century and maybe a few centuries before that.'

'I'll wait to hear from you, then.'

'OK. But if I don't call you by this time tomorrow, you can reach me on 102 9190, extension 1.'

Rick jotted it down on the palm of his hand. 'What's that? A cellphone?'

'Auburn, New York.'

Rick frowned at his phone in bewilderment, but Bill Pringle had hung up.

'Auburn, New York? What the hell did he mean by "Auburn, New York"?'

'Auburn, New York?' Noah repeated. He frowned, and thought for a while, and then he said, 'I know – that's where they invented the talking pictures – Auburn, New York. Some guy called Cross.'

'Well, they have a very famous jail, too,' said Rick. 'Back in the 1800s, the inmates weren't allowed to speak, *ever*. The Auburn System, they called it. It was supposed to stop them from plotting riots and breakouts. They all had to walk with one hand on the shoulder of the guy next to them, in this sliding kind of a sideways shuffle, with their faces turned towards the guards, in case they moved their lips. The Auburn Lockstep. They even named a dance after it.'

He paused, and looked down at the number on his hand. 'None of which explains why Bill Pringle's going there. But he says he's found out something important. The story of the century, that's what he called it.'

Only a few minutes later, Leon came in, carrying a sheaf of printouts. He looked flushed and excited.

'Found something?' asked Rick.

'You bet. I Googled for air crashes off Gibraltar in 1943, and I came up with this one, pretty much straight away.'

He sat down and laid a black-and-white photograph on the

table. It showed the silvery outline of a World War Two bomber, clearly visible on the bottom of the ocean under a few feet of water.

'This was July 4, 1943, right? It says here that the plane is a Liberator bomber, and it was supposed to be flying some Polish guy called General Sikorski from Gibraltar to Britain – him and his daughter and his chief of staff and some British brigadier and some British politician.'

'*Sikorski*,' said Adeola. 'My God!'

'You know who he was?' asked Noah.

'Wladislaw Sikorski? For sure. A great negotiator. A very respected politician in his time. Anybody who wants to go into foreign diplomacy has to learn about Wladislaw Sikorski. During the Second World War, he was premier of the exiled Polish government in London, and also commander-in-chief of all the Polish forces abroad.'

'Sure – I saw something about him on the history channel,' said Rick. 'Didn't some people think that the Russians killed him?'

'Some historians believe that the Russians were responsible, yes. In the early years of the war Sikorski signed a treaty with the Russians to end the Nazi-Soviet partition of Poland, and for a while he managed to restore diplomatic relations between Russia and the exiled Polish government. But of course, after the war was over, the Russians were never going to allow Poland to be taken over by such a popular man.'

'So what did they do?' asked Noah. 'Shoot the plane down?'

'No,' said Leon, holding up his printouts. 'It was Prchal!'

'You've found Prchal?'

'It's all here. Prchal was the name of the pilot. Edward Prchal.'

'You mean he was like a suicide pilot – crashed the plane on purpose?'

'No way. He was the only person on the plane who survived. He had a cut on his face and a broken bone in his right arm, but that was all. Everybody else had fatal head injuries – all ten of them.'

'Prchal,' said Noah, shaking his head. 'Prchal and his goddamned cigarette papers!'

'The British held this really thorough Court of Inquiry,' said Leon. 'The governor of Gibraltar said that he went out on to the runway around about ten o'clock in the evening to say goodbye to General Sikorski and his daughter. He knew this guy Prchal and he talked to him for about five minutes while the second pilot was warming up the engines. He said Prchal was like always, absolutely calm and normal.

'Anyhow, they switched off all the searchlights, so that the pilot wouldn't be dazzled when he took off. The plane took off, and because it was so dark, all they could see were its navigation lights. But the governor said that he suddenly noticed that the navigation lights were slowly starting to sink towards the sea.

'He and one of his aides both agreed that they could tell that it was Prchal who was flying, because after take-off he always put the airplane's nose down to gather extra speed before he climbed up to his cruising height. He said they waited for the lights to start to rise, but they never did. The aircraft flew out about three-quarters of a mile and then crashed straight into the sea.'

Leon turned the page. 'At the Court of Inquiry, Prchal testified that after putting his nose down to pick up speed, he found that the joystick was jammed and he was unable to pull the airplane up again. But after it was salvaged, five different technical experts examined the airplane in detail, and none of them could work out how the controls could have become stuck. However, when he tried to pull back the stick it somehow became stuck and would not move. The governor said that nobody could have sabotaged the airplane, because it had been guarded by a Commando and an RAF guard during Sikorski's entire visit to the Rock.

'But here's the clincher,' said Leon. 'The governor said that Prchal never wore his Mae West, ever. He always hung it over the back of his seat. In his evidence, Prchal insisted that he had done the same thing this time, but when he was picked out of the sea he was wearing his Mae West and every tap and fastening was properly fastened.'

Rick sat back in his armchair. 'Sounds like an assassination to me. Especially since he was carrying that medallion with him.'

'But there is no connection between Sikorski and me, none at all.'

Noah said, 'Maybe we're talking about assassins who kill

people for no other reason except they're trying to make peace. Sikorski, you, and who knows how many others they've bumped off – but nobody knows it was them.'

'I can't believe that. Who would benefit? It's not even as if they claim responsibility to further their cause. They're just like random killers.'

Rick dry-washed his face with his hands. 'Well, I don't know about you guys, but I'm pooped. Thanks for the meal, Silja. Thanks for the hospitality, Noah. And thanks for your detective work, scout.'

'Keep your eyes peeled,' said Noah. 'And don't get into any strange Liberator bombers.'

Adeola kissed him on both cheeks. 'I really appreciate your help, Noah. This could be a great risk for all of us.'

He looked at her for a moment. She had the most striking face he had ever seen. Her eyes were more like those of a carnivorous animal, and her lips pouted as if she were on the verge of saying something that would make a man's spine prickle. No wonder she could persuade politicians that there were better things in life than violence and aggression.

'Take care,' he told her, and kissed her back.

Fourteen

Silja went to bed almost as soon as Adeola and Rick had left, but Noah went out on to the terrace again for a last warm glass of wine. He had a headache and he felt battered and confused, but he didn't feel like going to sleep yet. He didn't want to have any more nightmares about Jenna.

He thought it was strange that he hadn't heard any more from the police about Jenna's murder. It had been reported briefly on the TV news, but the crash in which the two men in grey suits had been killed had received no mention at all. He almost felt as if it had never happened.

The night was humid and oppressive. Moths were beating

against the lights along the terrace railing, and on the horizon he could see the distant flicker of lightning. He was beginning to realize that the world was a very different place than he had always imagined it to be. It was like walking behind a movie set and finding out that a sunny suburban front yard was actually located in a huge, gloomy studio, where doors led to nowhere at all and staircases stopped halfway.

He finished his wine and went back into the kitchen. As he passed Leon's room, he saw that the light was still on. He hesitated, and then he tapped on the door and said, 'Leon? Everything OK? Don't you think it's time you got some shut-eye?'

There was a snorting sound. He opened the door and saw Leon sitting on the side of the bed, his face a mess of tears.

'Hey, buddy,' he said, and sat down beside him. 'You've lost your dad and your stepmom, but I promise you that you're not alone.'

Leon wiped his eyes with his sleeve. 'I can't believe he's dead. I feel like I could just go home now and he'd still be there.'

'You're never going to stop feeling like that. He's always going to be alive, so long as you remember him.'

'But why should anybody want to kill him? He was such a great dad.'

'I don't know for sure. Maybe it was all connected with this medallion thing, maybe it wasn't. But we'll find out, won't we? Look at all that good work you did this evening, finding out about that plane crash.'

Leon sniffed, and nodded.

Noah said, 'I'll see you in the morning, OK? Do you want a drink or anything?'

Leon suddenly and unexpectedly smiled. 'Do you know what my dad used to say? He said that everything's funny, in the end. Being born is funny; living is funny. Even dying is funny. I guess he's probably in heaven right now, telling jokes.'

Noah put his arm around Leon's shoulders. 'You can count on it. Bet the angels are wetting themselves.'

He crossed the bedroom as quietly as he could and slipped under the sheet. Silja had her back turned to him, breathing steadily. He lay there for a while, looking up at the ceiling. Right above his head, the jagged shadow of a yucca tree nodded backward and forward, like a predatory bird nodding on a branch.

He closed his eyes. He needed to sleep. He heard rustling, but he knew that it was only Silja, turning over. He needed so badly to sleep.

'*Chaos, and old Night,*' somebody whispered.

He opened his eyes. There was nobody there. The predatory bird was still nodding on the ceiling, Silja was still lying there with her pale shoulder raised. He wondered where he could have heard that phrase before. It sounded like Shakespeare, maybe . . . He would have to ask Leon to look it up for him. Maybe his subconscious mind was trying to give him a clue about something critical.

He slept. He dreamed that he was walking along the beach, and that a strong wind was blowing from the ocean. Lightning was flickering on the horizon, and every now and then there was an indigestive grumbling of thunder. Up above him, large predatory birds were circling, more and more of them, as if they were gathering for a kill.

About fifty yards ahead, he saw Jenna. She was wearing the wide straw hat that she had always worn during the last summer they had lived together, with a long white scarf tied around it, and the thin flowery dress with the puffy little sleeves.

He tried to walk faster, so that he could catch up with her, but whenever he was close enough to reach out and touch her shoulder, his vision blinked and jerked, and there she was, fifty yards away again.

Jenna! he called, but the wind was blowing against him and she obviously couldn't hear. *Jenna, wait up.* He looked up again and even more predatory birds were wheeling around.

He started to run, but there was something wrong with his leg, like Professor Halflight's, and he could only manage an awkward, disjointed gallop. *Jenna, wait up!*

He still couldn't make up any ground between them, but then he remembered what Rick had said about the Auburn Lockstep. Shuffle sideways, dragging one foot. He started to do it, and found that he could make much better progress. He did it faster and faster, his foot leaving long slide-marks in the sand, and within a few seconds he had almost caught up with her.

'Jenna!' he panted.

She turned around, smiling, but as she did so her neck opened up in a gaping red wound and her head fell off, landing in the sand with a soft thump.

He shouted out, '*No!*' and jerked upright. Silja immediately sat up, too.

'Noah – what's wrong?'

He stared at her. 'Sorry – sorry. I had another nightmare, that's all.'

'Jenna?'

'Sorry.'

She brushed the hair back from his forehead. 'You're so hot. Almost like you've been running.'

'I was. In my nightmare, anyhow.'

'It's only inside your head, Noah. It's only like a movie.'

'I know. Look, I'm sorry I woke you.'

Silja said, 'You need to relax yourself completely. When I was eighteen, you know, I saw my boyfriend killed on his motorcycle. I had nightmares just like you, over and over. In the end I went to see this therapist, and she taught me how to deal with them. First, relax. Then, talk to the person that you have lost, and explain to them how much you miss them, but you are now going to say goodbye. Then, turn around and walk away, and don't look back.'

Noah lay back on the pillow. 'And that works?'

'It worked for me.'

She stroked his forehead with her fingertips, and then she leaned over him and kissed his eyelids. 'You must lose all of your tension. Think of your mind like an hourglass, filled with black sand. The sand is running away, endlessly running away, and soon all of your mind will be empty.'

Her fingernails traced the shape of his face, and touched his lips. She kissed his eyelids again, and this time she delicately licked his eyelashes with the tip of her tongue, so that they were sealed with warm saliva. Then she kissed his lips, and ran her tongue across his teeth.

'The sand is running away,' she whispered. 'Endlessly running away . . .'

She caressed his neck, and his chest. 'Now, your heart is not beating so fast. Breathe deeper, and slower. Hold each breath for just a little while, yes?'

He felt her soft breast against his arm. Her nipple was crinkled tight. She slowly drew down the sheet, as far as his knees. He was wearing white-and-green striped boxer shorts, but he couldn't disguise the fact that his penis was already beginning to stiffen. Silja's fingertips did a light dance down his stomach muscles, and then wriggled their way underneath the elastic waistband.

He could have told her to stop. We're not lovers, he thought. We work together. We respect each other for how professional we are. Not only that, I'm supposed to be shocked. I'm supposed to be grieving.

But he realized that what Silja was doing for him was nothing to do with being lovers. She was doing it because they were friends, because she wanted to make him feel like a man again, and less like the survivor of a terrible tragedy. It was sexual, yes, but it was deeply therapeutic. It was a first step towards repairing his soul.

She grasped his penis and slowly rubbed it up and down until it was swollen hard. Then she tugged down his boxer shorts, and took them right off.

'You should think of nothing but yourself, and how good this feels. Concentrate completely on this.'

'Silja—'

'Ssh. This is your treatment. This is how you learn to say goodbye to your nightmare.'

She knelt up beside him, and took off her own white panties. In the dim light from the window, he could see that she was completely waxed, and there was a glisten of moisture in between her lips. Without any hesitation, she took hold of his hand and held it between her legs, so that he could feel how soft and wet she was. He slipped one finger inside her and she smiled.

'You see? Therapy can be pleasure for the therapist, too. In Finland they say "*Jos et loyda rauhaa itsestamme on turhaa etsia sita muualta.*' If you cannot find peace within yourself, it is no good looking anyplace else.'

'Here,' he said, trying to lift himself up on one elbow. But she pushed him back down.

'No,' she said. 'I am the therapist and you are the patient, and you must do whatever I demand.'

Without any hesitation, and with extraordinary grace and

flexibility, she sat astride him, facing him, with her knees fitting into his armpits. Then she arched herself backward, so far back that she could take his penis into her mouth, and swallow the whole length of it. He had seen her do the splits. He had seen her jump, and somersault, and cartwheel. But he had never seen a contortion like this. It was both unearthly and highly erotic, as if he were making love to a completely new species of creature altogether.

She dipped her head back rhythmically, sucking his penis deeper and deeper. Her bare, pouting lips were right in front of him, so he lifted his head from the pillow and licked her, too, tasting thin, slippery sweetness.

On the ceiling, the predatory bird nodded and nodded.

The darkness began to close in. Silja sucked and sucked, and it began to feel to Noah as if she were sucking his whole being out of him; his passions and his rages and his memories and fears. Suddenly he went into a foot-curling spasm, and climaxed. She kept on sucking him until he softened, and then she sat up straight.

'So. You feel better, yes?'

He looked up at her. He hardly knew what to say. She climbed off him, as easily and as athletically as she had climbed on, and lay down beside him, so close that he could feel her breath on his shoulder.

'Tell me,' he said, 'did somebody teach you to do that, or did you make it for yourself?'

'That is a secret. A therapist never gives away her secrets.'

He kissed her forehead, and then he kissed her lips. 'OK, Dr Fonselius, have it your way.'

But then she said, 'A man from a circus taught me. He was Greek. But he was very hairy.'

Noah put his arm around her and held her. He watched the predatory bird nodding for a while and then his eyes closed and he slept. If he dreamed, he didn't dream of Jenna.

Fifteen

Early the next morning, Noah was out on the terrace teaching Leon some stunt fighting moves.

'In the movies, see, punches only *sound* real. Most of the time, the stuntmen miss each other by a mile, and the SFX are put in afterward. But even when they're really grappling with each other, stuntmen are actually doing almost the exact the reverse of what it looks like they're doing. They're always taking care of each other and protecting each other from twisting their necks or straining their backs or hitting their heads.

'You take the Atomic Knee, right, when a stuntman picks somebody up and slams his crotch down on to his knee. What happens is, the guy who looks as if he's being lifted up actually *jumps*, and when he does come down, he makes sure that his feet hit the ground first. He grabs himself between the legs and staggers around in agony, but it only looks like his nuts have been pulverized.

'It's selling the move afterward. Looking like you're badly hurt when you're not. That's the secret of being a really great stuntman.'

Silja came out with three mugs of coffee, wearing Noah's black satin bathrobe with the embroidered dragon on the back, the one that he had been given when he was filming *Night of the Nineteen Ninjas*.

'Leading Leon astray?' she asked.

'Teaching him some basic moves, that's all. No reason why a graduate in Jewish Studies shouldn't be able to do a Sunset Flip.'

'So what are we going to be doing today?' asked Silja.

'Rick's supposed to be calling me later, once he's heard from his pal in the Secret Service. And Leon's going to be surfing the Net. I'll tell you what – I'd like to know some more about this professor of yours, Leon – Julius Halflife, or whatever his name is. When you think about it, he was just about the only person who knew that your dad was asking about those two medallions, wasn't he?'

'And you think, what?' asked Silja. 'That *he* has links with terrorists, and assassins? Some old Jewish university professor with a gammy leg?'

'Who knows? Maybe he innocently mentioned it to somebody who innocently mentioned it to somebody else and in the end the wrong people got to hear about it. But it's worth checking out, don't you think?'

'I suppose so, yes.'

After a half-hour of teaching Leon how to drop kick and stomp and fell his opponents with a flying elbow, Noah went into the house to take a shower.

Before he went into the bathroom he turned and looked at Leon out on the terrace. Leon was practising simulated punches and karate chops, and kicking at the chairs. '*Hah!* Hah! *Ahuga!*' He had so much pent-up aggression. It would give him some relief to take it out on the furniture.

Silja was in the bedroom, sitting in front of the dressing table, brushing her hair. 'You're very good with him,' she said. 'He has so much anger.'

'He's not the only one.'

Silja turned around and looked at him with those icy-sky eyes. 'In Finland, we learn to keep our anger inside ourselves, frozen, until it is time to thaw it out.'

'Remind me not to upset you, then.'

Noah was still in the shower when he heard Silja shout out, 'Noah! Noah, come quick!'

He turned off the faucet and listened. 'Silja?' he called. 'Silja, what's wrong?'

There was no answer, so he reached out for his big burgundy towel, wrapped it around his waist and went out into the kitchen. Through the open doors to the terrace, he could see Silja standing by the table, one hand raised.

'Silja?'

She still didn't answer so he went outside. At the far end of the terrace, next to the flagpole, were the spidery man with the small head and the blond man who had cut Jenna's throat. The blond man was gripping Leon's curly hair, and as the flag stirred in the morning breeze, Noah saw the sharp glint of an upraised knife. Leon was wide-eyed with panic.

'Let him go!' Noah barked. 'Do you hear me, you murdering creep? Let him go!'

'Bastards,' croaked Noah's parrot. 'All of them. Bastards.'

'Let him go?' said the spidery man, stepping forward with a smile, although his eyes were concealed behind his sunglasses. 'Why should we let him go? Not in our interests at all.'

'He's only a kid, let him go. He doesn't have anything to do with any of this.'

'Oh, really? You'll have to let me be the judge of that.'

'How the hell did you get in here?'

'Through the front door, Mr Flynn. This young man was polite enough to open it for us, when we rang.'

'It wasn't his fault,' said Silja. 'They told him they were police, with news of his parents.'

Shit, I should have warned him, thought Noah.

'Screw you,' said his parrot.

The spidery man said, 'You managed to escape from us last time, Mr Flynn, but you won't escape from us now. It's a pity that you've involved this innocent young man, as well as this beautiful young lady. But, well, you know what they say. No good crying over dying. Comes to all of us, sooner or later.'

'Look, you can take me, but leave the kid alone,' Noah urged.

'Mr Flynn,' smiled the spidery man, tugging at his knuckles, 'you know as well as I do that confidentiality has to be absolute. We can't take any risks at all. Now, let's get this over with.'

The blond man pulled Leon's head back, exposing his prominent Adam's apple. As he did so, however, Silja suddenly started to run towards him – not run, *sprint*, so fast that the blond man reared backwards in alarm.

As Silja ran nearer, however, it became obvious that she wasn't running directly towards him, but towards the terrace railing six or seven feet to his right. Even Noah couldn't think what she was doing. *Don't tell me she's going to escape by throwing herself clear off the terrace. That's a sixty-foot drop, through pine trees, down a steep rocky slope . . .*

Silja jumped, and did a back spring, twisting herself sideways in mid-air. She grabbed the flagpole with both hands and swung herself right around in a semicircle, kicking the blond man square between the shoulders. He crashed down on to the terrace like a felled tree, and his knife skated across the polished oak floor.

Noah didn't need any prompting. Stretching open his mouth and letting out his famous Noah Roar, he launched himself at the spidery man and gave him a Flying Elbow. Not the safe, harmless Flying Elbow that he had been teaching Leon – but a vicious slam in the middle of the chest with the bony angle of his arm. The spidery man was thrown back against the living-room window, and cracked his head on the wooden frame. His sunglasses went flying.

The blond man was trying to pull himself back up on to his knees, but Silja kicked him square in the back of the head, and he fell forwards again.

Noah seized the spidery man's shirt front and banged his head against the window frame two or three times.

'OK,' he panted, 'I want to know who you are, and I want to know who you work for, and I want to know exactly why you've been trying so goddamned hard to kill us.'

The spidery man looked up at him with concussed, unfocussed eyes, but said nothing. Noah reached down into the man's belt and hoicked out his gun, a dull grey Ruger automatic. He also pulled up the legs of his pants to make sure that he wasn't carrying any back-up weapons strapped to his ankles.

'Come on,' he repeated. 'I want to know who you are, you toads, and I want to know *now*.'

The spidery man shook his head and coughed but still didn't speak. Noah went across to the blond man, who was lying face down with Leon's red-and-white baseball boot pressed against his left ear. He gave the man a heel kick in the side of the ribs, and then another, and then said, 'How about you, scum? You killed my girlfriend right in front of my eyes. Any reason why I shouldn't cut your nuts off and stuff them down your throat?'

'Up yours, asshole,' the blond man snarled back at him.

'I think maybe now we should call the police,' said Silja. 'What are we going to do with them, otherwise? And if this is the man who killed your Jenna—'

'Let me call Rick first, see what he says. Leon – want to go into the living room and bring me the phone?'

'Sure thing,' said Leon. But he was only halfway across the terrace when there was a deep, soft explosion, and a huge ball of dirty orange fire came rolling out of the living-room doors. Noah felt a wave of compressed heat, and raised his hand to shield his face.

Silja said, 'My God! My God, what's happened?'

'Leon?' shouted Noah, above the funnelling roar of the flames. 'Leon, are you OK?'

Leon turned around, his face flushed with heat. 'They had a briefcase,' he gasped. 'When they came in the door, one of them had a briefcase.'

There was another explosion, much louder this time. The living-room windows were blown across the terrace in a glittering shower of glass, and the flaming drapes were blown out after them, waving and burning like dragons' tongues.

Noah gave the blond man another furious kick and looked round at the spidery man. 'What the hell was that? What the *hell* did you do?'

The spidery man painfully climbed to his feet, holding on to a chair for support. Blood was sliding out of both nostrils and into his mouth. 'Destroying the evidence, of course, Mr Flynn, once we'd disposed of you. Three unfortunate people burned beyond recognition in Laurel Canyon house conflagration. Pity it didn't work out that way, but you don't always get what you want.'

Noah's house was now burning fiercely, with flames pouring out of every window and dark grey smoke teeming out from underneath the shingles.

'I swear I'm going to kill you for this,' said Noah. Everything that he and Jenna had built up together, every fabric that she had chosen, every drape that she had hung up, it was all whirling around him in a storm of black ashes.

'You won't kill me, Mr Flynn,' said the spidery man, his voice barely audible over the popping and crackling of timber. 'If I fail, there are others who will get to me first. But not you.'

Without warning, he turned and limped across the terrace, towards the railing. Before Noah could reach him, he had rolled himself over the top of it, and dropped down into the canyon. Noah glimpsed his grey-suited body bouncing and cartwheeling between the tree trunks. There was a faint crash of underbrush, and then he was gone.

'*Noah!*' shouted Silja – and, as he turned around, the blond man was struggling to his feet, violently pushing Leon to one side. Noah tried to block him off, but the blond man feinted and sidestepped, and dodged around to the far side of the dining table.

Noah pointed the Ruger at him and released the safety catch. 'On your knees,' he ordered him. 'Hands behind your head.'

'On my knees? What do you want me to do for you?'

'I said, on your knees, you bastard!'

But the blond man ignored him, and took three surging strides towards the railing. He vaulted over it, his arms waving and his legs pedalling, and disappeared with a splintering of branches amongst the pines. Noah swung the gun after him but he didn't shoot. He and Silja went to the railing and looked over. They could still hear branches breaking, but they couldn't see the blond man at all.

'Jesus,' said Noah. 'Even I wouldn't try a stunt like that.'

There was another smaller explosion inside the house, and a bang as Noah's pc imploded. Flames were beginning to lick up under the shingles now, and there was no question of them trying to put out the fire themselves. In the distance, they could hear the wailing and honking of fire trucks.

Noah looked down at the burgundy towel around his waist. 'I'll be ten seconds,' he said. He took off the towel and quickly drenched it in water from the brass faucet at the side of the terrace. He splashed his body with water, too. Then he wrapped the towel around his head and ducked back into the house.

'For God's sake, be careful!' called Silja.

'Don't worry! Done this a hundred times before!'

'In a Nomex suit, not naked!'

It was fiercely hot inside the house, and filling with acrid smoke, but Noah kept low as he hurried along the corridor to the bedroom. He opened the door, went straight across to his closet and pulled out shirt, pants and shoes. He also went to the dressing table and collected his wristwatch, his wallet, his car keys and his cellphone.

Coughing, he scurried back out again. Silja looked at the

red-and-purple Hawaiian shirt he had retrieved and said, 'You nearly died for *that*?'

'Come on,' he told her. He went over to Marilyn's perch and unchained the parrot's leg. Marilyn flapped and squawked and protested, but he kept his grip on her. Then he led Silja and Leon around the side of the house to the parking area in front. They were just coming through the ivy-entangled gate when the first fire truck arrived, its lights flashing and its klaxon blasting.

Two firefighters dropped out of the fire truck and came hurrying towards them, their rubbers making a loud wobbling noise.

'Anybody still in there?'

'No, everybody's safe.'

'Anything else we should know about? Do you have any photographic chemicals in there? Any movie stock, anything explosive?'

Noah shook his head. 'Only my entire life, that's all.'

Sixteen

They had to wait for over an hour, sitting on the low stone wall under the bougainvillea, while two police officers took a statement from each of them. One police officer was short and Hispanic, with black furry forearms, his face beaded all over with perspiration. The other was tall and gingery with a large nose and close-set eyes. To Noah, they looked more like movie extras than real police officers. The officer with the close-set eyes kept asking the same questions over and over, in a flat, expressionless drawl, and writing the answers down with childish slowness, with the tip of his tongue clenched between his teeth.

'Before the fire started, did you hear an explosion of any nature?'

'An explosion, yes. Like, *boofff*.'

'*Boofff?*'

'Well, it could have been softer, you know. More like *woofff.*'

'Which was it, then? *Boofff* or *woofff?*'

'*Woofff,* I'd say. But not quite as drawn-out as that. More like *whoof!*'

The Hispanic officer wiped his forehead with the fur on his arm. 'You didn't notice any individuals acting at all suspicious around here, any time before the fire started?'

Noah shook his head. 'I was out on the terrace. You can't see the front of the house from the terrace.'

'Only reason I ask, sir, is that there's a grey sedan illegally parked up the road a ways, with no license plates and so far as I can see, no VIN number.'

'Haven't seen a soul,' said Noah.

'Nobody come to your door or nothing, asking to call the auto club?'

'Nope. Nobody.'

Noah had never liked lying. His father always used to slap him on the back of the head if he caught him out in a lie, hard. Apart from that, this whole situation was getting way too dangerous. Jenna had died, Mo had died, Trina had died, and now he and Silja and Leon had come close to being killed. Maybe it was time to tell the police about the medallions and the men in grey suits.

'There's one thing—' he began.

'What's that?' asked the gingery police officer, but Silja narrowed her eyes at Noah, and gave him the briefest shake of her head.

'No, nothing,' said Noah. 'Forget it.'

Once the police officers had moved out of earshot, Silja came and stood close beside him. Without looking at him, she said, 'Adeola warned us not to trust anybody at all, remember? Even the police.'

'I know. But we could have had our throats cut, for Christ's sake. And look at my goddamned house. I mean, look at my goddamned *house.*'

'It's terrible. I'm so sorry. But the safest thing for now is to act like we know nothing, and saw nothing.'

'Screw you,' said Marilyn, and then imitated the warbling of Noah's cellphone.

In fact, his cellphone *was* warbling. He answered it, and it was Rick.

'Noah? Can you meet us at the Bel Air? I think we might be making some progress.'

'OK . . . but you'll have to give us twenty minutes or so. We've had a slight problem.'

'What's the matter? You sound upset.'

'Oh, I'm upset. We were paid a visit by a couple of unwelcome friends this morning. Friends in grey suits.'

'Same people? What happened?'

'Can't tell you now, cops are still here. But mayhem isn't the word for it.'

'You're all safe, though?'

'Shaken, for sure, but not stirred.'

'OK, come down as soon as you can. A guy called Ted Armstrong will meet you when you get to the entrance. Tell him that you want to speak to Mr and Mrs Trebuchet.'

Noah went over to the police officers and asked them if he and Silja could leave. The gingery one said, 'We're going to need a location, sir, where you'll be staying for the rest of the day.'

'With friends. Guy called Mo Speller, 548 Lincoln Boulevard, Santa Monica.'

'OK, sir. We'll probably need to talk to you again.'

'Not sure if I can tell you any more than I've told you already. I was taking a shower and the whole goddamn house went up, that's all. If you ask me, it was a natural gas leak. Can't think what else.'

'Sir – you'd be surprised what people know without them knowing that they know it.'

'Excuse me?'

'Witnesses, that's what I'm talking about, sir. They see things happen, but at first they don't understand the significance of what they're looking at. A little while later, though, when they've had time to think it over, it all fits together. Like, *bing!* a light bulb switches on, right over their heads.'

'Bing?' said Noah.

'That's right, *bing!* We call it "delayed interpretation".'

There was a slow, interrogative quality in the officer's tone of voice that made Noah feel uncomfortable, as if the officer suspected that he hadn't been telling him the whole truth.

He'd said 'delayed inter-pre-*tation*' as if it were a question. There was something in the way that the officer was staring at him, too, with those close-set eyes.

Come on, Noah, he told himself, you're being paranoid. He lifted his hand and said, 'So long, then, fellas.' He was trying to look nonchalant, but he was acutely conscious of how stiffly he was acting it.

Adeola said, 'My God, they do mean business, don't they? Your *house*! You were so lucky you managed to escape.'

'I don't think luck had much to do with it,' said Noah. 'It was Silja. Never saw anything like that. One swing round that flagstaff and wham! The guy was knocked flat.'

Adeola reached her hand out and took hold of Silja's hand. Two tall women, one the colour of burnished bronze, the other as white as milk. 'You must teach *me* how to swing round flagstaffs. Think how much I could impress the diplomats at those UN conferences in New York.'

They were sitting in one of the newly-refurbished Spanish cottages in the grounds of the Bel Air Hotel. The walls and ceiling were panelled in pale yellow and the furniture was gilded and ornate. A huge spray of fresh flowers stood in the centre of the coffee table, filling the room with the fragrance of sweet peas and roses.

The back door to the garden was open, but a solid-looking man with cropped white hair was sitting in an armchair, keeping an eye on it, while an even more solid-looking man with a bald head was sitting by the front door, reading the sports pages.

'I heard from Bill Pringle around eleven thirty this morning,' said Rick. 'He had breakfast at The Watergate with his old friend from the Secret Service Archive. His friend is almost one hundred per cent sure that there's another medallion in the archive, exactly the same as the others.'

'Did he tell you who it used to belong to?'

'No. But he said that his friend was going to go round to the archive later this afternoon, to check on the medallion and make sure that it *is* identical. Then he'll call me again.'

'OK,' said Noah. 'So what do we do in the meantime?'

'There's very little we *can* do,' said Adeola. 'I intend to ring around some of my Middle Eastern contacts, to see if I can find out any more about those two attempts on my life. It's possible that one of them has heard something on the diplomatic grapevine. Leon – you might use my computer to do some more research into what the medallions might actually mean.'

'Sure,' said Leon. 'And I'll see if there's any more dope on Professor Halflight, too. I mean – if he turns out to be some secret terrorist mastermind – how cool would that be?'

'Question is,' Noah put in, 'what happens if we find out who these people are? If we can't even trust the cops, who's going to help us?'

'What does an animal do, when it is cornered?' asked Adeola.

'It takes a dump?'

'It turns around, and it attacks its attackers. And that is exactly what *we* are going to do. We have no choice. We have to find out who these people really are. We have to hunt them down before they hunt *us* down.'

'And then what?' asked Noah.

'I don't know. It depends who they turn out to be, how influential they are. It depends if they have friends in high places. If necessary, we will have to kill them.'

Noah looked at Silja uneasily. Adeola caught his look and said, 'Noah – you have seen what they are capable of doing. Obviously they have no compunction whatsoever about killing *us*. For them, human lives have no value, not even their own. We may be faced with no alternative.'

'So we're forming ourselves into a hit squad?' said Noah. He turned from Silja to Leon to Rick to Adeola. 'Some fricking hit squad! Look at us!'

The solid-looking man sitting by the garden door turned to Rick and said, 'Hey – you're forming a hit squad? We'll join your hit squad, Ted and me. Life's been pretty damned boring, since we retired. Let's face it, one human being can only play so many games of double-deck pinochle in his lifetime, without going loopy.'

'Thanks, Steve.'

The rest of the day passed slowly and quietly. Adeola closeted herself in her bedroom so that she could make phone calls to her contacts in Egypt, Iran, Syria and Palestine. One of her friends in the government offices in Qatar told her that, two or three weeks before the Dubai explosion, he had picked up rumours that DOVE negotiators might be the target of terror attacks. But the information had been so sketchy that he hadn't thought it worth passing on. After all, DOVE received death threats from dozens of different terrorists and political pressure groups, on almost a daily basis.

Noah played double-deck pinochle with Rick and Ted and Steve, while Silja gave herself a pedicure and polished her nails. Leon sat on the couch, frowning at Adeola's laptop, and occasionally making notes.

At lunchtime they ordered room service: club sandwiches and shrimp salad, and a bagel with cream cheese and lox for Leon.

In the middle of the afternoon, Leon said, 'I can't find anything more about the medallions. But this *Emu Ki Ilani* thing keeps on coming up. Back in the days of King Nebuchadnezzar, in 605 BC, it was like a whole political and religious concept – "to become like the gods". Nebuchadnezzar wanted to keep every nation in turmoil, always struggling against each other, so that mankind would never become complacent and lazy.'

'What's wrong with complacent and lazy?' asked Steve. 'I *like* complacent and lazy.'

'Anything about Professor Halflight?' asked Noah.

'Some. But it's not very consistent. One website says he was born in Munich in November of 1938, and that his name was originally Julius Halblicht. But Wikipedia says he was born in Queens, New York, in August of 1937 and his name was originally Julius Halbrecht.

'Whichever it was, he was educated at the Solomon Schechter High School in New York, and then the Bar-Ilan University in Tel Aviv. He graduated in 1961 but after that there's nothing about him at all, where he went or what he did. He just kind of surfaces in 1984 as professor of Jewish history at the Hebrew Union College in Los Angeles, and in 1993 as professor of Jewish history at UCLA.

'I did find a picture of him, though, in 1993, on Google Image. Here, look.'

Leon clicked on to the Google image library and showed them a blurry black-and-white photograph of Professor

Halflight sitting in a wheelchair. He must have been at a convention or a conference somewhere, because there were several square tables visible in the background, each with a flag on them, and name cards. He was much thinner than he was now, and he was wearing dark glasses and a neatly-trimmed beard. He was leaning forward and listening attentively to a man of about forty-five with black slicked-back hair, but the man's face was completely obscured by the flag in front of him.

'Does it say where this was taken, or who the other guy is?' asked Rick.

'No. It just says 1993.'

Rick examined the photograph more closely. 'There's a mirror behind him, and you can see some buildings and vehicles outside, and a couple of road signs. You want to make a print of this, Leon, and blow it up as much as possible? Maybe we can work out where this was.

'And keep at it. You're doing real good.'

Noah stayed beside Leon for a while.

'You OK?' he asked him.

Leon nodded. 'At least this has given me something to keep my mind off it.'

'You should call your uncle, ask about your dad's funeral arrangements.'

'Do you think I'll be able to go?'

'I don't know. Maybe we can think of a way. We don't even know if the coroner has released his remains yet. But we'll have to be careful. These guys are looking for you just as much as they're looking for me and Silja.'

Leon looked pale and tired. But he lifted his head and said, 'I don't mind so much about burying my dad, so long as I can bury the people who killed him.'

At 5 p.m., Bill Pringle called back.

'How did your friend make out?' asked Rick.

'Oh . . . pretty good.'

'Did he find another medallion?'

There was a lengthy pause, and then a cough, and then Bill said something indistinct.

'Bill? Is everything OK? Did your friend find another medallion?'

'Erm, sure. Everything's fine. I think – I think you need to come to DC in person.'

'Can't you tell me over the phone? Or email me?'

Another cough.

'Bill, are you sure that everything's OK?'

'Of course. But what I said earlier, about people listening. You know, Echelon.'

'You haven't had any trouble, have you?'

'Everything's fine, good buddy. Everything's hunky-dory. But you really need to come here in person, so that I can explain this to you.'

'What's to explain? Just tell me who the medallion belonged to. All I really need is a name.'

'Rick, this is the only safe way we can do this, OK?'

Rick took the phone away from his ear and frowned at it. He had never heard Bill Pringle sound so shrill before. Bill was normally a quiet, steady, wry kind of guy, but now he sounded almost as if he were begging.

'OK,' said Rick. 'I'll catch the redeye, see you for breakfast in the morning.'

Bill hung up without saying anything else.

'Is everything all right?' asked Adeola.

'I'm not sure. Bill says that his friend has found another medallion, but he wants me to go to DC tonight so that he can tell me about it face to face. He says it's too much of a risk, telling me over the phone.'

'You need to be very careful about this, Rick,' said Adeola.

'I'll tell you what,' said Steve, 'I'll come along, too, if that's OK. Watch your back for you.'

'Me, too,' said Noah. 'If there's going to be any trouble, I don't want to be here, sitting on my hands, considering I started this whole mess, by bringing up that medallion in the first place. Should have left it where it was.'

'No, Noah,' said Adeola. 'If there is one thing that I have learned from all of my work in politics, it is that you have to face up to the worst that can happen before you can hope for the best.'

Seventeen

They caught the 9.15 p.m. America West flight from Burbank and arrived at Ronald Reagan airport in Washington at 7.30 the next morning.

After they had made their connection at Phoenix, Noah had managed to sleep for over two hours, and if he dreamed he didn't remember any of his dreams when he woke up. But as they taxied up to the finger, Rick said, 'You sure like to talk in your sleep, don't you? Quite some conversation you were having with somebody. Kept talking about KOs.'

KOs? thought Noah. Or had it been *chaos*?

It was a grey, humid day, with clouds hanging low all across the capital, like filthy sheets. They rented a metallic red Chevy Lumina and drove south on Route 1 to Groveton. A fine rain began to prickle the windshield.

Steve, sitting in the back seat, leaned forward and said, 'Let's do a straight run up the street, see if there's anything that don't look quite right.'

They reached the corner of Alexandria Street, where Bill Pringle lived. It was a quiet, unassuming street of two-storey houses, most of them painted white or grey or pale blue, with creepers on their front porches, and children's bicycles lying on their front driveways. The paper boy had already delivered: outside almost every house a copy of the *Washington Post* was flapping damply on the grass.

Bill's house was number 1103. There were two cars parked outside the garage, a Dodge Intrepid and a five-year-old Honda Civic. The drapes were open but as they drove past they saw nobody in the front living room, nor the bedrooms upstairs.

There was a dark green Ford Explorer with tinted windows, parked by the curb about a hundred yards away from Bill's house.

'What do you think about that?' Steve asked Rick. 'If that's a resident, how come he hasn't parked in his own driveway?'

'The licence-plate is local,' Rick observed. 'And there's a "baby on board" sticker in the back. I can't see any self-respecting terrorist driving around with *that* in his window.'

They turned into Bill Pringle's front yard and climbed out of the car. Rick went first, with Noah and Steve staying well behind him. Steve kept glancing up and down the street, and giving nervous little sniffs and shrugs.

Rick rang the doorbell and they heard it chime inside the house. He was just about to ring again when the door opened and Bill Pringle appeared.

'*Rick*,' he said, almost as if he hadn't been expecting him. 'And you brought some friends, too.'

Noah glanced at Rick to judge his reaction to Bill Pringle's appearance. Bill was in his early sixties, as skinny as a scarecrow, with wild white hair and heavy-rimmed spectacles. He hadn't shaved that morning, because his deeply-cleft chin was sparkling with white stubble. He was wearing a grubby plaid shirt and baggy jeans, and carpet slippers.

'You – ah – want to come in?' he asked them.

Rick hesitated. 'Everything OK, Bill?'

'Sure. Sure. Come on in.'

'You're sure that everything's OK, Bill? Looks to me like you haven't slept.'

Bill didn't answer, but stepped back into the hallway, and made a beckoning gesture with his finger.

Rick went in after him, followed by Noah and Steve. The hallway was cramped, with a barometer hanging on the wall, and an old-fashioned hallstand, with pegs for hats and coats. There was a stale, warm smell in the house, as if the air conditioning had been switched off and the windows kept shut.

As soon as Bill led them through to the parlour at the back of the house they understood what was wrong. Bill's wife, Kathleen, was sitting at one end of the beige leather couch, wearing only a dark maroon bathrobe, her grey hair in curlers. Her face was a picture of misery and exhaustion. On the other end of the couch sat a young woman of about thirty-two or thirty-three, who from her looks, Noah immediately took to be Bill and Kathleen's daughter. She was wearing a summer dress with tiny red-and-yellow flowers on it, but the red ribbon around the neckline was torn, and there was an angry crimson bruise on her left cheekbone, so that her eye was almost completely closed.

Between the two of them, in what was almost a parody of domestic contentment, slept a large tortoiseshell cat. But immediately behind the couch stood two men in light grey suits. One looked like a boxer, with a shaved head and a broken nose. The other could have been a hairdresser, with a greasy, chestnut-collared pompadour and a narrow, rat-like face. The hairdresser had his arms folded, but in his left hand he was holding a dull grey Beretta automatic.

'Good morning, gentlemen,' said the hairdresser, in a tensile North Virginia accent. 'We've been waiting on you for quite some hours now.'

'Oh, Bill,' said Rick.

Bill Pringle lowered his head and said nothing. But the hairdresser came around the couch and said, 'Poor Bill, he didn't have too much choice now, did he? So don't you go being too censorious, sir. If you were married to such a lovely woman, and you had such a lovely daughter, what would *you* do if somebody were to threaten to blow their brains all over your rug?'

Rick said. 'What's the deal?'

'Deal? Who said anything about any deal?'

'Then what do you want? Because whatever it is, you're welcome to it.'

The hairdresser came closer. He had a large wart at the side of his nose, and his teeth were brown and crooked. He smelled strongly of lavender oil.

'All I want, sir, is silence. Nothing more. Nothing *less*, though, neither.'

'You can have it,' said Noah. 'You want us to promise never to say anything to anybody about those medallions? OK, we promise. We'll back off, and forget we ever saw them. We'll never mention them again, as long as we live.'

'Then you know why we're here?' said the hairdresser.

'Like I said – whatever it is those medallions mean – whatever it is they represent – we're prepared to forget about them. I swear to God that you'll never hear from us again.'

Bill said, 'Please. My wife isn't well. Whatever this is all about, there's no profit in it for us. This gentleman here says that we'll forget it. I give you my word of honour, we'll both forget it. So long as he remembers the number I gave him.'

The hairdresser looked from Bill to Rick to Noah to Steve, and he didn't blink once. Then he walked back around the couch, taking a silencer out of his pocket as he did so. He screwed the silencer on to the muzzle of his Beretta, then cocked the gun with his thumb, and pointed it directly at the back of Kathleen Pringle's head. The Pringles' daughter let out a high-pitched breath, and Bill pleaded, 'No, please! *Please!*'

'What did you expect?' asked the hairdresser. 'You didn't think that your word of honour was going to cut it? Did you seriously expect me to go back to the people who sent me here, and tell them that your mum-ness is one hundred percentile guaranteed, because you *promised*? What do you think they would say to me, if I did that?'

'I think they'd be genuinely upset,' remarked the boxer. He had the childish lisp of a man with no front teeth.

'Well, me too. So I'm sorry about this, but you don't leave me any alternative. Henry, let's get this over with.'

The boxer reached into his belt and produced a long, triangular-bladed knife.

Noah said, 'Hold it! Hold it!' But the boxer stepped up behind Kathleen Pringle and took hold of a bunch of her hair curlers in his left hand, pulling her head back and exposing her throat.

'*No!*' shouted Bill Pringle. He made a jerky rush forward, like a marionette whose strings have become entangled, and tried to stumble around the side of the couch. But with complete calmness, the hairdresser lifted his automatic, levelled it, and shot Bill at point-blank range in the face. There was a sharp, compressed whistle, and the back of Bill's head was sprayed all over the wallpaper behind him, and halfway over a family photograph.

Kathleen Pringle screamed, and tried to stand up. The boxer pulled her back down again. Her daughter reached across for her, catching at her sleeve. '*You can't! You can't do this!*' The tortoiseshell cat opened its eyes and looked up, plainly annoyed at being woken up.

The hairdresser moved across, trying to push the daughter away. But the instant he was blind-sided behind the boxer, Noah lunged forward and seized hold of the cat. The cat screeched in fury, its legs scrabbling, but Noah took hold of the end of its tail and swung it around in the air – once, twice – and then he threw it straight into the hairdresser's face.

The hairdresser yelled out, '*Shit!*' and toppled backwards, with the cat clawing wildly at his cheeks. He fell awkwardly into the green velveteen drapes behind him, just as Noah bounded over the couch and dropped his full two-hundred-pound weight on top of him. He caught hold of the hairdresser's left wrist and wrenched it backwards, so that he could hear all of his tendons snapping, like elastic bands. The hairdresser lost his grip on his Beretta, and Rick bent over and picked it up, pointing it between his eyes. The cat rushed out of the room as if all the demons in hell were chasing it.

The boxer backed into the corner by the window, holding up his knife. Rick said, 'You want some advice, buddy? Drop it, before I drop you.'

But the boxer shifted the knife from one hand to the other. 'You think you have the balls?' He pronounced it 'ballth', which somehow made it sound more threatening.

Steve said, 'Come on, feller. Put it down.' He carefully stepped over Bill Pringle's body and moved around the couch. Kathleen Pringle was whimpering in shock, and her daughter was holding on to her tightly.

'What you going to do, man? Shoot me in cold blood? You're not going to shoot me in cold blood.'

'Try me,' said Rick, aiming the Beretta at him.

Steve picked up a green brocade cushion from the couch, and held it up in front of him. The boxer stabbed at it, and changed hands with his knife again.

Noah approached him from the other side.

'I'm going to gut one of you,' said the boxer. 'Come on, ladies, which one of you is it going to be?'

Steve dodged towards him, and then to his right. The boxer slashed at his cushion, and a blizzard of feathers blew out. He lurched around to face Noah, but Noah was much too quick for him. He side-stepped behind him, seizing his left wrist and twisting it up between his shoulder blades. Then he grabbed his right wrist, and jammed it upward.

The point of the boxer's own knife went vertically straight into his lower jaw, just behind his chin, penetrating his tongue and crunching into his palate. His eyes widened, and blood spurted out from between his lips. He said, '*Mmmmfff, mmmmfff, mmmmfff,*' and spun around, trying to tug it out. He fell against the wall, and then knocked over a side table with a lamp on it.

Rick went straight up to him and shot him in the ear. Blood splashed over the wall like a huge crimson chrysanthemum. Then he went back to the hairdresser, who was still lying on the floor behind the couch.

Noah said, 'Jesus, Rick. You're not going to shoot both of them?'

'I thought we decided it was kill or be killed. We're a hit squad, remember?'

'Jesus. Yes, but Christ!'

Rick hunkered down beside the hairdresser and pointed the Beretta at his nose. The hairdresser flinched, and lifted one hand as if to shield himself.

'You're going to tell us who you are, and who sent you?' Rick asked him.

'Are you serious?' said the hairdresser.

'Oh, for sure. I'm serious.'

'And if I tell you? What – you'll off me anyhow?'

'I'll think about giving you a head start.'

The hairdresser lowered his hand. It had been a futile gesture, in any case. He gave Rick and Noah a tilted, rueful smile.

'I'm sure glad my mom can't see me now. She always wanted me to be a veterinarian.'

'She still alive?'

'Uh-hunh. Died of ovarian cancer, when I was eleven.'

Noah said, 'Why don't you tell us who sent you? What do you have to lose?'

The hairdresser dabbed the cat scratches on his cheeks with his fingertips. 'It won't do you any good, even if I tell you. You're better off changing your names and going to live some-place where nobody knows you.'

'Those medallions,' said Noah.

'Sure, they're part of it, like the swastika was part of the Third Reich. But, like I say, you're better off not knowing. They'll find you, no matter what you do, and then—' He made a throat-cutting gesture.

'They always do that? Cut people's throats?'

'It's symbolic. People with their throats cut can't speak any more.'

'How about castration?' asked Noah, sharply. 'One of my friends was gelded, as well as having his throat cut.'

'That's symbolic, too. A man with no nuts can't go spreading the seeds of doubt.'

Rick said, 'One more time, buddy. Tell us who sent you.'

Noah turned to Steve and said, 'Steve – how about taking Mrs Pringle and her daughter out of the room? Mrs Pringle – are you OK?'

Kathleen Pringle was grey-faced and still shaking. Steve helped her to stand up, and led both women through to the kitchen.

The hairdresser said, 'You might as well accept it. There's no way I'm going to tell you any more. So you'd better do whatever it is your conscience tells you.'

Rick looked at Noah, but the Beretta was still aimed at the bridge of the hairdresser's nose and his hand was rock steady.

'I'm coming, Mom,' said the hairdresser, and Rick shot him in the head.

Eighteen

It was a hot, brassy morning in Los Angeles. Adeola went with Ted that morning to the Hyatt Regency Century Plaza, where the International Peace Convention was being held, to meet two senior directors of DOVE, and to attend a welcome buffet for the 270 delegates.

She wore a long white flowing dress of see-through muslin, and a white turban decorated with bronze leopard pendants from Benin.

Alvin Metzler was waiting for her in his suite overlooking the Avenue of the Stars. Alvin was DOVE's political director of mission, a small, neat, trimly-bearded man with a nose like an anteater and a fondness for lightweight designer suits and very bright blue socks. John Stagione was there, too, the security director, a former FBI bureau chief with wavy grey hair and a sallow complexion like spotted liverwurst.

'You disappeared under our radar for a couple of days,' said John Stagione, in his harsh, congested voice, splitting a pistachio nut with his thumbnail.

'Rick was taking care of me – Rick and two friends of his.'

'Oh yes?'

'You don't have to worry. They were ex-Secret Service.'

'Ex-Secret Service or not, you should have let me vet them first. Even old friends can be turned. Retired Secret Service officers, finding it hard to live on their pensions – everyone has their price.'

'As dedicated as I am, John, and as much as I love you all, I do occasionally need *some* time to myself.'

'Thing is, Adeola,' said Alvin Metzler, 'we have an eye-watering amount of capital invested in your current missions. Our investors aren't going to be very happy if someone knocks you off and screws up a mission as potentially profitable as the Ethiopian deal. I mean – as you're aware – peace is a business like any other.'

He paused, and then he added, 'Not only that, we'd be extremely distressed on a personal level to lose you.'

'Oh, thanks. But I have no intention of making myself a target, Alvin, believe me. I'm a conciliator, not a martyr.'

'Of course. But we've decided to intensify your personal security. John has arranged for six close-protection body-guards to keep a twenty-four-hour watch on you, in six-hour shifts.'

'For how long?'

'Until we find out who's been trying to paint you out of the picture,' said John Stagione.

'Or at least until your current missions are complete,' Alvin Metzler added.

'Well, I appreciate your concern,' Adeola told him. 'But I'm not too sure that I'm going to be able to live like that.'

'I'm sorry, Adeola, this is non-negotiable. The trust have discussed it and we simply can't risk anything going wrong, not at this juncture.'

Adeola said, 'All right, if that's the way it has to be. Does Rick know any of this protection team?'

'Ah,' said John Stagione. 'That's where I've had to make some changes. I'm moving Rick to intelligence duties.'

'You mean you're demoting him?'

'I'm moving him back into the office, that's all.'

'But come on, John, I don't trust anybody else, not like I trust Rick. I want *him* to take care of me.'

John Stagione scratched the back of his neck. 'From what I hear, Adeola, he's being taking care of you over and above his job description.'

'That's no business of yours.'

'Oh, it is, I'm afraid. Any personal relationship between a DOVE negotiator and a member of her protection staff is a security risk. It can lay both of you open to all kinds of untoward pressures.'

Alvin Metzler said, 'We're going to give Rick a couple of months' downtime, Adeola. He's been under a whole lot of strain lately, especially after losing so many of his team in Dubai, and in Ireland. Remember that he's still officially under investigation by the *Garda Síochana*.'

'I want him to stay with me. I insist.'

'I'm sorry, Adeola. It's a decision made by the whole trust and it has to be final.'

Downstairs, in the largest of the Century Plaza's convention rooms, delegates from twenty-three different countries were mingling at an informal buffet. Most of them wore dark business suits: others were dressed in flamboyant national costumes, saris from India and kente cloths from Ghana; Arabian haiks and jellabas.

It had been somebody's idea to give the buffet a Cajun theme. Underneath the sparkling chandeliers, the long tables were crowded with shrimp and blackened catfish and corn-fried oysters, as well as spiced chicken and jambalaya and filé gumbo. In the far corner, a quartet in floppy blue shirts were playing zydeco music with fiddles and accordion.

Adeola knew many of the delegates already, especially the Middle Eastern diplomats. With Ted keeping close beside her, she talked to the junior foreign minister from Algeria, the development minister from Qatar, the trade secretary from Egypt. In the far corner of the room, though, she saw a good-looking man of maybe forty-two or forty-three, with dark, combed-back hair, rimless glasses and a suntan, and although she thought she recognized him, she couldn't immediately think of his name.

She excused herself from the Egyptian trade secretary and negotiated her way across the room. The man was standing by himself, nursing a glass of white wine. He looked not unlike a young Louis Jourdan, almost too smooth and too handsome to be attractive. He was wearing a well-cut navy blue coat and a pale blue silk necktie with some kind of gold insignia on it.

Adeola went up to him and said, directly, 'We've met, haven't we?'

He didn't even look at her. 'No, we haven't. I'd have remembered.'

She held out her hand with all the jangly bangles on her wrist. 'Adeola Davis. I'm sure I've seen you before.'

He turned to her. His eyes were unusually black. He clasped her hand between both of his, and slowly shook it. 'Adeola Davis, from DOVE? Yes . . . I read about you in *Newsweek*. Globe-trotting freelance peace negotiator extraordinaire.'

'That's one description.'

'It's an honour to meet you, Adeola Davis. Without you, the world would be a much more miserable place than it is already. Can I get you a glass of wine? Or a mint julep? I think they're even serving a blue mamou.'

'I'm fine with Evian, thanks. So why do I think I know you?'

'I've been featured in a few magazines, I guess.' His voice was deep and measured, with a hint of a Southern accent, which Adeola couldn't quite place. Louisiana, possibly. 'Hubert Tocsin. I was the winner of last year's Round-Bermuda Yacht Race. And the year before that.'

'Don't tell me that's your only credential for being here.'

'Of course not. But I like to boast about it, all the same.'

'So what are you doing here? I saw you across the room and I thought you looked kind of lost.'

Hubert Tocsin looked around at the peace delegates, and gave an odd, self-deprecating smile. 'As a matter of fact, I'm the devil in the company of angels. I'm the owner of Tocsin Weapons and Rocketry Systems, of Escondido, and the current president of the Association of American Arms Manufacturers.'

'*Now* I know you,' said Adeola. 'You made that speech,

didn't you, at the United Nations, about arms being necessary for world peace?'

'That's the one. I'm flattered you remember.'

'I wouldn't be flattered, if I were you. I disagreed with
every word you said. And I mean *vehemently*, with a
capital V.'

Hubert Tocsin laughed. 'I wouldn't have expected you to
feel any other way. But I guess the difference between you
and me is that you're an idealist and I'm a realist.'

'Mr Tocsin, I've been to Angola, and I've been to Beirut,
and I've been to Somalia, and I've witnessed your reality first
hand. Believe me, it isn't pretty.'

'Well, don't let's fall out over our different world view, not
in the first five minutes of meeting each other. I know what
you're telling me, Ms Davis, and I fully understand your
distress. But as far as I'm concerned, a well-armed world is
the lesser of two evils. Look at the Hutus. They didn't need
smart bombs to slaughter each other. All they needed was
prejudice and hatred and machetes, and you can't ban prejudice and hatred. Or machetes, for that matter.'

A waiter came past with a tray of fried shrimp, and Hubert
Tocsin took one. 'I have a special weakness for fried shrimp,'
he smiled. 'I ought to take you to Mulate's, in New Orleans.
They also serve a crawfish *étouffée* to die for, and a great
blackened alligator, if you have a taste for blackened alligator.'

'The weapons maker invites the peace negotiator out for
dinner?' asked Adeola.

'Why not? I could spend the evening making swords and
you could spend the evening beating them into ploughshares.'

Adeola looked at him acutely. 'So what exactly *are* you
doing here?'

'I'm here because I was invited. I'm here because peace is
just as much my concern as yours, even though we both believe
in different ways of achieving it.'

'You got that right.'

Hubert Tocsin put down his wine glass and took hold of
her hand again. 'I really respect what you do, Ms Davis. I
just want you to know that.'

'I wish the feeling were mutual, Mr Tocsin, but it isn't.'

Hubert Tocsin shrugged. 'That makes me a little sad, I have
to admit.'

'I saw a fifteen-month-old boy lying in the dirt in Beirut, with both legs blown off at the knees. That made *me* sad.'

Hubert Tocsin kept on smiling, and kept on holding her hand, but Adeola saw something in his face that made her feel suddenly chilled, as if the sun had disappeared behind a cloud.

She rejoined Ted, who was standing at the end of the buffet table with his mouth full of spicy Cajun sausage. 'Everything OK?' he asked her. 'You look kind of pissed.'

'No . . . I'm fine. I met somebody I didn't expect to meet, that's all.'

'That guy in the sport coat? Who he?'

'Let's put it this way. You see all these people gathered here today? One way and another, Hubert Tocsin has probably killed a thousand times more people than this.'

Outside, in the hotel lobby, John Stagione was waiting for her, looking impatient and sweaty, with a stocky young Korean man in a black suit and a black shirt. He had shiny black hair parted in the centre and long scimitar-shaped sideburns.

'Adeola, this is Hong Gildong. He's going to be taking care of you for the next six hours.'

Hong Gildong bowed his head and shook her hand. 'Pleased to make your acquaintance, Ms Davis,' he said, in immaculate English. 'Rest assured I will make my presence as unobtrusive as I possibly can. But if there is anything you require from me, all you have to do is say the word.'

'Well, thank you,' said Adeola, turning to Ted in amusement.

Ted said, 'Guess you won't be needing *me* to run close-protection any more. Obtrusive kind of a mook like me.'

'You've been terrific, Ted, don't worry about it. You and Steve both. I'll see you later, anyhow, when Rick and Jonah get back.'

'Where is Rick?' asked John Stagione. 'I've been calling him on his cell all morning but he's not answering.'

'Went to see a friend, that's all,' said Adeola. 'I'll have him call you.'

'I have my SUV here,' said Hong Gildong, gesturing towards the curb.

At that moment, with a faint ringing sound, one of the bronze pendants dropped from Adeola's turban and rolled across the sidewalk. The fine silk thread necklace that was holding it had broken.

She picked it up, and unwound the necklace from her head-dress. Another pendant must have dropped off without her noticing it, because she had only five left. They were only copies of the fifteenth-century originals from the reign of Oba Ewuare, but they were beautifully cast, and they had been given to Adeola by the Nigerian ambassador to symbolize her 'speed, her grace, her beauty, and like the leopard itself, her remorselessness'.

'Hold up a minute,' she said, and went back across the lobby to the convention room. The reception was beginning to break up now, and the few delegates left were standing around in small knots, finishing their discussions and saying their goodbyes. But Hubert Tocsin was still there, in the same corner, and he was talking to a black man in a grey suit.

As she came nearer, Hubert Tocsin caught sight of her, and the black man turned around, too. It was Captain Madoowbe, from the Ethiopian security forces, with his ritually-scarified, pockmarked cheeks. He gave her a grin crowded with orange teeth.

'Captain Madoowbe. What a pleasant surprise.'

'Ms Davis, the pleasant surprise is all mine. I am here in the LA with His Excellency Ato Ketona Aklilu.'

'I wasn't aware that you and Mr Tocsin were acquainted.'

Hubert Tocsin laid a hand on Captain Madoowbe's shoulder. 'Oh, you'd be surprised what friends you can make, in the arms business. Once I had breakfast with Fidel Castro's brother, Raul, and dinner with the Most Reverend Diarmuid Martin, the Primate of Ireland, both on the same day.'

'I've dropped one of these pendants,' said Adeola. 'You can't see it anywhere, can you? It's a reproduction, but I'd hate to lose it.'

Hubert Tocsin and Captain Madoowbe looked around the carpet. Suddenly, Captain Madoowbe bent down and picked up the missing pendant from underneath one of the buffet tables. 'Here, Ms Davis. I have always had a keen eye.'

'Thank you, Captain,' said Adeola.

There was another moment of high tension, although Adeola didn't know what it was that was causing the stress between herself, Hubert Tocsin and Captain Madoowbe. It was almost like standing next to an electricity substation, the atmosphere so charged Adeola felt as if sparks might crackle between them.

Hubert Tocsin looked at her as though he were expecting her to say something else. She was deeply curious to know what he and Captain Madoowbe were talking about, but it was obvious that they were waiting for her to leave before they resumed their conversation. She walked out of the hotel and Hong Gildong opened the Landcruiser's door for her.

'You've found your leopard, Ms Davis?'

'Oh, please, call me Adeola. And what's *your* real name?'

Hong Gildong smiled. 'You know Korean, then.'

'I know that "Hong Gildong" is just an anonymous name, like "John Doe".'

'Hong Gildong will do. I am an anonymous sort of man.'

They pulled away from the front of the hotel. As they did so, Adeola's cellphone rang and it was Rick.

Nineteen

R ick tapped on the bedroom door. Linda Pringle said, 'Come in.'

Inside, the flowery green drapes were drawn to keep out the late-afternoon sun. Kathleen Pringle was lying in bed asleep, the back of her hand half-covering her face. Her daughter was sitting beside her in an armchair, her eyes swollen, but looking much more composed now.

'She went off all right, then?' asked Rick.

'I think she's too shocked to cry. I think I am, too.'

'I'm so sorry for what happened. You should never have gotten involved in any of this.'

He looked around the bedroom. It was small and stuffy, with green speckly wallpaper and a framed print of Jesus above the bed.

'You'll be safe here, anyhow,' he told her. 'Phil and Grace, they're good people. They'll take care of you.'

'What about Dad? What about those men?'

'Steve will take care of them. That's one of Steve's specialties: making problems disappear.'

'But that's my dad. I don't want him just to disappear.'

'I know. And if I know Steve, he'll have fixed something, so you can say goodbye properly, when this is all over. Listen – why don't you come downstairs and have a drink? We can leave the door open in case your mom needs you.'

Tiredly, Linda stood up and leaned over to kiss her mother's hand. Then she followed Rick downstairs to the living room. Steve wasn't back yet, but Noah was sitting with Phil and Grace Bukowski.

Phil was in his mid-sixties, bald, with prominent false teeth, while Grace was much larger than he was, a big woman with dyed-brown curly hair that was much too abundant for her age, and badly-drawn eyebrows, and a long face like a placid horse.

As skinny as he was, Phil had once been in charge of the close-protection team that looked after President Jimmy Carter, and completely unknown to the media or the public, he had stopped a .22 bullet that had been fired at the president from long range on the golf course at Pine Hills, Georgia. He was tough, and he was wiry, and he was unfailingly loyal, which was why he had agreed to take care of Kathleen and Linda Pringle until it was safe for them to go home again.

Rick sat down in one of the cream leatherette armchairs, and Grace brought him a cold bottle of Miller. On the table next to him there was a cluster of framed photographs of grandchildren, some of them with Phil's imp-like looks, and others resembling horses.

'Cute kids,' said Rick.

'Nine of them we got now,' Phil told him. 'And a tenth due in September.'

'Jesus. The whole damn world's going to be overrun with Bukowskis.'

'Your mom OK now?' Grace asked Linda.

'She's sleeping, thank God.'

Rick said, 'Your dad . . . did he ever tell you the name of this friend of his, from the Secret Service Archive? The one he met at The Watergate?'

'Sure,' said Linda. 'Wallace Rudge. Dad had known him

for years. They used to go fishing together. Wallace was writing a book about the Secret Service.'

'I know Wallace,' said Phil. 'Good, steady guy. You want his phone number?'

Wallace Rudge lived in Falls Church, only seven miles away. Rick called him but the line was busy. Ten minutes later he called again but the line was still busy. After forty-five minutes, he said to Noah, 'Either this guy's wife is on the phone, or there's something wrong. Why don't we drive over there?'

Noah swigged the last of his Miller and said, 'Why not?'

It was almost 7.45 p.m. by the time they turned off the Dulles Toll toward Tyson's Corner, and the sun was shining directly into their eyes, so that they had to lower their sun visors.

Wallace Rudge lived in a 1950s brown-brick apartment block on George C. Marshall Drive, mostly hidden from the road by oak trees. Rick parked in the visitors' area at the back of the block, but before he went to the front doors, he walked over to the residents' parking section. The space marked 5C was occupied by a faded red Honda Accord.

'Well, somebody's home, even if it isn't him.'

They went up to the main entrance and Rick pressed the bell for apartment 5C. They waited, but there was no reply. Rick pressed the bell again. Still no response.

'This isn't right,' said Rick. 'His car's still here, his phone's off the hook.'

He jabbed every single bell. After a while, a man's voice came over the intercom. '*Deirdre? That you?*'

Without waiting for a reply, the man pressed the door-release buzzer, and Rick pushed the door open.

They took the elevator up to the fifth floor. The apartment block was hushed except for the muffled sound of *Friends* on somebody's television, with intermittent bursts of laughter. They walked along the dull green carpet until they reached apartment 5C at the very end, next to a hammered-glass window with dead flies on the sill.

Rick knocked. Then he pressed his ear against the door and listened.

'I can hear something. Sounds like a faucet running.'

He knocked again, and called out, 'Mr Rudge! Mr Wallace Rudge! Friends of Bill Pringle's here!'

Still no reply. He pushed the door and it swung open, silently. The lock was broken and the security chains had been cut, so that they were dangling loose.

Rick drew back his windbreaker and tugged out an M9 semi-automatic pistol.

'Where the hell did you get that?' asked Noah.

'Phil lent it to me. Precautionary measure.'

Rick dodged into the hallway, with Noah crouching well behind him. The Rudges' apartment was cramped and old-fashioned, with red sculptured carpets and tapestry-covered armchairs and couches. On the walls hung amateur oil paintings of rivers and forests and local churches, all of them signed *Nora Rudge*.

Noah walked across the living room and picked up the fallen telephone receiver. He held it up to show Rick, but he didn't have to say anything.

'Mr Rudge!' Rick shouted again. They could hear a faucet running, maybe in the bathroom, but nobody answered.

Noah said, 'They killed my friends in their bathroom, Mo Speller and his wife. Maybe you'd better take a look.'

Rick scuttled crabwise across the corridor. He nudged open the bathroom door with the muzzle of his M9, and then pushed the door wider and looked inside.

'Well?' asked Noah.

Rick stiffly stood up, leaning against the door frame for support. 'Looks like the same thing's happened here, man. It's wall-to-wall blood.'

'Oh, Christ.'

Rick took a quick look in the bedroom, and the kitchen, but there was nobody there. Whoever had murdered Wallace and Nora Rudge, they were long gone. He pushed his M9 back into his belt and came back into the hallway.

'Time to call in the cops?' asked Noah.

'Uh-hunh, Not yet, man. These guys seem to know what we're going to do even before we do. So don't let's rule out some tip-offs from the CIA, or the FBI, or the local law enforcement agencies.'

Noah nodded his head towards the bathroom door. 'Were they—?' he asked Rick, and made a throat-cutting gesture with his finger.

Rick nodded.

'Shit, that's terrible. That's terrible.'

'How do you think *I* feel? If I hadn't called Bill Pringle, and asked him to look into it—'

'He must have found out something important,' said Noah. 'Otherwise they wouldn't have—Shit.'

'Come on,' said Rick, gripping his arm. 'We need to get out of here, quick. We've probably left a shit load of forensic as it is.'

'But don't you think we ought to, like, search the place? Look for any notes that this Rudge guy might have left?'

'You think the guys in grey suits wouldn't have done that already? They're trying their damndest to keep a secret here, Noah. Besides, I think that Bill left me a clue already – even before he went to see Wallace Rudge at The Watergate.'

'So, what clue?' asked Noah, as they walked back into the living room at Phil and Grace's house.

'Don't you remember? Bill was promising those guys that he was going to keep quiet about the medallion, only a few seconds before they shot him. He said, *"This gentleman here says he'll forget it . . . so long as he doesn't forget the other number I gave him."*'

'I don't get it. What other number?'

'He must have meant the number he gave me last night, the Auburn number.'

'Maybe you should try calling it,' said Phil, and handed him the phone.

'I did. But as far as I can work out, it isn't a telephone number at all. The code for Auburn is 315, not 102, and it's not a cellphone number, either.'

'He didn't give you any other hints, apart from that number, and the name Auburn?'

'That was it. And he was very specific that it was Auburn, New York.'

'Maybe we should call Leon,' Noah suggested. 'He could check it out on the Internet for us.'

'Leon?'

'He found that Prchal character for us, didn't he?'

'Well, OK . . . maybe it's worth a try.'

Rick called Leon at the Bel Air, on the conference phone. 'Leon? It's Rick. You online?'

'Sure. I've been trying to find out who that guy is with Professor Halflight. I think I've identified the location. It's the Manchester Grand Hyatt, on Market Place, in downtown San Diego. But I haven't been able to identify the guy yet.'

'Who's there with you?'

'Adeola, and Silja, and Adeola's new bodyguard.'

'She has a new bodyguard?'

'Erm—'

Adeola broke in. 'Rick, don't worry about that for now. Alvin Metzler assigned me some extra protection, because of the Peace Convention.'

'Are you sure?'

'I'm sure I'm sure. I'll talk to you about it when you get back.'

'OK,' said Rick. 'I need to talk to Leon. Leon, that Professor Halflight stuff . . . can you drop that for now, and see what you can find re Auburn New York . . . related to the number – here it is – 1029190.'

There was a pause, and then Leon said, 'Not too much. All I have here is like New York stock market numbers.'

'Wait a minute,' said Rick. 'Bill said 1029190 – extension 1. Try an extra 1 on the end.'

Leon typed in the extra 1, but it produced nothing more than a grave-marker number in St Mary's Cemetery, Auburn.

'St Mary's Cemetery?' said Noah. 'Maybe we should find out who's buried there. Maybe *that's* the connection.'

Leon tried to access the cemetery's grave-marker listings, but 10291901 could only give him the family name Robbins.

'Looks like we'll have to fly to Auburn and dig 'em up,' said Noah.

'Hmm – sounds like a pretty obscure clue to me, even for Bill,' said Phil.

'Bill? I wouldn't put it past him,' said Rick. 'He *was* a cryptologist, as well as being a security analyst. He used to work for the code-breaking section.'

Over the phone, Adeola said, 'You mentioned a famous prison in Auburn, didn't you, Rick? Maybe that number he gave you was the identity number of one of the inmates.'

Leon typed in *Auburn Prison* but there was no Internet record of prisoners' identity numbers.

'In fact, it says here that the governors of Auburn Prison

did everything possible to take away their inmates' individuality. They weren't allowed to speak, and they all had to dress in identical black-and-white striped uniforms, like those prisoners in the old silent movies.'

'Hmm,' said Rick. 'Could be it's an account number, at one of the Auburn banks.'

More keyboard-rattling. Then, 'Tompkins Trust Company, HSBC – that's just about it. And neither of their account numbers starts with 102.'

'Wait up a second,' said Noah. 'My bank registration number, the one I use for online banking, it's the same as my birthdate, right, that's how I remember it. Oh-nine-oh-nine nineteen-seventy. Look at this number. This could be a date, too. October twenty-ninth, nineteen-oh-one.'

Leon typed '*Auburn, October 29 1901*'. Almost immediately, he said, 'This could be it. "October 29 1901. The execution at Auburn Prison of Leon Czolgosz, for the assassination of the president, William McKinley."'

'Rick – you have to read this,' said Adeola. 'I'll bet you this is what Bill Pringle was trying to tell you about.'

Leon typed at the keyboard some more. 'There's even a prison mugshot of him. Leon C-z-o-l-g-o-s-z, however the hell you pronounce it. And there's some biographical stuff underneath.'

'Read it,' said Rick.

'OK . . . "Leon Czolgosz was of Polish origin" – yeah, he sure *looks* Polish. "He was born in 1873, in Detroit. He suffered a nervous breakdown when he was twenty-five years old, and quit his job.

'"In the summer of 1901, he rented a room above a saloon in Buffalo, New York, and bought himself a .32 Iver-Johnson revolver for $4.50.

'"On September 6 1901, he approached President McKinley at the Pan-American Exposition in Buffalo, and shot him in the abdomen at point-blank range.

'"President McKinley died a week later, of shock. Leon Czolgosz was given a trial that lasted only eight hours and twenty-six minutes, and was found guilty in thirty-four minutes. He was electrocuted on October 29 1901, with three jolts of 1,700 volts each.

'"His last words were, 'I killed him because he was the enemy of the good people – the good working people.'

'"Sulphuric acid was poured into Czolgosz's coffin before it was sealed."'

'I don't think I know a damn thing about President McKinley,' said Noah. 'Was there any special reason why this Show-gosh guy should have wanted to assassinate him?'

'Who knows?' said Adeola. 'But just like General Sikorski, McKinley was a very skilful diplomat. A great compromiser. He was the first president who really dragged the United States out into the big wide world. Up until McKinley, Americans had been very inward-looking, very isolationist. But McKinley got us involved in foreign trade and international politics. It was McKinley who annexed Hawaii, and the Philippines.'

'See what it says here?' put in Leon. '"He might have survived, if his doctors had managed to get the bullet out. There was one of the very first X-Ray machines at the exhibition where he was shot, but nobody thought to use it."'

'If Czolgosz has any connection to Prchal,' said Rick, 'that means this terrorist organization goes way back to the beginning of the twentieth century. And maybe even further. And who knows who else they've assassinated.'

'Sure,' said Noah. 'But how are we going to prove it?'

'Wallace Rudge must have known of some material evidence. Maybe we should pay a visit to the Secret Service Archives, see what we can find.'

'Will they let us in?'

'Are you kidding me? Absolutely not. We'll have to find our own way in.'

Twenty

They waited until the last employee had left her desk at the First Columbia Insurance building and click-clacked on her court shoes to the elevator.

'OK,' said Rick, as they heard the elevator whine. He led Noah down to the end of the shiny marble-floored corridor, until they reached the window. Both of them were wearing blue overalls from the Potomac Office Cleaning Company and matching blue baseball caps, which they had found in the super's storage closet in the basement.

The First Columbia Insurance building stood right next to the Secret Service Library and Archive at 948 H Street. It was set slightly at an angle to the Secret Service building, and a few feet further back, and its window ledges were six or seven inches higher. All the same, it was so close that they could see a Secret Service librarian sitting in his shirtsleeves, sorting through two folders of filing, and they could almost read the label on his file.

At the rear, the two buildings were less than ten feet apart. The windows of the Secret Service building had been painted over in solid grey gloss.

'That's the archive section, in back,' said Rick. 'Hardly anybody ever goes in there. I mean, it's just like historical stuff. Cardboard boxes with Sirhan Sirhan's bloodstained T-shirt in it. James Earl Ray's forged Canadian passport, stuff like that.'

'There have to be alarms on those windows, surely.'

'Of course there are. But they're not activated until the library closes for the night. And somebody's almost always working late, like that guy there.'

They walked further along the corridor until they reached the last window. Rick opened the black canvas bag that he had brought with him and took out a broad-bladed chisel. He rammed it into the side of the bronze window frame, and levered the frame backward and forward. The catches had been permanently screwed into place, but it didn't take him more than two or three minutes to bend the screws until they snapped. The window swung inward, and they felt the warm draft of traffic fumes rising up from the street below.

Noah leaned over and looked down seventy-five feet to the narrow triangular space between the two buildings. A high wall with metal spikes on top of it separated the space from the H Street sidewalk, and the space itself was cluttered with trash cans.

'Hmm. Usually I have a mattress to fall on, or packing cases.'

'Hey – you're not counting on falling, are you?'

'No. But, you know, accidents happen.'

'Think you can do it?' Rick asked him.

'Well . . . it won't be easy. But, yes.'

'Don't do it just to prove something to me, man. This isn't a pissing contest.'

'I wouldn't. I'm doing this for Jenna, and Mo Speller, and Trina, and your friend Bill. Not to mention Wallace Rudge and his wife.'

Rick took a Capewell retractable grappling hook out of his bag, unfolded its four claws and handed it to Noah. Then he unwound a coil of nylon climbing rope, tying one end of it to the grappling hook and the other end around his waist.

'There's thirty metres of rope here, so you can rappel to the ground if you need to.'

Noah climbed up on to the window ledge. Rick held his legs to balance him while he swung the grappling hook around and around, and then threw it up to the parapet of the Secret Service building. He missed the first time, and the grappling hook clattered back down.

He swung it again, faster, and let out more rope. Then he hurled it upward and it caught on the guttering. He tugged it two or three times to make sure that it was firm, and then he turned to Rick and said, 'OK, let's go for it. You only live once.'

Rick handed him the chisel, which he tucked into his belt. He leaned back as far as he could, and then he swung himself across the gap between the two buildings, and landed with a complicated thud on the ledge of the window opposite.

The ledge was barely wide enough for Noah to kneel on, and there was only the narrowest rim across the top of the window frame for him to get a grip. For one long, vertiginous moment he was sure that he was going to lose his balance and fall. He didn't even dare to look back at Rick, because he could feel his centre of gravity teetering from one side to the other, and it was a long, nasty drop to the ground.

'You OK?' called Rick.

He didn't answer. Gripping the rope with his left hand, he edged himself a few inches backwards so that the sole of his right foot was wedged against the window frame. That steadied him, and allowed him to shift his right knee a little closer to the window, and make him feel more secure.

'OK now,' he said. 'Just give me a second, and I'll try to get this window open.'

Fortunately, it was a sliding window, which opened upwards. Still gripping the rope to keep himself from falling, he lifted the chisel out of his pocket and worked it into the gap underneath the frame. He managed to push the chisel in about an inch, but when he tried to pull the window up, he found that it wouldn't budge.

'What's the problem, man?' Rick asked him.

'Damn thing's jammed solid. Wait up.'

Inch by inch, he pulled himself upwards into a crouching position. He couldn't believe that he was so afraid of falling. In movies, he was always toppling off buildings and trampolining himself off cliffs. But in movies, he knew that he was going to land softly and safely, in a stack of packaging. As the old saying went, it ain't the falling you need to worry about, it's hitting the goddamned ground . . .

The top of the window frame was too low for him to stand up completely straight, but he was able to lift his left foot and place it on top of the chisel handle. Then he bore down on the chisel with all the weight he could muster without losing his balance.

At first, nothing happened. He twisted the rope around his hand so that he could hold on to it more tightly, and then he stamped down on the chisel handle again. There was a splitting sound, and then a loud creak, and the window opened a half-inch. The chisel dropped out and fell into the darkness.

'Shit,' he said, but the window was open now. Carefully, he knelt down again and insinuated his fingers into the gap. It took three hard tugs, but at last the window slid upwards, and he was able to climb inside.

He looked around. He was in a long, gloomy storeroom, with rows of cardboard boxes and box files arranged on grey metal shelving. There was a strong smell of old paper and lavender floor wax.

He turned back to the window. 'Everything OK?' Rick asked him. He gave the thumbs-up. Rick pulled the rope tight and then swung himself across, clumsily grabbing at the window ledge.

'Jesus! Ouch! And you do this for a living?'

Noah helped Rick to clamber in through the window, and then Rick immediately slid it shut. 'Just in case somebody decides to switch on the alarms before we've found what we're looking for.'

Taking a small flashlight out of his pocket, Rick checked the boxes closest to them. 'These are recent. Look – *Francisco Martin Duran, 1994*. He was the guy who took twenty-nine potshots at the White House, trying to kill President Clinton.'

He slid the long cardboard box off the shelf and opened the lid. Inside was a trench coat in a plastic bag, a stack of dog-eared notebooks, a collection of Polaroid photographs, a wristwatch, a cheap brown wallet, and a Chinese SKS assault rifle.

'See? The Secret Service keep pretty much everything that characterizes any particular case.'

Noah peered into the box. 'No medallion?'

Rick gave the box a shake. 'Not in this case. Wouldn't have expected one, either. Duran wasn't part of any terrorist group, so far as we could work out. He believed that the White House was connected to some kind of alien mist.'

They walked further along the corridor, with Rick flicking his flashlight at every box they passed. Most of the names Noah didn't recognize, but a few stood out. *Dan White, 1978*, the former policeman who had shot and killed Mayor George Moscone and Supervisor Harvey Milk in San Francisco. *Talmadge Hayer, 1965*, who had confessed to taking part in the shotgun assassination of the black power leader Malcolm X in New York. *Collie Wilkins, 1965*, accused of shooting civil rights activist Viola Liuzzo in Alabama.

'Rogues' gallery,' Rick remarked. 'You have to learn all about these screwballs, when you're training for close protection. It's supposed to help you pick out a would-be assassin. Creepy, isn't it, to think that those boxes contain their actual possessions?'

They walked up and down five rows of shelving before they came to the boxes related to the 1900s. Right at the very end, on the top shelf, they found a dark brown plywood box with a faded label on it, and the inscription *L. Czolgosz, 1901* written in italics in purple ink.

Rick lifted the box down and set it on the floor. Inside was a pale brown tweed coat, carefully folded and wrapped in tissue paper, even though it was worn-out and dirty. Underneath the coat there was a black hand-knitted sweater, with fraying cuffs, a grubby grey shirt with no collar, and a pair of dark brown corduroy pants.

A pair of cracked brown leather shoes had also been neatly wrapped up, in a copy of the *Buffalo Express*, so old that the paper had turned amber.

There were twenty or so letters and pages of notes, some of them written in blunt pencil, but a few of them written in a smaller, much more feminine hand, in ink. Rick picked one of these up and read it.

'*Dear Leon,*
  '*You ask me what an unemployed man should do to survive. I say he should ask for work. If they do not give him work, he should ask for bread. If they do not give him work or bread, then he should take bread.*'

Rick showed the letter to Noah. 'Look at the signature – Emma Goldman.'

Noah shook his head. 'Doesn't mean anything to me.'

'Emma Goldman was a famous anarchist – or *infamous* anarchist, I should say – and one of the early feminists, too. Red Emma, they called her. She was all in favour of birth control for women, dodging the draft, and assassinating capitalists. Not necessarily in that order of importance.'

'So maybe this Czolgosz guy wasn't just a lone screwball.'

'Hard to say, from this. But Emma Goldman's boyfriend was sent to prison for trying to kill Henry Clay Frick.'

'Who?'

'Big industrialist, in the 1890s. Gave millions to the arts, but when his workers tried to strike, he hired Pinkerton men to open fire on them. It was a different world then, Noah.'

'Maybe not so different,' said Noah. 'These bastards are still trying to kill Adeola, aren't they?'

Rick said nothing, but lifted out a grey cotton bag, with a drawstring. He shook it, and it sounded metallic. The drawstring was knotted so tightly that he had to cut it with his clasp knife. He tipped it up, and the contents spilled on to the floor: Leon Czolgosz' personal effects.

They sorted through them. There were three dollars and eighty-one cents in coins, two pencils with metal caps on them, a tortoiseshell comb with several broken teeth, a small screwdriver of the type used for fixing spectacles, and a heavy circular object wrapped up in greaseproof paper.

Rick passed it to Noah and Noah carefully unfolded it. It was a tarnished silver medallion, identical to all the others, decorated on one side with arrow-like cuneiforms, and inscribed on the other side with the name C Z O L G O S Z. Noah said, 'There. Guess that proves it, doesn't it, without a doubt? Czolgosz was connected to Prchal, and Prchal was connected to those Arab guys who tried to kill Adeola, and all of those guys who killed Jenna and Mo and your friends, too.'

'Wallace must have seen this at some time, or found it listed in the archive. I'm just amazed that nobody has ever made the connection before,' Rick said.

'Why would they? It's not like Czolgosz and Prchal and those Arab guys had the same, like, political agenda. One was a communist and one was a Soviet agent and the other two could have belonged to any bunch of mad Muslims you can think of. Maybe Adeola was right. Maybe they assassinate people for no other reason except to keep the world in a constant goddamn state of turmoil.'

They heard voices somewhere outside the archive, and a door slamming. Rick said, 'I think it's time we got the hell out of here, don't you? Keep the medallion. I'll put everything else back in the box.'

He quickly refolded Leon Czolgosz' clothes and returned the box to its place on the shelf. Then he and Noah made their way back towards the window, their soft-soled shoes squelching on the polished floor.

They were halfway to the window when Rick stopped, and pointed his flashlight at a large cardboard box marked with red capital letters.

'Will you take a look at this?' he said. 'Lucien Sarti.'

They heard more voices outside the door, and the jangle of keys. 'Come on,' Noah urged him. 'It sounds like they're coming in.'

But Rick had already pulled the box labelled *Lucien Sarti, 1972* off the shelf, and started to pick at the thin green ribbon that was tied around the lid.

'For Christ's sake, Rick,' said Noah. 'What's so important about Lucien Sarti, whoever he is?'

Rick gave up trying to untie the ribbon and cut it with his knife. He quickly lifted the lid and rummaged inside. The box contained a black suit, a white shirt, and several folders full of documents, as well as two strips of black-and-white passport photographs, showing a dark-haired man with bulbous eyes, a large nose, and a weak chin.

'Lucien Sarti,' Rick repeated. 'He was killed by the cops in Mexico. I never realized they brought his stuff back here.'

He rummaged around some more, coming up with a small spiral-bound telephone book, crowded with dozens of numbers; a penknife with a broken blade; and a necktie clip in the shape of a horse's head with an orange agate stone for an eye. There was something else, too: and Rick lifted it out of the bottom of the box as if he had discovered the Holy Grail. A silver medallion, with cuneiform patterns on the front, and the letters S A R T I on the reverse.

Rick shone his flashlight into his own face, so that Noah could see his expression.

'What?' said Noah. Outside the door to the archive, a man coughed, and another man said, 'Give me a couple of minutes, OK? I have to put all these records back.'

'*What?*' hissed Noah.

'Lucien Sarti was a hitman for the drug-trafficking mob in Marseilles, in the 1960s.'

'So?'

'He was one of the prime suspects in the assassination of JFK. Years afterward, he even confessed to it. Two shots were fired from behind the presidential limousine. But Sarti said that he fired the third shot, from the grassy knoll – an explosive bullet that hit Kennedy from the front, and killed him.'

He lifted up the medallion and let it spin.

'And just look what we have here.'

Twenty-One

'So, then, we have proved this connection between these different assassins,' said Silja, lighting up another cigarette. 'But what can we do about it? It seems to me that the more we discover, the greater the danger we are placing ourselves in.'

They were sitting around Adeola's cottage at the Bel Air, surrounded by the remains of the Mexican meal they had ordered on room service – chicken fajitas and carnitas duck and *poc chuc* with pasilla guacamole. They were drinking cold beer with wedges of lime.

'You're right,' said Rick. 'I was wary about going to the cops, even before we went to DC. But finding that medallion in Lucien Sarti's box—'

'I'm not so sure I understand about that,' said Silja. 'What does that tell you?'

'It tells me everything. Lucien Sarti worked for the Mafia in Marseilles and it was the Mafia who had JFK assassinated. But all of the law enforcement agencies were involved in it too, to a greater or lesser extent – the CIA and the FBI and the Dallas police. That's why they were so insistent that Lee Harvey Oswald shot him. It's always a whole lot more convenient to blame your classic lone gunman with a screw loose . . . that's happened in almost every assassination you can think of. It's especially convenient if you can also arrange to have him whacked before he can go to trial.'

'But what about the Warren Report?'

Rick smiled and shook his head. 'Nobody with any expertise in ballistics was convinced for a moment. The shots that hit Kennedy and Governor Connally had far too low a trajectory to have been fired from the schoolbook depository, and how the hell did Oswald manage to shoot Kennedy from the front?

'A guy called Thomas Killam was one of the first to point the finger at the Mafia, only a few days after JFK was shot. Well – you don't forget a name like "Killam", do you, not in this context? But Thomas Killam was found in an alleyway a few months later, and guess what? His throat had been cut wide open, same as your friends.

'So – no – I don't think it's a great idea to go to the cops, not yet. It only needs a word to be whispered in the wrong ear.'

'All the same,' said Adeola, 'how are we going to find these people unless we let them find us first?'

'That's something we'll have to sleep on. But Silja's right.

The more we know, the more danger we're in. We're really going to have to watch our backs.'

Early the next morning, Noah was woken by somebody persistently shaking his shoulder. He rolled over and almost fell off the couch.

'Jesus – I forgot where I was for a moment.'

He sat up, squinting against the sunlight. Leon was standing over him in his cuneiform riddle T-shirt and a baggy pair of boxers, his curly hair tangled like a fright wig.

'Noah? Sorry to wake you, man, but you have to see this.'

'What? What the hell time is it?'

'Five thirty. I've been up all night. You really have to see this.'

'OK . . .' Noah stood up and shuffled after him into his bedroom. Silja, on the other couch, was still fast asleep, with a multicoloured blanket pulled right up over her head.

Leon sat down at his desk, where he had been working on Adeola's laptop. On the screen was a black-and-white photograph of a hotel lobby crowded with men in suits. In the foreground a tall, handsome man was receiving some kind of award, and shaking the hand of an older man with a high, silver pompadour.

'So? Who's this?' asked Noah.

'Adeola asked me to check up on a guy called Hubert Tocsin. He owns an arms company in Houston, and he's president of the Association of American Arms Manufacturers.'

'Any reason?'

'She met him yesterday, that's all I know.'

Noah read the caption under the photograph. '"Loew's New York Hotel, Lexington Avenue, New York, 06/15/89. Hubert Tocsin, chairman and ceo of Tocsin Weapons and Rocketry Systems, is presented with the Wernher von Braun Award for Technological Excellence." So?'

'Two things. I can't be sure, but look at Hubert Tocsin's hair. He *could* be the guy in that photograph with Professor Halflight in San Diego. Tocsin Weapons and Rocketry Systems is based near San Diego, and they look pretty much alike, don't you think? But – look in the corner of *this* picture.'

Noah examined the photograph more closely. On the left-hand side of the lobby, two men were deep in conversation.

Although their faces were partially blurred by reflected flash from the mirror behind them, Noah recognized one of the men immediately. He was tall, and stooped, with an unmistakable lion-like head. Professor Julius Halflight.

The other man was much shorter, thickset and swarthy, with a skullcap and a jazzy shirt that was open at the neck. Around his neck, in his woolly black chest hair, hung a shining medallion.

'Is that what I think it is?' asked Noah.

'Yup. I've blown it up, and you can clearly see the cuneiforms.'

'Do you have any idea who he is, this character?'

'Oh, yes. That's why I woke you.'

'And?'

'I've been looking through every mugshot of every well-known assassin for the past fifty years. This is El Sayyid Nosair, who shot Rabbi Meir Kahane at the Marriott Hotel on November fifth, 1990.'

'You're kidding me!'

'No, I can show you dozens more pictures of him, if you like.'

'Well, well. I wonder what the good professor could have found to talk about with *him*.'

'Not much, apart from assassinating Rabbi Kahane, unless it was the price of toilet cleaner. Nasair worked as a janitor at the Manhattan Criminal Court.'

Leon brought up a *New York Times* report from 1990. 'See? When he went for trial, they tried to make out that Nosair was just another lone fruitcake. But there were two co-conspirators, at least – somebody who bought the gun for him, and somebody else who told him who he was supposed to shoot.'

'You've done good work there, Leon,' Noah told him. 'I don't know where this Tocsin guy fits into this, but it looks like your Professor Halflight is up to his neck in it, for definite.'

Leon looked grave and tired. 'Yes,' he said. 'And you know what that means?'

'Yes. It means that it was Professor Halflight who arranged to have your dad and your stepmom murdered. Or – at the very least – he must have tipped off the people who did.'

'I don't understand,' said Leon. 'My dad never did any harm to anybody, ever.'

'I know. But we'll make sure that Professor Halflight gets what's coming to him, I promise you.'

'Oh, yes? How?'

Adeola said, 'Maybe I can act as a Judas goat. Bring them out into the open. Because there's one thing we know for certain: they want to kill *me*. If I walk around freely when I go to the Peace Convention—'

'Out of the question,' said Rick. 'Far too risky. And far too unpredictable.'

'Rick is right,' agreed Hong Gildong. 'We want them to show themselves, but we must be in complete control of the circumstances. Otherwise they could kill you with a remote-control bomb or a sniper's bullet from a thousand yards away and we would never find out who had done it.'

'Rick – I've been thinking,' said Noah. 'Maybe I could, like, *join* them.'

'Join them? How are you going to manage that? For starters, they know what you look like.'

'I know. But supposing I approach them and they don't recognize me.'

'I don't understand. How could they possibly not recognize you?'

Noah turned around to Leon and said, 'Show them, Leon.'

Leon clicked Adeola's laptop, and the face of a Latino-looking man appeared, with a heavy moustache and brambly eyebrows.

There was a lengthy silence. Eventually, Rick said, 'OK, I give up. Who the hell is that?'

'That's me,' Noah told him. 'That's how I appeared in *Border Patrol*, doing the stunts for Pasqual Hernandes.'

'Well, terrific make-up job, I have to admit. But would it fool anybody in daylight?'

'Oh, sure. The foam prosthetics around the neck and chin are absolutely minimal. It's mainly hair and colouring. And you see how my ears stick out? It's amazing how much you can change somebody's appearance by making their ears stick out.'

Adeola said, 'You're suggesting you disguise yourself like this, and approach these people, and ask to join them?'

'It's an idea, isn't it? Now we know for sure that Professor Halflight's involved.'

'Come on – you really don't think that he'd recognize you?'
'I talked to him for less than ten minutes. Most of the time,
he had his back to me. I'll be dark-skinned, I'll look thirty
pounds heavier, I'll talk with a foreign accent. I can do any
accent you like. You vont German? You want Italiano?'
'It's insane,' said Rick. 'It's a really original idea, I'll grant
you, but it's total madness.'
'Did *you* recognize him?' Silja challenged him, pointing at
the picture.
'Well, no, I didn't—'
'Let me tell you, I was on a set once and Noah's only make-
up was a brown curly wig and brown contact lens in the eyes,
and he was walking with his shoulders hunched up so that he
looked so much shorter. I did not realize that it was Noah at
all until he came right up to me and said hallo.'
'But even if Halflight *does* fall for your disguise, why
should he recruit you for Emu Ki Ilani? I mean – look at the
lengths those bastards go to, just to prevent anybody from
guessing that they exist.'
Noah lit two cigarettes and passed one to Silja. Hong
Gildong reached out for one too.
'That's what I've been thinking about,' said Noah. 'Setting up
an assassination, it has a whole lot in common with setting up
a movie stunt. You have to calculate the timing, the risks involved,
the angles, the coordination between the people you're going to
use, and you have to make allowances for the unexpected.'
'Go on,' said Adeola.
'Almost every time, no matter what the location, they arrange
their assassinations in pretty much the same way. They work
out the logistics very carefully, but they recruit some stray
nutjob to commit the actual killing, so that it never looks like
some kind of organization's involved.
'Sometimes, when you're setting up a movie stunt, you
have to use the talent instead of a trained stunt-person, and
so the stunt is much more difficult to get right. But you make
allowances for the talent's inexperience, and you factor in a
far wider safety margin.'
'OK,' said Rick. 'But I still don't see how you can get to
join them. Why would they want to recruit you?'
'They might, if I assassinated somebody on their hit list.'
Adeola frowned. 'The only person we know for sure that

they want to assassinate is *me*. You're going to kill me, just so Emu Ki Ilani will accept you as a member?'

'You've got it.'

'Well, I'm sorry to think that you consider me so dispensable.' But Rick was smiling. He leaned back in his chair and said, 'I see where this is going.'

'I was thinking of kidnap,' said Noah. 'Followed by the release on the Internet of a highly-graphic video, showing Adeola's execution. A shot between the eyes, maybe. We might even manage a beheading.'

'A kidnap would certainly be the best way of doing it,' Rick agreed. 'We wouldn't even have to produce a body.'

'So who exactly is going to kidnap me?' asked Adeola.

'Some Middle Eastern fanatic, I guess,' Rick extemporized, 'from some splinter group that nobody's ever heard of.'

Adeola nodded. 'Palestinian would probably be the most convincing. I tried to talk to some Palestinian freedom fighters at the end of last year, but they refused to consider any kind of compromise. They spat at me and called me a Western whore.'

'Perfect,' said Rick. 'And before he executes you, this fanatic could appear on the video, ranting against capitalism and Western tyranny. A few days after which, he could contact Professor Halflight and ask if he could join Emu Ki Ilani and assist them in their struggle.'

'Can you talk like a Palestinian?' Adeola asked Noah.

'I told you, I can do any accent you want. I can do Greek. I can do Inuit.'

'Can you *look* Palestinian?'

'My friend Mitchell DeLorean is the best motion picture make-up artist in Hollywood. Did you ever see *The Gods of Mount Olympus*? Mitch won more than half a dozen awards for that. The movie was shit, but the make-up was sensational.'

Hong Gildong said, 'You will need to work this out with very great precision. The kidnap must be seen by independent witnesses and must appear to be one hundred per cent authentic. And whatever happens, you cannot afford to be apprehended. I have some friends who may be able to assist us with this.'

'You're going to need a watertight background story, too,' said Rick. 'I don't doubt that Professor Halflight and his pals have the facilities to vet you all the way back to the moment the doctor cut your umbilical cord.'

'I can help you out with that one,' said Steve. 'I have a friend in immigration. We can pick some stray Palestinian who's staying in this country without papers and gone on the lam. Somebody like that won't exactly be rushing forward to protest that he's innocent of kidnap and first-degree homicide, will he?'

Adeola said, 'All right. I think I understand what you're planning to do. I will disappear, presumed murdered. I'm not sure if this is ethical, and it will certainly cause a great deal of distress to my family and my friends and the people I work with at DOVE—'

'But?'

'But – if it's the only way of stopping these people, how can I disagree with it? I have so many dead friends who deserve justice. All that worries me, Noah, is what you're planning to do, once Emu Ki Ilani have accepted you – always supposing, of course, that they *do* accept you.'

'I hadn't really thought about that, not in any detail. I guess the first thing is to find out who the head honchos are, and how the organization works, and who they plan to knock off next.'

'And then?'

Noah pulled a face. 'It depends.'

'What if they do allow you to join them? Won't they expect you to kill somebody else? What if they demand that you assassinate somebody, or kidnap them and shoot them or cut off their head? What will you do then?'

Noah looked queasily from Rick to Silja to Hong Gildong. 'I don't know. I think I'll cross that particular swamp when I come to it.'

Twenty-Two

Mitchell DeLorean was delighted to turn Noah into a Palestinian fanatic. In fact, he was almost too enthusiastic. 'I could give you this amazing scar, all the way down the side of your face, and make your teeth look seriously rotten. And maybe you could have this one milky eye.'

'Mitch, we're not making *Aladdin and his Wonderful Lamp* here. I just want to look vaguely Middle Eastern. And the most important thing is that I'm not recognizable as *me*.'

'Sure, sure,' said Mitchell, walking around Noah in a circle, sizing up his profile, and flicking at his hair. Mitchell was a small, restless man – bald, with a deeply-suntanned head and protuberant ears, and a heavy black Stalin moustache. He was wearing a silk shirt with lilac swirls on it, very tight Massimo Dutti jeans and Cuban-heeled boots. For all that he acted so effeminate, he had a ravishing young wife – Nadia Greene, who had appeared in several episodes of *Coast Patrol*, most of which had required her to stand on the prow of a coastguard cutter in a diminutive yellow bikini, and say nothing.

'I don't need to make your face any darker, because you already have a suntan. But I need to change the *quality* of your skin tone. You need to look like a person who is naturally dark, but doesn't go out in the sun a whole lot.'

'OK. That sounds good.'

'I'm going to give some interesting moles on your forehead, too. Those will distract anybody who talks to you, so that their recognition process is thrown off. That was one of the reasons why women in the eighteenth century used to wear beauty spots . . . the spots caught people's attention and stopped them from realizing how homely the women were.

'I can give you some bushy black Muslim-style face fungus, and a bump on your schnoz. A bump on the schnoz, that's *amazing* for changing your appearance. Why do you think cartoonists always draw people with such big noses? Your nose is easily the most significant part of your facial identity. I made a huge prosthetic hooter for Brad Pitt once, for some picture about down-and-outs, but he refused to wear it. He didn't mind looking like he'd slept in a dumpster for three weeks, living on fish heads, but there was no way he was going to walk around looking like Jimmy Durante.'

Rick said, 'Before you agree to do this, Mitch, you have to understand that you won't be getting any credit for it, no matter how brilliant it turns out.'

'Sure, sure. Noah told me this was some kind of secret hush-hush thing.'

'It is. But it's also highly likely that you'll see it on TV, and in the media.'

'Really? But I still can't say that I did it?'

Rick shook his head. 'If you do, you could be putting yourself in danger. You have to know that before you say yes.'

'You don't think I can keep schtum?'

'Of course I do. If Noah trusts you, then I trust you. But if and when you do see it, the chances are that you'll find it a shock. All I can say to you is that nobody will get hurt, even if it looks like they are.'

'OK . . . ' said Mitchell, although he began to sound dubious. 'When you say "*danger*" . . .?'

'If you never say a word about this to anybody, ever, there's no reason why you should have to worry about it.'

'Noah?' asked Mitchell.

Noah shrugged. 'It's up to you, Mitch. But like Rick says, if you forget you ever did it, and never mention it to nobody, not even to Nadia, then everything should be OK.'

'Can I ask you . . . is it the Mob?'

'Something like that.'

'Well . . . why not, in that case? Some of my best friends are wise guys, believe it or not. I did all the make-up when Vinnie Proietti's eldest daughter got married.'

'Vinnie the Grin?'

'That's him. We're neighbours. He's always inviting us round for linguine.'

Three days later, as the Peace Convention was coming to a close, the sky over Los Angeles turned a dark, corroded green, and lightning flickered in the hills.

The final speech was given in the main conference room by Mahfoud Ould N'Diayane, the UN Secretary General. As he spoke about the need for greater tolerance between the world's religions, there was a deafening crash of thunder overhead, and rain began to clatter against the windows.

Adeola turned to Alvin Metzler and said, 'Sounds like God doesn't approve of religious tolerance.'

'You weren't always so cynical,' smiled Alvin Metzler.

'I don't think you can help it, after people have made serious attempts to kill you.'

Mahfoud Ould N'Diayane said, 'I would ask you to leave this convention today with one thought in your minds: that worldwide peace can only be achieved if we look at the world through each other's eyes. Put on your enemy's spectacles, and look at yourself in the mirror.

'Maybe, in that mirror, you will see somebody who is much more aggressive and intolerant than you thought. Maybe you will see somebody who needs to learn that the ways of other people – even if they are different – are not necessarily wrong.'

'"Put on your enemy's spectacles"?' Alvin Metzler repeated. 'Holy cow. Is he a diplomat or an optometrist?'

Adeola gave him a quick, nervous smile. Now that the convention was breaking up, she knew that it wouldn't be long before she was 'kidnapped'. But Rick and Noah had insisted that it came as a surprise, when she was least expecting it, so that she would look genuinely startled. She knew, too, that there was a high element of danger in what they were doing. The convention was swarming with federal agents and police and armed security guards.

The convention hall gradually emptied. Adeola went over to talk to Christophe Corthouts, the Belgian foreign secretary, and then to Przemek Romanski, from Poland. As Przemek Romanski kissed her hand, she looked sideways and saw Hubert Tocsin standing only five or six rows of seats away from her, chatting to a striking young woman with a very white face and a black raven's wing of hair. He was wearing a soft black mohair sport coat, with a flame-red carnation in the lapel.

Hubert Tocsin caught her eye. He excused himself to the white-faced young woman and came over to her.

'Well, well,' she said. 'Mr Tocsin again. Have you had a good convention?'

'Saleswise, yes, not bad at all. Our super-smart bombs have generated a gratifying amount of interest, especially from the Syrians.'

'*Super*-smart bombs? I thought ordinary smart bombs were bad enough.'

'At Tocsin, Ms Davis, we're always trying to find new ways to minimize collateral damage.'

'You mean you're trying not to blow up too many innocent bystanders.'

'If you like. The super-smart bomb makes political sense, as well as humanitarian sense.'

'I don't know how you can use the words "bomb" and "humanitarian" in the same sentence, Mr Tocsin, let alone "sense".'

'Are you coming to the farewell dinner tonight?' Hubert Tocsin asked her. 'I'd very much like to discuss this with you some more. I like a woman with fire.'

'Yes, I'll be coming. But I'll probably be sitting next to the Iranian ambassador. He's much more interested in world peace than you are, Mr Tocsin.'

Hubert Tocsin gave her a radiant smile, but in his eyes she saw that that she had seen before. He was like an alligator, watching her, unblinking, from a sandbank.

Hong Gildong came up to Adeole and gently took hold of her elbow.

'Time to leave, Ms Davis. The SUV's right outside.'

'Thank you,' she said, and then, 'Goodbye, Mr Tocsin. And good luck with your super-smart bombs.'

Hong Gildong steered her through the crowded hotel lobby, giving a running commentary into his throat mike.

'We are approaching the front doors now, right-hand side. OK. There are two men in dark glasses immediately to the left of the revolving door. You've marked them? OK.'

They pushed their way out through the swing doors. For security reasons, Adeola had long ago stopped going through revolving doors. It was too easy to jam revolving doors, and there was your intended victim, caught like a rat in a jelly jar.

It was chaos outside the hotel. Beyond the shelter of the portico, it was raining hard, and thunder was still rumbling overhead. Peace convention delegates were milling around, shaking hands and saying their goodbyes. TV crews were interviewing some of the most controversial personalities. SUVs and limousines were nose-to-tail, all of them trying to manoeuvre as close as they possibly could to the front steps. Bodyguards of twenty different nationalities were looking warily all around them – Japanese, French, Ghanaian – every one of them wearing dark suits and dark sunglasses.

'Looks like the *Men In Black* fan club,' said Adeola.

Hong Gildong pointed across to the far side of the hotel portico. Adeola's silver Grand Cherokee was waiting for her, with another of her new security team, Peter Silverman, standing by the rear door. Peter was a skinny, hard-bitten type from Omaha, Nebraska originally, whose mouth was always puckered up as if he were sucking on a lemon.

They negotiated their way through the narrow spaces between the Lincoln Town Cars and Escalades. Adeola said, 'Can we make a detour on the way back? I need to stop at Mickey Fine's Pharmacy, to pick up some of that skin cream.'

'No problem,' said Hong Gildong. They had almost reached the Grand Cherokee now, and Peter Silverman was opening the door for her.

At that instant, however, a figure in a maroon tracksuit and a black ski mask came running at full pelt through the portico. The figure knocked into Hong Gildong, so that he collided with the Escalade right behind him and sprawled on the ground. Then it seized Adeola, crooking one elbow around her neck and holding up a large hunting knife.

Peter Silverman reached into his coat and tugged out his gun.

'Let her go!' he yelled. 'Let her go *now*, and hit the ground!'

There were shouts of confusion from the delegates on the steps. Three or four bodyguards drew their guns, too, and began to weave their way towards them between the lines of cars. A uniformed cop shouted out, 'Stay back! Everybody stay back!' Then, 'Drop the knife, feller! Do you hear me? *Drop the goddamned knife!*'

The figure in the maroon tracksuit heaved Adeola towards the open door of the Grand Cherokee, using her as a shield. Peter Silverman kept his gun trained on them, but he obviously couldn't risk a shot.

The uniformed cop made his way around the assembled cars until he was less than fifteen feet away from Adeola and her abductor.

'Come on, fella, you don't stand a chance! Just drop the knife, will you?'

The figure in the maroon tracksuit said nothing, but if it *had* answered, Adeola knew what it would have sounded like. As tall and strong as the figure was, Adeola could feel breasts pressing against her back.

The uniformed cop came closer, and now he was joined by a second cop with a sandy moustache and three other men with guns who looked like FBI agents.

'Drop the knife on the ground and stand back!' one of them demanded. 'You have a count of three, then we're going to take you out!'

'Don't shoot!' gasped Adeola. She was genuinely breathless.

'One!' rapped the FBI agent.

'Don't shoot! Don't shoot!' Adeola begged him.

'*Two!*'

At that moment, there was more shouting and more clamour. One of the uniformed cops said, 'What the hell—?' Then, 'Back off! Back off! You can't come in here! Back off!'

As if it had been swamped by an incoming tide, the portico was suddenly flooded with dozens of young Korean men in green-and-white T-shirts, some of them holding up home-made placards. They poured in between Adeola and the police, and all around the Grand Cherokee, shouting, 'No more nuclear! Kim Jong Il! No more nuclear!'

The FBI agent screamed out, 'Get these fucking lunatics out of here!' and the uniformed police yelled, 'Back off! Back off!'

But the Koreans kept on milling around, chanting and clapping. '*No more nuclear! No more nuclear!*'

The police tried to force their way through the crowd, but it was impossible. They seemed to be everywhere, jostling each other and waving their placards.

'No more nuclear! Kim Jong Il! No more nuclear!'

The figure in the maroon tracksuit climbed up into the back seat of the Grand Cherokee and wrestled Adeola in after her. Adeola made a show of kicking and struggling, but the figure dragged her inside and slammed the door. Immediately, the driver gunned the engine, and the Grand Cherokee slewed out of the hotel portico, and into the hammering rain.

They drove along the Avenue of the Stars at nearly eighty miles an hour, and took a right through a red light on to Olympic Boulevard, accompanied by a chorus of angry horns. Then they sped eastward, as far as La Cienega, taking a left and then a right and then another left. They skidded around the corner at Edinburgh and Melrose at nearly sixty, so that the Grand Cherokee slid sideways across the road and mounted the sidewalk.

As they bounced back on to the road, Adeola said, 'At this rate, you won't have to *pretend* to kill me.'

Noah turned around in the driving seat and said, 'Sorry . . . a few more blocks and we'll be changing vehicles. Then I can drive more sedate.'

Silja had dragged off her ski mask. Her cheeks were flushed and her hair was stuck to her scalp. 'I didn't hurt you?' she asked.

'Not at all. But you were scary.'

'I think Hong Gildong might have some bruises, but he told me I should hit him hard.'

'Was that his idea? All those Korean demonstrators?'

Noah laughed. 'You know who they are? The Korean Cycling Club of Los Angeles. I'll bet you didn't even know that it existed. But Hong Gildong's sister is married to one of their coaches.'

'They were taking one hell of a risk, weren't they? My God, they could have been shot!'

'No, not a chance. A peace demonstration against nuclear proliferation in North Korea? You think the LAPD are going to start firing at people like that?'

'Amazing,' said Adeola. 'And did you see how many TV cameras and press photographers there were? I'm going to have the most publicized kidnapping in history.'

Noah turned into De Longpre Avenue. He slithered to a halt behind a pale green metallic Chevrolet Classic Caprice, and immediately said, 'Out! This is where we change cars, and we're going to change them again when we get to North Hollywood.'

As they climbed out of the Grand Cherokee, there was an ear-splitting crack of thunder right over their heads, and the rain was dancing madly on the sidewalk. There was nobody around to see them hurry from the SUV, run to the Chevy, and pull away from the curb with twin fountains of spray.

Noah drove as if he were playing a computer game – smooth and fast, swerving from side to side, running red lights, never easing off the gas for a moment. They had a near-miss with a Wal-Mart truck on Cahuenga, with a barrage of blaring and swearing and middle fingers stuck up, but this was the kind of driving that Noah had been trained to do, always looking for the chances, always looking for the narrowest of opportunities, using the rain-slick road surface to slide and ski and get himself ahead.

He was nearly six minutes ahead of schedule when he slid sideways into Otsego Street in North Hollywood, and jammed on the brakes.

'Just like you said,' Adeola told him. 'That was very sedate.'

'We're on the run, Adeola,' said Noah. 'Every second counts.'

A black Dodge Caliber was parked on the opposite side of the street. Noah climbed out of the Chevrolet, ran across the road, and opened the doors.

Silja frog-marched Adeola after him, so forcibly that Adeola had to half-jump with every step. It was unlikely that anybody was watching them, especially in the middle of a downpour like this, but if there were any witnesses, Adeola's kidnap had to look completely convincing.

'Where are we going now?' asked Adeola, as they turned south again, towards the Ventura Freeway. The rain was clearing away now, and the sun was coming out again, so that the road surfaces were dazzling.

'A little house up in Scholl Canyon, in Glendale,' Noah told her. 'Belongs to a friend of mine, Dave McCray. He spends most of his time filming at Cinecitta, in Rome.'

'Do you really think this kidnap is going to work?'

'Let's take a look at the TV news tonight. Then we'll know.'

Silja said, 'My father used to tell me, you can run in your thoughts, but you won't get anywhere.'

Noah glanced back at Adeola. 'Very philosophical, these Finns. All those long, dark winter nights, know what I mean?'

'And those summers,' put in Silja, 'when the sun never sets. You would be surprised what people can do in the middle of the night, if the sun is still shining.'

'Maybe we can take a trip to Finland one day,' said Noah. 'Then you can show me.'

Twenty-Three

'And this evening,' said Larry Coleman on NBC News, 'incredible live pictures as a peace delegate is abducted right under the noses of police and FBI agents at the International Peace Convention in Los Angeles.'

'Adeola!' called Rick. 'You don't want to miss this!'

The TV news coverage of Adeola's kidnap was even more extensive than they had hoped for. It appeared on almost every news programme around the world, from CNN to Al-Jazeera. Every station showed the same jerky footage: Adeola being seized by a tall figure in a maroon tracksuit; then the stand-off with the uniformed police officers and the FBI; followed by the flood of Korean cyclists in green-and-white T-shirts, chanting and brandishing their banners.

'I can't believe it,' said Adeola. She had been washing her hair, and it was all wound up in a tall white turban. 'The way I remember it, it seemed to last for ten minutes, at least. But look – it all happened in a split second.'

'Most of the best stunts do,' said Noah. 'You remember them for ever, but in screen-time they're nothing at all. Even the car chase in *Bullitt* only lasted for nine minutes and twelve seconds, yet most people would swear that it lasted for more than twenty minutes.'

Larry Coleman continued: 'Police have located Ms Davis's abandoned SUV on DeLongpre Avenue in Hollywood. Crime scene investigators are examining the vehicle for any clues as to who might have kidnapped her.

'So far, however, police have admitted that they have no leads. There has been no word from her abductors; no indication whatsoever why this outstanding peace negotiator should have been so dramatically snatched and driven away.'

'Hey – outstanding peace negotiator,' said Rick. 'How would you like a drink?'

'Love one,' said Adeola.

Alvin Metzler was on television now, looking upset and harassed. 'As you know, a suicide bomber made an attempt on Adeola Davis's life in Dubai, and there have been other attempts which I am not at liberty to reveal.

'So we at DOVE are seriously concerned for Ms Davis's safety. If her abductors are watching this, I want you to know that we're prepared to listen to any grievance you might have. We're prepared to talk about our aims and our peace projects, and sort out any misapprehensions.'

'You're prepared to negotiate with terrorists?' asked Larry Coleman.

'I didn't say that. But more than any other organization in the world, DOVE understands that every story has more than one side to it, and of all DOVE's representatives, Adeola understands that the most.

'We value her. We care for her. And we want to have her back where she belongs.'

Adeola pressed her fingers to her forehead. 'Oh, Alvin, I'm so sorry.'

Rick came into the living room with a glass of Zinfandel for her. 'He'll get over it, when he finds out you're safe and well.'

'He'll have to see me being killed first. How do you think he's going to feel about that?'

They spent a quiet evening watching television and playing poker. Adeola won hand after hand, until Noah said, 'That's me done. If I'm going to die, I don't want to die broke.'

'She's too good at reading people,' said Rick. 'Apart from which, she has the most inscrutable face since the Sphinx.'

He looked across at Adeola and for the first time Noah realized that there was more to their relationship than protector and protected.

'So when is this Palestinian nutjob going to announce that he's holding her?' Noah asked.

'Not before tomorrow morning. Maybe later. The longer we leave it, the better. It'll rack up the tension, and the cops will think that he could have taken her a whole lot further away. Even flown her out of the country. Which will make us that much more difficult for them to track down.'

'OK . . . so we'll be shooting the video Thursday? I just
need to know, so that I can arrange for Mitch to come around.'
'Thursday would be good.'
Adeola was shuffling the cards. 'A little disturbing to know
that I only have thirty-six hours left to live. Have you decided
yet how you are going to kill me?'
'Bullet between the eyes, if that's OK with you. It's the
least complicated. And the cheapest.'
'I see. I have to die on a budget.'

After Rick and Adeola had gone to bed, Noah and Silja sat
out on the lamplit veranda at the back of the house, smoking
and looking out over the twinkling lights of Glendale.
'How the hell did we get ourselves into this, Silja?' said
Noah.
'Too late to worry about that. All we have to do now is
make sure that we get ourselves out of it.'
They heard sirens somewhere in the distance. At first they
sounded as if they were coming closer, but after a while they
gradually faded away.
Noah said, 'I'm supposed to be at Paramount on Thursday
morning, to have a meeting about a new Nick Burton picture.
Pirates in space, something like that.'
'Pirates in space! It all seems so ridiculous now.'
'You think so? Compared with all of this, it seems totally
rational.'
Leon came shuffling out, holding up a DVD. 'Hey – I've
downloaded some Palestinian accents for you. I found a couple
of interviews with Ahmed Sa'adat. He was the Secretary
General of the Popular Front for the Liberation of Palestine,
but the Israelis kidnapped him in Jericho, and put him on
trial.'
'Thanks. You've really helped out, you know that?'
Leon sat down on the step. 'I only wish there was more I
could do.'
'Come on, dude. Your dad would be proud of you.'
'I'd rather he was still alive.'
'I know. He was always quoting Woody Allen, wasn't he?
"I don't want to achieve immortality through my work. I want
to achieve immortality by not dying."'

*   *   *

Noah practised his Palestinian accent all the next morning, until he sounded more like Ahmed Sa'adat than Ahmed Sa'adat. 'This is Armed Front for Freedom of Palestinian!' he shouted, crossly, at the mirror. 'APPF! – I mean, shit, AFFP! We have your negotiator, Ms Adeola Davis! This is Armed Front for Freedom of Palestine! We have your negotiator, Ms Adeola Davis!'

It was still unseasonably hot, and all of them were beginning to grow tense and impatient, and to question the sanity of what they were doing.

'What are you going to do if Professor Halflight isn't interested?' said Adeola.

'I don't know,' said Noah. 'I'm just assuming that he will be.'

'But if he's not? What if he makes out that he doesn't know anything about Emu Ki Ilani, and those men in grey suits are still coming after you?'

'I guess we'll have to leave the country, and give ourselves new identities. I always fancied living in the South of France.'

'And Silja? And Leon?'

'Let's just take this one step at a time, shall we?' said Rick. 'Look – it's nearly time we made contact with DOVE.'

'I'm not too sure I can do this,' said Noah.

'You have to. We've gone this far. We can't give it up now.'

Noah took a deep breath. He sat down on the sagging beige leather couch, and Rick handed him a sheet of notepaper and a disposable cellphone, which Steve had bought for them yesterday, in Anaheim.

He lit a cigarette and then punched out the number of DOVE headquarters in New York. The phone rang for a long time before an operator eventually picked up.

'DOVE, can I help you?'

Noah cleared his throat. 'This is Armed Front for Freedom of Palestine. We have your negotiator, Ms Adeola Davis.'

'I'm sorry?'

'Jesus,' said Noah, under his breath. Then he repeated himself, speaking more slowly and emphatically.

'You have seen TV news?' he asked the operator.

'Yes, sir. I know what's happened to Ms Davis.'

'We have her. The AFFP. So far she is alive and well. But we have demands. You must meet our demands or she will be executed.'

'Sir – can I put you on hold for a moment?'

'We are AFFP! I mean, AFPF! We have demands!'

'Sir – I need to put you through to somebody in authority.'

'I am speaking to *you*. You can tell your bosses what we want. Immediate withdrawal of all Israeli forces in Palestine. Immediate demolition of separation wall.'

'Sir—'

'That is all. No discussion. Now it is one o'clock. I will call again at six o'clock. You will say yes to our demands or Ms Davis will be executed.'

'Sir—'

'That is all.'

Noah switched off the cellphone and tossed it on to the glass-topped coffee table. 'Christ almighty. I sounded like Eddie Murphy!'

'No, you didn't,' said Adeola. 'You sounded exactly like one of those Palestinian freedom fighters I was talking to. *Exactly*. Macho. Intolerant. That poor girl must have been shaking in her shoes.'

At 6.15, Eastern Standard Time, Noah called DOVE head-quarters again.

'This is Armed Front for Freedom of Palestine. I am ready for your answer. Yes or no?'

'Sir – I'm going to put you through to a gentleman who is authorized to negotiate with you.'

'There is no negotiation. Yes to our demands, or no?'

'Excuse me,' a man's voice broke in. 'May I ask to whom I am speaking?'

'AFFP. Armed Front for Freedom of Palestine. We have Ms Adeola Davis. You know our demands. Withdrawal of all Israeli forces from Palestine. Demolition of separation wall declared illegal by International Courts of Justice. Yes or no?'

'Please, hold up a moment,' the man asked him. 'I have to confess to you that none of us have ever heard of the Armed Front for the Freedom of Palestine.'

'We are secret organization, that is why. Secret. AFFP.'

'OK . . . and you're saying that you abducted Ms Davis?'

'We have Ms Adeola Davis. Yes to our demands, or she will be executed.'

'How do we know that you really have her? Can I speak to her?'

'Of course.'

Noah passed the cellphone to Adeola. Adeola closed her eyes tight and tried to sound fearful.

'Ms Davis?'

'Yes, this is Adeola Davis. Please, help me. They say they're going to kill me if you don't give them what they want.'

'Ms Davis, this is Special Agent George Windom of the FBI. I'm a trained hostage negotiator. I'm going to do everything I can to get you out of this situation quickly and safely. Don't panic. We have hundreds of officers looking for you, and one way or another we'll make sure that you come to no harm.'

'They say you have twenty-four hours. Then they're going to kill me.'

'Adeola? This is Alvin. You just need to hang on in there. We're all thinking of you. We're all rooting for you.'

'Can you give us any idea where you are?' asked Special Agent Windom. 'Are you still in Los Angeles, or have they taken you someplace else?'

'I don't know. I don't know where I am.'

Noah snatched the cellphone away from her. 'Listen! We are AFFP! We have demands! You say yes to our demands, or you will never see Ms Adeola Davis again, only on death video! You have till six o'clock, evening time tomorrow! Then I call you again! Then you say yes!'

'Sir – could you tell me your name, so that we can talk man-to-man?'

Noah put his hand over the phone. 'Adeola – he's asking me what my name is. What's my name?'

Adeola thought for a moment. Then she scribbled on his crib sheet 'Abdel Al-Hadi'.

'I am Abdel Al-Hadi,' said Noah. 'I am leader of AFFP. You say yes to our demands!'

'You have to understand, Mr Al-Hadi, that what you're asking for isn't going to be easy. The Israelis never give in to any kind of threat, even if it means the loss of an innocent life. And Ms Davis is nothing if not innocent.'

'She is guilty! She is a hypocrite and a whore! She is a two-legged spider, who spins out a web of sticky lies!'

'You know that's not true,' retorted Alvin Metzler. 'She speaks for everybody who wants peace, whether they're Israeli or Palestinian or any other nationality. You need to release her, Mr Al-Hadi, and then we can talk about the things you want to achieve.'

'Six o'clock tomorrow!' Noah insisted. 'Then you say yes – or then she will die!'

He switched off the phone. Rick shook his head in admiration. 'You're living this part, man. You should have been a character actor, instead of a stuntman.'

'I'm a two-legged spider?' said Adeola. 'First time I've ever been called that!'

'Sorry,' said Noah. 'Guess I got a little carried away there.'

That night, bundled up on his couch, Noah dreamed of Jenna again. This time, he was walking across the Piazza San Marco, in Venice, and it was raining. Jenna was fifty or sixty yards ahead of him, wearing a thin white dress that was almost transparent. As she walked, she scattered scores of pigeons, which settled again as soon as she had passed.

Jenna! he called, but his voice was dead and flat and he knew that she couldn't hear him. Three hundred feet above him, the bells rang from the campanile, and the bells sounded equally dead and equally flat, as if they were tolling a death knell.

It began to rain harder, and he stumbled into the chairs outside one of the outdoor cafes. A waiter in a long apron shouted at him. *'Chaos! Chaos!'*

Noah waved to the waiter to show that he was sorry, but by the time he had picked up the fallen chairs, Jenna had disappeared around the corner. He hurried after her, just in time to see her walking between the two granite columns outside the Palazzo Ducale, one of which was topped by a statue of St Mark, and the other by a statue of St Theodore, and the sacred crocodile of Egypt.

He knew that it was unlucky to walk between the columns, because this had once been a place of execution.

Jenna! he shouted. But hundreds of pigeons exploded into the air in front of him, and he lost sight of her altogether.

'You're shouting in your sleep again,' said a hot whisper, close to his ear.

What?

'I said, you're shouting in your sleep again.'

He opened his eyes. Although it was two o'clock on the morning, there was a full moon shining through the window and the living room was unnaturally bright. Silja was kneeling on the floor next to him, naked, her ash-blonde hair sticking up in a halo of white flames.

'I'm sorry. I was dreaming. I thought I was in Venice . . .'

'Venice? Very romantic.'

'I don't like Venice. For some reason it always gives me the creeps.'

Without being invited, Silja lifted his blanket and climbed on to the couch on top of him. 'I was thinking that it would be sad for us to die without ever making love.'

He stared up at her. Their faces were only inches apart. 'You think we're going to die?'

'I am quite sure of it. This kidnap plan is all going to go wrong. It is a crazy plan. How can it go right? Those men in grey suits will cut our throats the same way they killed Jenna and Mo Speller and everybody else, and nobody will ever find out what happened to us. And nobody will care, either.'

'I didn't know Finns were such pessimists.'

'No – realists.'

She kissed him, and then she kissed him again, sliding the tip of her tongue into his mouth. She tasted as if she had been eating sweet white grapes. She stroked his face with her finger-nails, delicately touching the sides of his eyes and outlining his lips, over and over, as if she wanted to remember what they felt like for the rest of her life.

He took hold of her narrow, boyish hips. Her skin was silky but she was completely lean and he could feel the sexual taut-ness in every muscle. Her nipples crinkled tight and brushed against his chest. Between her legs, his penis rose harder and harder, until he felt as if it had been fashioned out of solid ivory, instead of flesh, with every vein exaggerated and the head polished to a perfect shine.

Silja reached down with one hand and parted her hairless lips. She lifted herself up a little, so that the head of Noah's penis was positioned between them. Then, very slowly, she lowered herself on to him, until he was buried inside her as far as he could possibly go.

She was warm inside, and very slippery, but more than that

she had absolute control over her vaginal muscles, so that she could rhythmically squeeze him, almost as strongly as if she were massaging him by hand. She squeezed, and squeezed, and at the same time she looked into his eyes as if she were daring him to roll her over and thrust himself into her.

'Is this love, Noah?' she asked him.

'Do you want it to be?' He had a catch in his throat, and he had to clear it.

'I don't know what I want. I don't know what this is. But how does it feel? Do you like it, when I do this to you?'

'I'm too old for you. You know that.'

'I don't know anything.'

She stopped squeezing him, and started to ride up and down. With each upstroke, his penis came completely out of her, and then plunged back in again. She was so strong that she seemed to have no physical weight at all. There was no sound in the living room but their steady breathing, and the sound of *shlip, shlip, shlip*, with every stroke.

Noah could feel his climax rising. 'Oh, shit,' he said. It was far too soon.

Without hesitation, Silja lifted herself off him, and took hold of his penis in her right hand. She gripped the shaft, and pressed the ball of her thumb hard against the thin line of skin directly below the opening. She kept up the pressure until, gradually, Noah's climax began to subside.

'All right now?' she asked him.

He nodded, and she climbed on top of him again.

'The old Masters and Johnson squeeze technique,' he said, smiling up at her. 'I read about it in *Playboy*.'

'In Finland we call it "Braking the Sledge".'

They made love for over twenty minutes, until Silja bent forward and silently quaked. It wasn't a shared orgasm. All Noah could do was hold her while she shuddered and shuddered. The full moon had moved around the house now, and the living room was dark.

Eventually she rolled over and lay close to him, caressing his face.

'You're right,' she said, 'you're too old for me. But I love you. I love your body. I love the clockwork inside of your head.'

'Clockwork?'

'Yes. All those little cogs and wheels, always whirring. You are not a stupid man at all, are you? But you don't think the same way as the rest of us, do you? You believe that every problem in life can be solved by a stunt.'

Twenty-Four

All the next day, the news channels repeated the story of Adeola's abduction, and the demands that had been made by 'a hitherto unknown splinter group of Palestinian freedom fighters, led by a fanatic calling himself Abdel Al-Hadi.'

The police had found the metallic green Chevrolet in Otsego Street, but now they had to admit that the trail had gone cold. Police commissioner Pearson Drake said, 'Nobody saw the kidnappers abandon the vehicle, and we have absolutely no idea where they might have gone next. Some intelligence sources suggest Canada, but we can't be sure. All we can do is wait for them to contact us again.'

'Can you tell us exactly what demands the kidnappers are making?' asked Gwen Durango, for CNN.

'At this stage, no I can't, because it isn't within our power to give them what they want, and we have to negotiate with a third party.'

'Is it money? Or the release of political prisoners?'

'I'm sorry, I simply can't tell you. But we're expecting to hear from Mr Al-Hadi again at six o'clock EST, and at that time I may be able to comment further.'

Adeola was sitting back in a wicker armchair heaped with Moroccan-style cushions, holding a glass of pomegranate juice. 'I've had a terrible thought,' she said. 'Supposing they give in? Supposing the Israelis give us everything we asked them for – withdraw their forces and tear down the wall? What do we do then?'

'It's a good thing I know that you're joking,' said Rick.

'I almost wish that I weren't. What an achievement that would be!'

Silja cooked them a meal of stuffed vine leaves and tomato sauce, which they ate out on the veranda. Noah's friend Dave McCray hardly ever came back to Los Angeles these days. The pool had been drained and the yard was wild and overgrown.

They talked very little, and they kept the television news on low. Noah sat on the step next to Leon and told him about the time he had worked on a Jackie Chan movie.

'Hilarious. You want to try doing a powerslam when you're laughing your goddamned head off. Almost broke both legs.'

At the same time, he was watching Silja as she walked around the yard, picking pink roses from amongst the weeds, and waving away the bees. For all of her strength, she looked so white and vulnerable. He couldn't decide if he was protecting her, or taking advantage of her, or if she was the one who was taking advantage of him.

She saw him looking, and she waved. He wished he had a camera. Then he was glad that he didn't. If anything happened to her, he didn't want to be reminded of a moment like this.

The afternoon passed with dreamlike slowness, as if all the clocks in the house had been drowned in honey. Adeola stayed inside the house, but Rick sat outside in a dilapidated deckchair, with his eyes closed against the sun. At last the minute hand on Noah's watch crept around to 3.00 p.m., Pacific Time, which meant that it was 6.00 p.m. in New York. Time for Abdel Al-Hadi to give his ultimatum.

'Mr Al-Hadi, this is Special Agent George Windom again. How are you today?'

'I am very angry! The Armed Front for Freedom of Palestine is very angry!'

'Well, I'm sorry to hear that. We've been doing everything we can today to come up with some kind of a compromise for you.'

'Compromise! Did I ask you for compromise? I made demands! Will you meet my demands?'

Special Agent Windom took a deep, audible breath. 'I'm sorry, Mr Al-Hadi. The demands you made are simply not in our power to bestow. We've talked to the Israelis, but they're not prepared to give in to either of them. They reserve the right to deploy their forces in Palestine, as and when their own security requires it, and the separation wall stays, at least for the foreseeable future.'

'Then we have no more to talk about.'

'Mr Al-Hadi . . . maybe we have. The Israelis are holding two freedom fighters from the United Jihad, and they'd be prepared to release them in exchange for Ms Davis, if that could be arranged. So you'd certainly achieve something positive out of this situation.'

'What do I want with two freedom fighters from United Jihad? AFFP has all the freedom fighters it needs. I said, withdrawal of forces and demolition of wall. Nothing else will do.'

'Mr Al-Hadi—'

'You say yes to my demands?'

'Mr Al-Hadi—'

'You say yes? Tell me now! Yes or no?'

'Mr Al-Hadi, I can't. All I can do is appeal to your humanity.'

'Do I sound human? Too late now. Finish! Adeola Davis will be executed. You will see for yourself.'

Noah switched off the cellphone and handed it to Rick.

'That's it,' said Rick. 'Adeola has to die.'

They took a sheet out of the linen closet, unfolded it, and draped it across the end wall of the living room, as a backdrop. Leon found some Arabic slogans on the Internet – 'Death to All Betrayers' and 'Palestine Will be Free.' He also devised a symbol for the AFFP, an AK47 in a clenched fist, with a crescent moon.

He painted these on to the sheet in thick tomato catsup, because they had forgotten to bring any paint.

Noah arranged two desk lamps so that they would shine directly on to the wall. He wanted the lighting to be bright, but amateurish. Steve had borrowed a JVC Everio video camera, which Noah set up on a tripod.

When they had finished, Adeola said, 'It looks depressingly authentic, doesn't it? Can you imagine the dread that hostages must feel, when they're dragged in front of a set-up like that?'

'Let's have a drink,' said Rick.

*   *   *

They passed another restless night. Silja slept with Noah again, but they didn't make love, just held each other close. Noah heard Leon sobbing in the bedroom, but after a few minutes he fell silent.

The full moon shone on the sheet hanging on the wall. The catsup had dried as dark as blood.

Mitchell arrived at 7.45 the next morning, driven by Steve. He was wearing a yellow satin shirt and tight white sailcloth jeans, and carrying a large make-up case.

As soon as he came into the house and saw Adeola sitting at the kitchen counter, drinking coffee, he did an exaggerated double take and said, '*Whoah!*'

'Mitch,' said Noah, 'this is Adeola Davis.'

'Don't I know it! I've seen you on the news! You were kidnapped by terrorists!'

He looked around. 'Well, obviously you weren't. You were kidnapped by stunt persons instead! Which is probably worse. Noah – what the hell is going on here?'

'I can't tell you the whole story, Mitch, but we needed it to look like Adeola had been abducted, and now we need it look like she's been executed.'

'My God, Noah. What have you gotten yourself into?'

Noah put his arm around Mitch's shoulders. 'It's really better if you don't know.'

'I'm not so sure I should do this. I mean, isn't this conspiracy or something?'

'Nobody's going to get hurt, Mitch. But it's very important that everybody believes that Adeola has been murdered.'

'And this Middle Eastern person you want me to make you up as, he's the murderer?'

'You got it.'

Mitchell said, 'You're not doing this to shake anybody down for money, are you? This isn't a scam?'

'You've been living next door to the Mob for too long. It's more like a political thing.'

'Hmm, well, OK . . .' He put down his make-up case and flicked the catches. 'I guess I owe you for that *Mission Impossible* job.'

Rick said, 'You can make it look like Noah's shot her, right?'

'Right between the eyes. That's what you wanted, isn't it?

But I'll start with you first, Noah. You're going to take a whole lot longer.'

It took Mitchell nearly three hours to turn Noah into Abdel Al-Hadi. He applied latex moldings to Noah's neck, and a latex bump to the bridge of his nose. With a sponge and pale foundation cream, he subtly altered the colour and tone of his skin, so that he looked as if were Palestinian, but rarely went out in the sun. He glued on bushy eyebrows and a thick black beard, and darkened his iron-grey hair. He gave him dark brown contact lenses.

Finally he painted on a pattern of prominent moles, all across his forehead, like a star chart.

Noah came out of the bedroom and confronted Silja, Adeola and Rick. 'What do you think?'

Silja shook her head in amazement. 'I don't believe it. Is it really you? It *sounds* like you. But – my God!'

Noah took a step towards her, but Silja jumped back and said, 'No! Don't come near me!'

Adeola couldn't help laughing. 'It's incredible, it really is. I never would have recognized you, not in a thousand years.'

Rick simply pressed his hands together and bowed his head. '*Salaam*,' he said. 'A pleasure to meet you, Mr Al-Hadi.'

Noah looked at himself in the mirror on the opposite side of the room. There was Abdel Al-Hadi, with his beard and his moles and his umber-coloured circles under his eyes. He *was* Abdel Al-Hadi. As he approached the mirror to inspect Mitchell's handiwork more closely, he walked with shorter, shuffling steps, and his shoulders were rounder, like somebody who had spent their whole life feeling resentful and oppressed.

Mitchell came out of the bedroom, wiping his hands on a towel. 'OK, then. You happy with that?'

'You're a genius, Mitch. Now, all we need is a bullet hole for Adeola.'

Mitchell said, 'Come on, then. I promise you this won't hurt a bit.'

He led Adeola through to the bedroom and sat her down in front of the dressing-table mirror. From his case he produced a jar of embalmer's wax, a box of greasepaints and a bottle of stage blood.

'I always make my own blood,' he told Adeola, as he rolled

and warmed the wax between the palms of his hands. 'Ninety-eight per cent sugar alcohol, two per cent red food colouring powder – Candyland brand is the best. Looks messy but doesn't stain your clothes.'

He carefully fashioned a thin envelope of wax, and spooned a small quantity of blood into it. Then he tied a very fine nylon line to the middle of a shirt button, and placed the button in the blood. He sealed the wax envelope, smoothed it over, and stuck it to the centre of Adeola's forehead, using grease-paint to match her skin colour.

By the time he had finished, it was almost impossible to tell what he had done to her, even close up.

'Thanks, Mitch,' said Noah. 'You want to stick around and see us make this video?'

Mitchell was packing his bag. 'The less I know about what you lunatics are up to, the better.'

'See you again in a couple of days, then.'

Adeola knelt on the floor in front of the bed sheet and held her hands behind her back as if she were tied up. Noah adjusted the lights so that they shone on her face bright and flat.

Rick hunkered down beside her. 'Are you sure you're OK with this? You don't have to go through with it if you don't want to. I'm pretty confident that I can keep you safe, even if we don't go after these bastards.'

'I'm not doing this just for me,' said Adeola. 'Of course I don't want to spend the rest of my life not knowing from one second to another when somebody's going to shoot me, or blow me to bits, but this is for Nesta and for Reuben and for Charlie.'

'OK. So long as you're sure.'

Leon crouched down behind the video camera and adjusted the focus.

'I want it slightly blurry,' Noah told him. 'Just enough so you won't be able to see the fine detail.'

Silja carefully picked up the end of the thin nylon line that protruded from Adeola's forehead, and stood close beside Leon, holding the line taut.

'Everybody ready?' asked Noah.

'Ready as we'll ever be.'

'Then . . . *action!*'

Noah walked in front of the camera, holding up a sheet of paper in one hand and Rick's SIG-Sauer automatic in the other.

'This is Armed Front for Freedom of Palestine!' he declared, waving the paper. 'We have made just and fair demands! But now it is clear that the international community is not prepared to listen to us, nor to make any concession to our just and fair demands!

'Because of this, we are making a gesture of revenge against the international community. This woman, Ms Adeola Davis, represents the tyrannical interests of Western capitalism, and now you will see the consequences of such political alignment.'

He pointed the automatic at Adeola's forehead, and said, 'What do you say to those who have used you as a pawn? What do you say to US government and their running dogs?'

Adeola looked directly at the camera. 'Please . . .' she said. 'Whoever is watching this, please contact the AFFP and try to meet them at least halfway. Talk to them. Please don't let them kill me.'

'You think your masters will listen to you?' Noah sneered at her. 'They murder thousands of women and children without any qualm. Do you think they are concerned about *you*?'

'Please,' said Adeola. 'Killing me, that won't do you any good. They'll come after you. They'll hunt you down, and they'll punish you, and they'll probably punish scores of other Palestinians, too – innocent Palestinians – out of revenge.'

'Do you think we care?' said Noah. 'We are overjoyed to die for what we believe in. Are you?'

'I believe in peace,' said Adeola. 'But I believe in life, too.'

Without any more hesitation, Noah shot her. There was a deafening bang from the blank round in Rick's automatic, and at the same time Silja yanked the nylon thread that protruded from Adeola's forehead. The shirt button flew out, leaving a perfect bullet hole, spurting with blood.

Adeola dropped sideways, and Noah defiantly held up the gun.

'The people of Palestine will be avenged! Our land will be ours again! God is great!'

They watched the recording three times over, to make sure that it would stand up to expert scrutiny. Even though they had set it up themselves, they were still shocked by its impact, and afterwards they sat in silence.

'I wasn't too nonchalant, was I?' asked Adeola at last. 'Maybe I should have cried or gone hysterical or something.'

'Not at all. Have you ever seen any of those beheading videos? There's no screaming or shouting. Just a few minutes of struggling, like kids in a schoolyard. They all look so matter-of-fact, and that's what makes them so horrible.'

'OK, Leon,' said Noah. 'You're the computer expert. Let's send this out to the news networks.'

While Leon contacted CNN, Silja poured them all a glass of wine. Noah tugged off his beard and peeled the latex bump from the bridge of his nose, while Adeola scraped the embalmer's wax from her forehead.

Noah had expected to feel excited, after making the video, but he was unexpectedly depressed. He took his wine out on to the veranda and lit a cigarette.

'Are you all right?' Adeola asked him, from the doorway.

'Yeah, I guess so. But I keep thinking of all those hostages who get killed for real, by people who don't even know them, for causes they don't know nothing about.'

She came out and leaned against the railing beside him. 'Why do you think I do what I do? It's horrifying, talking to fanatics. I gave up trying to appeal to their sense of humanity long ago: they simply don't have one. They see their cause and nothing else. All I can do to stop them from murdering innocent people is to make it more profitable for them not to.'

Rick came out, too, and took hold of Adeola's hand – rather possessively, Noah thought.

'Hey,' said Rick. 'You sure don't *feel* dead.'

That evening the news of Adeola's murder was featured on all the TV news networks, although only a few of them showed the actual moment when 'Abdel Al-Hadi' blew a hole in her forehead.

Alvin Metzler came on to the screen, and he looked deeply distressed. 'I want to say how much we're going to miss Adeola, and what an outstanding contribution she made single-handedly to world harmony.

'In her memory, I am personally going to make sure that the accords which she was negotiating in Ethiopia are carried through. DOVE is prepared to divert millions of dollars of extra funds to achieving a political and social settlement in the Horn of Africa, and also to several other diplomatic initiatives which Adeola was working on, in other parts of the world.

'It's the least I can do to honour her courage, her self-sacrifice, and her devotion to peace. She was a beautiful, gifted woman, and I still find it almost impossible to believe that we're never going to see her again.'

Adeola wiped the tears from her eyes with her fingers. Rick put his arm around her and gave her a squeeze. 'He *likes* you. Listen to him, he really likes you.'

'Oh, sure. Now I've passed away he likes me.'

Twenty-Five

Professor Halflight was limping through the cloisters of Royce Hall when a man in a short black hooded jacket stepped out in front of him.

'Professor Halflight?' the man asked him, with a strong Middle Eastern accent.

Professor Halflight stopped, leaning heavily on his lion's-head cane. 'Yes?' he demanded. 'If it's lecture notes you're after, you'll have to wait till tomorrow. I flew in from Israel less than two hours ago, and I'm feeling exceedingly jet-lagged. Leave your name with my secretary.'

He tried to swing himself forward again, but the hooded man moved to the left, and wouldn't let him pass.

'Is there something else?' said Professor Halflight. 'You don't want my wallet, do you, because I can assure you that it's not worth stealing. I have about thirty dollars and a maxed-out Visa card.'

'Professor, I need to have talk with you.'

'Well, as I say, leave your name with my secretary, and we can arrange a mutually convenient time.'

'Is *now* not convenient?' The man dragged back his hood. 'You see who I am? You recognize me?'

Professor Halflight stared at him for a very long moment, with his mouth puckered, as if he were trying to identify the taste of a rather inferior wine.

Then he said, 'Put your hood back up. Come with me.'

The man in the black jacket followed him through the cloisters. When Professor Halflight reached the Department of Middle Eastern Languages and Culture, however, he didn't take the man through his secretary's office. Instead, glancing over his shoulder to make sure that he wasn't being watched, he unlocked a side door, and led the stranger directly into his study.

The man in the black jacket walked around the room, nodding in admiration. 'So many books. So many photographs. Very great status!'

Professor Halflight lurched across and pointed with his cane at a black-and-white photograph of himself shaking hands with a man in an Arab headdress. 'Me and Abu Ammar.'

The man in the black jacket nodded even more enthusiastically, but didn't reply.

'Better known as Yasser Arafat,' Professor Halflight explained. 'But then you knew that.'

'Of course! Yasser Arafat! He was my hero.'

'So who are you?' asked Professor Halflight. 'And what's this group of yours? I haven't been able to turn on a TV or open a newspaper for the past three days without seeing your rather less than prepossessing face.'

'My name, sir, is Abdel Al-Hadi. I am the leader of the Armed Front for the Freedom of Palestine. We have the same aims as yourself.'

'Mr Al-Hadi – you are responsible for the murder of a well-known international peace envoy. I am a professor of languages and ancient culture. I fail to see how you can think that our aims are in any way coincident.'

Abdel Al-Hadi kept on nodding. He went up to the window and touched the leaves of the tall, spiky plant on the window ledge. 'Asphodel,' he said.

'That's right.'

'Food for the dead. They grow in my father's garden, in 'Bayt Hanun.'

'I'm a very busy man, Mr Al-Hadi,' said Professor Halflight. 'I think you need to come to the point.'

Abdel Al-Hadi reached into his pocket and produced the silver medallion which Rick had taken from the would-be assassin he had killed at Parknasilla. He held it up high so that, as it slowly rotated, Professor Halflight could clearly see the cuneiform writing and the name K A Z I M I.

'*This* is the point, Professor. This medallion. When she was down on her knees begging me to spare her life, Ms Davis told me all about this medallion, what it means, where it came from. She said that if I wanted to further my struggle, I should come to you, because you know all about the people who wear such medallions.'

Professor Halflight walked around his desk, dragged out his chair, and sat down. 'What on earth made Ms Davis believe that I could be involved in anything like that? I teach dusty old history to sweaty young students.'

'Ms Davis did much research. She found pictures of you with known assassins. I saw these pictures for myself.'

'Fakes, probably.'

'No, professor. She had much other evidence. Like the killing of a man called Speller, and his wife. And other killings. She believed that if she told me how I could join Emu Ki Ilani and wear one of these medallions, I would spare her.'

Professor Halflight raised one eyebrow. 'But you *didn't* spare her, did you? You *shot* her. You murdered her, publicly. In front of a worldwide audience.'

'The value of liberation is much greater than the price of any life, Professor.'

'So you're here, *why* exactly?'

'As I say, to join you. To strike at our oppressors.'

'I see. How many of you are there, in the Armed Front for the Freedom of Palestine?'

'I am the leader.'

'Yes, but how many of you are there altogether? Ten? Fifty? Two hundred?'

'So far, just myself. And sometimes my friend Safwan.'

'Just yourself? You've organized an armed front with just yourself?'

'And sometimes my friend Safwan. It was he who drove the SUV, when we kidnapped Ms Davis.'

'One man hardly constitutes a front.'

'But I am armed, and I have shown you what I am prepared to do. I have killed Ms Adeola Davis, which you were unable to do. Even if the AFFP is only one man strong, it is strong like a lion, and it has proved itself.'

Professor Halflight unscrewed a tortoiseshell mechanical pencil and scribbled a note on a sheet of paper. Then he said, 'How long have you been in the United States, Mr Al-Hadi?'

'Seven months, nine days.'

'Do you have papers?'

Abdel Al-Hadi shook his head. 'I was making application for asylum.'

'Where did you first land, when you arrived in America?'

'Newark. I fly from London. Before that, from Lisbon.'

'All right. I also need to know where you were born, and when, and where you were educated. Are you married? Do you have any relatives in the United States? Where have you been living since you got here? Do the immigration authorities know where you are?'

'You are making a check on me.'

'You're a very perceptive man, Mr Al-Hadi. Yes, I'm making a check on you.'

'I am Abdel Al-Hadi, from the Armed Front for the Freedom of Palestine.'

'So you say.'

'It is true! I have proved myself! I have personally killed Ms Adeola Davis. All the world has seen this!'

'All the same, I like to know who I'm dealing with. The world is a hall of mirrors, Mr Al-Hadi, a hall of mirrors! In my seventy-two years I have yet to meet a single person who has turned out to be anything like *who* or *what* they first presented themselves to be.'

'Very well, OK. Yes. I give you my answers. I was born in Cairo, 16 January 1971. I was educated at Cairo University at Fayoum, first-class degree in hydraulic engineering. You asked married? I have never been married. In the United States I have two cousins who have aluminium siding business in East Orange, New Jersey, Mohammed and Raouf. First I live in New Jersey, too. Then I move to Los Angeles.'

'Very good,' said Professor Halflight.

'Very good?'

'You answered all of my questions correctly.'

'What? How do you know this?'

'Because I initiated a background check on you as soon as I saw your little home movie. You kidnapped and assassinated one of the prime targets on the international hit list, yourself, personally, right under the noses of some of the best security guards that the world has to offer. You don't think that I wouldn't be interested in a man like you?'

Abdel Al-Hadi blinked. 'So – if I had not come here today—?'

'That's right. In a day or so, once I had gotten over my jet lag, I would have come to find *you*.'

'So you are interested that I should join you?'

Professor Halflight tossed down his pencil and stood up. 'There's something you need to understand, Mr Al-Hadi. This movement which you call Emu Ki Ilani does not specifically support Palestine against Israel, or Eritrea against Ethiopia, or Iran against the United States. It does not specifically support Islam against Christianity or indeed anybody against anybody.'

'I do not understand this.'

'To understand it, you have to understand the ancient history of Babylonia, under King Nebuchadnezzar.'

Abdel Al-Hadi frowned suspiciously, but said nothing.

Professor Halflight picked up his stick and slowly paced around his study. 'Nebuchadnezzar ascended to the throne of Babylon six hundred and five years before the birth of Christ. He carried on the military adventures that his late father had begun – especially to the west, against the Egyptians, and in 597 he captured the city of Jerusalem.

'Eight years later, the Egyptian pharaoh Apries tried to retake Palestine, but again Nebuchadnezzar laid siege to Jerusalem and this time he destroyed the city and brought down the Temple, and to make sure that he kept Jerusalem under his thumb, he took some of its most prominent and influential citizens into exile. Hence, "by the waters of Babylon we sat down and wept, when we remembered thee, o Sion." Psalm one-thirty-seven.

'Nebuchadnezzar was one of the first military leaders to realize that the best way to subdue your enemies is to keep

them in a constant state of chaos and dissent. Divide and rule.
If any of his enemies looked as if they were likely to make
peace with each other, he would send assassins to kill those
who were responsible for negotiating the treaties. After each
assassination, he made sure that each side would blame the
other, and peace would be averted.

'But it was more than that. Nebuchadnezzar also grew to
understand that when men are at peace, they fail to evolve,
and they fail to fulfil the potential that was given to them by
the gods. They become complacent, lazy, and reactionary.
Think of the Amish. In the twenty-first century, these peaceful
people are still riding around in horse-drawn buggies? Is that
an insult to the intelligence that they were given by the god
they claim to worship, or what?

'Many historians say that Nebuchadnezzar went mad. But
I believe that he was one of the few people who could clearly
see human destiny for what it was meant to be.

'With his priests, and his advisers, he formed a secret society
known as Nakasu, which in Babylonian simply means "to
slaughter". For each member of this society, a medallion was
forged – a sort of Babylonian dog tag, if you like – about five
hundred, I believe, possibly more. Down the centuries these
medallions were passed from one member of Nakasu to
another, with their names being engraved, and erased, and re-
engraved. Many medallions, of course, have been lost. But at
least fifty have survived.'

Professor Halflight heaved his way across the study to Abdel
Al-Hadi and stood so close that Abdel Al-Hadi could see the
brambly white hairs protruding from his nostrils.

'The mission of Nakasu is to keep mankind at war, for ever,
until they become like the gods. It is their holy vocation. If
men do not fight, they cease to develop. Those who try to make
peace are the true enemies of human aspiration, and that is why
they have to be eradicated. Nakasu has been doing that since
biblical times.'

Abdel Al-Hadi said, 'You don't care *who* you assassinate?
You don't care which side they're on?'

Professor Halflight stared at him for a long time, almost as
if he suspected that he was wearing a disguise. But then he
smiled and said, 'Absolutely right. All we want to do is to
keep the world in a permanent state of chaos. Chaos is the

only way forward. Otherwise, we atrophy. Physically, intellectually and economically. And spiritually, too.'

Abdel Al-Hadi said, 'If I join you, then, you might ask me to assassinate any leader who is trying to make peace? Even Palestinian?'

'That's right. We even had a plan to kill Yasser Arafat, after he made the Oslo Accords with Israel in 1993, when the Palestinians grudgingly recognized Israel's right to exist. But our man was arrested before he was able to get close, and we never got another chance.'

'And who else? Tell me. You say that Nakasu have been assassinating people since biblical times? I mean, for instance, like who?'

'Mr Al-Hadi, if I told you every single one, we would be here, you and I, for a week.'

'Plizz. Tell me some names.' Abdel Al-Hadi's Palestinian accent suddenly sounded very thick. He was conscious that 'for instance, like who?' might have been too American.

Professor Halflight looked at the clock on his desk. 'Why don't you come back to my house? I can freshen up, and have some breakfast, and we can continue our discussion there. Besides – I feel much more comfortable about the security, back home. You know what they say about walls having ears. Not to mention phones having bugs and mirrors having concealed video cameras.'

'I don't know.'

'You can trust me, Mr Al-Hadi, I assure you. Like I trust you. You don't think I would have told you anything about Nakasu, if I didn't? You eliminated Adeola Davis, which has saved us a great deal of complicated planning and expense. You have just the right combination of fervour and gall and sheer bloody-minded stupidity, if you don't mind my saying so. Believe me – we can use a man like you.'

Twenty-Six

Professor Halflight drove a half-mile up Nichols Canyon, and then turned into a down-sloping driveway. He parked in front of a two-storey cedar-wood house that looked as if it had been architect-designed in the late 1960s, with a flat roof and a deck that ran around three sides of it, and huge picture windows with slatted blinds.

As they climbed out of the professor's big silver Mercedes, Abdel Al-Hadi looked up and saw that somebody was sitting out on the deck, staring down at them – a very white-faced woman, with a dark brown headscarf. But Professor Halflight didn't acknowledge her. He heaved himself up the wooden steps and opened the front door and led the way inside.

The house was gloomy because all of the blinds were three-quarters closed, and there was a stale smell of last night's dinner. The walls were painted a dull magnolia, and were covered in dozens of Arabic prints and documents, all of them framed in dark brown wood.

Professor Halflight ushered Abdel Al-Hadi into a wide open-plan living room, with a dark polished floor and faded Persian rugs. All of the furniture was Middle Eastern, too: a green velvet ottoman with its stuffing hanging out like a disembowelled horse; and several leather armchairs with frayed fringes.

Abdel Al-Hadi heard the sharp flip-flap of slippers, and a diminutive Mexican woman appeared, wearing a black dress and a brown apron. If she was happy to see Professor Halflight back home, she didn't show it.

'Ah, Berta. I could use some breakfast. Coffee, and juice, and *huevos rancheros*. What about you, Mr Al-Hadi? Maybe some tea?'

'Hot water for me only, please. Maybe a squeeze of lemon.'

'OK. Hot water it is. And have Miguel bring my cases out of the car, would you?'

Berta said nothing, but flip-flapped away again. Professor Halflight took off his coat and pulled off his bright lavender necktie and tossed them both on the ottoman. Abdel Al-Hadi could see himself in the large, mottled mirror on the other side of the room. Although the air conditioning was rattling away furiously, the living room was stifling, and he was growing increasingly uneasy about his black hair dye.

'My partner will be down shortly,' said Professor Halflight. 'I'm sure she'll be delighted to meet the man who rid the world of Adeola Davis.'

'That was your partner, on the deck, when we arrived?'

'Fariah is housebound, I'm afraid. She was seriously injured, not very long after we met.'

'I am sorry.'

'Well, yes, but her misfortune only made the both of us more determined. She shares my belief in the critical necessity for the human race to be in constant turmoil. In fact, she is probably even more fervent about it than I am. I met her when I was studying ancient history in Tel Aviv. She was young, strong, beautiful. What I possessed in intellect, she possessed in political conviction and total – *total* – fearlessness.

'She took me to Jordan and together we joined the freedom fighters, Fatah, and they gave us guns and explosives. But we didn't just attack Israelis, she and I. We had our own agenda. Ha! We were like Bonnie and Clyde! We shot at buses. We blew up civilians. We made a point of attacking any local politician who was trying to make peace between the Israelis and the Jordanians, no matter who they were. That was when we were contacted by Nakasu.'

'Nakasu, they came looking for you?'

Professor Halflight nodded. 'In the same way that I would have come looking for *you*. Hitmen, you see, are two a penny, but assassins are not so easy to find – true assassins, anyhow. Assassins have to be *driven*. They have to be obsessed. They have to have a special madness, yet a terrible single-mindedness, too.'

'So you join Nakasu?'

'Of course. Nakasu was everything that Fariah and I had been waiting for, without realizing it. We had *heard* about them, of course, because of our studies of ancient Babylon. But we hadn't realized that after all these centuries they were still so active, and we had never guessed how widespread they were, in every country and every culture.'

Professor Halflight limped to the window, and angled the blind so that the sunlight shone into the living room in vertical bars.

'Fariah and I, we felt as if the scales had fallen from our eyes, and that it had been revealed to us why we were born. We had been born to save mankind from itself, from its own paralyzing sloth. We had been born for no less a purpose than the saving of human civilization.

'However, there was a personal price we had to pay. In August 1966, we blew up a house in Moshav Givat Yeshayahu, a few miles south of Beit Shemesh. The bomb went off prematurely. I lost my left kneecap, and most of my calf muscle. My dear partner lost both legs below the knee, and one arm, and also her face.'

As if Professor Halflight's partner had been listening to this conversation, and waiting for her cue, there was a whining noise as an elevator came down, and a door at the far end of the living room juddered open. Abdel Al-Hadi turned around, and there she was, sitting in a wheelchair, in semi-darkness, although her face had an eerie shine to it.

There was a higher-pitched whinny, as she steered her wheelchair out of the elevator and made her way towards them. She was wrapped, what there was of her, in a dark brown shawl with beige flower patterns on it. Her single hand, resting on top of the wheelchair control knob, had only three fingers. Her face was covered by an expressionless mask made of glossy cream celluloid. Behind the mask, her eyes shifted restlessly, like two blowflies busily laying eggs in her eye sockets.

'Fariah,' said Professor Halflight, 'this is Mr Abdel Al-Hadi.'

Abdel Al-Hadi bowed his head. 'I am honoured to meet you, madam.'

'Julius showed me your video,' Fariah croaked. 'You did well, to kill Adeola Davis. You should be proud.'

'It was unfortunate that she had to die, madam. But nobody would listen to our demands.'

'She was a *peacemaker*,' said Fariah, as if that was the most disgusting imprecation she could think of. 'Cursed are the peacemakers, for they shall condemn the human race to eternal compromise.' She let out a guttural laugh, which almost immediately degenerated into a bout of coughing.

'*Berta!*' called Professor Halflight. 'Berta! Bring water! Quick!'

Berta came flip-flapping into the living room carrying a plastic flask of water with a drinking straw attached. Professor Halflight poked the end of the straw into Fariah's mouth slit, and she sucked, and coughed, and made cackling catarrhal noises, and sucked again.

Eventually, she said, 'I'm all right now. Thank you, my love. Thank you.'

Abdel Al-Hadi hesitated for a moment, in case she started coughing again, but then he said, 'Tell me about Nakasu, Professor. You say there are many of them, in many different countries?'

'All over the world. In government agencies, in security forces, in universities, in business. You can hardly call them an organization, any more than you could call al-Qaeda an organization. But just like al-Qaeda they are utterly determined and they are prepared to sacrifice everything for what they believe in, and they will never be discovered and rooted out.

'Fariah and I have been associated with Nakasu for over forty years now. We have become connected with men and women of a hundred different nationalities and a thousand different political persuasions. But they all have shared our belief in chaos. Now, we are Nakasu's spiritual and cultural leaders, she and I. If somebody has to die, it is *our* decision.'

Abdel Al-Hadi said, 'Then the two of you – you rule the world – more than if you are king or queen or president?'

'I don't think it's entirely an exaggeration, to say that. In a way, we *do* rule the world. Nakasu has ruled the world for two-and-a-half thousand years. It's all a question of eliminating the right people at the right time.'

Fariah began to cough again, and Professor Halflight reinserted the drinking straw into her mask. More sucking noises, almost enough to turn Abdel Al-Hadi's stomach. He wished he hadn't chewed on that garlic clove after breakfast, but Mitchell had recommended it to give him 'authentic Palestinian breath'.

'A disguise is so much more than a stick-on beard and a false nose,' Mitchell had told him. 'You have to *smell* like the person you're pretending to be, too. Or, in your case, stink.'

Professor Halflight kept on feeding Fariah with noisy sips of water. Without taking his eyes off her, he said to Abdel Al-Hadi, 'You asked me earlier to give you some names.'

Abdel Al-Hadi shrugged, as if to say, Well, you can if you like, but if you don't want to—

'When I tell you,' said Professor Halflight, 'you will understand how influential Nakasu has been in changing the course of human history. In 2003, for example, there was the Swedish Foreign Minister Anna Lindh, who was stabbed in a department store in Stockholm, and died later of her wounds.'

'Yes. I remember this.'

'Ms Lindh, you see, was a tireless campaigner for international peace. Almost single-handedly she prevented a civil war between Kosovo and Macedonia, and she was still working on a new understanding between the Palestinians and the Israelis when Fariah and I decided that it was time for her to stop interfering in the natural order of things.

'A very successful operation, that one. We used a poor mad fellow called Mikailoviç, who didn't know what day of the week it was.

'Then there was Zoran Djindjiç, the prime minister of Serbia, also in 2003. And Yitzhak Rabin, the prime minister of Israel, in 1995, I think it was. And Olof Palme, the prime minister of Sweden, in 1986, and Indira Gandhi, in 1984.

'I won't pretend that Nakasu can take the credit for every single assassination over the past two-and-a-half thousand years. For instance, we had nothing to do with the killing of Earl Mountbatten, when his boat was blown up off the coast of Ireland. That was the IRA. But John F. Kennedy and Robert Kennedy, yes. And King Faisal of Iraq in 1958 . . . what wonderfully chaotic consequences *that* assassination has eventually brought us!

'And perhaps the jewel of all assassinations . . . the shooting of Archduke Franz Ferdinand of Austria, in 1914, which directly led to World War One, and the loss of thirty-seven million lives. But think how the world has advanced since then!'

Abdel Al-Hadi was silent for a very long time – so long that Professor Halflight leaned forward on his cane, cocked his head sideways and said, 'You want more names? There are dozens more. King Umberto I of Italy, in 1900. President James A. Garfield, in 1881.'

'You are right,' said Abdel Al-Hadi. 'You *have* changed history.'

'Yes, Mr Al-Hadi. But we have done something much more important than that. We have made sure that mankind moves forward. *Emu ki ilani*, as you rightly translated what it says on the medallion: to rise up, to move forward; to develop, to mature; to become like the gods.'

'So? I could join you? I could become a member of Nakasu? I could change history, too? I could become like the gods?'

'Let me show you something,' said Professor Halflight. He opened the top drawer of his desk and produced another medallion, exactly similar to the one that Abdel Al-Hadi was holding. He passed it over so that Abdel Al-Hadi could examine it.

On the reverse, the letters P A U L were engraved.

Abdel Al-Hadi handed the medallion back. 'Who is Paul?'

Professor Halflight didn't answer, but took a glossy colour photograph out of his drawer. It showed a catastrophic automobile wreck, someplace at night, in a tunnel. Firemen had cut the entire roof off a smashed-up black sedan, so that paramedics could attend to a woman who was sitting on the rear seat.

Her face was covered with an oxygen mask, but there was no mistaking the bright blonde hair.

Abdel Al-Hadi looked up in disbelief. 'This, also, was Nakasu?'

Professor Halflight took the drinking straw out of Fariah's mask slit, and it was still attached to a long spider's web of saliva.

'It was the landmines, that's why she had to go.'

'I don't understand.'

'My dear Mr Al-Hadi, the wonderful thing about landmines is that wherever you plant them they create a constant atmosphere of fear and uncertainty. In spite of that, they require absolutely no maintenance and they're outstandingly good value for money. Every month, all around the world, two thousand people are killed or injured by landmines. Yet your average landmine will cost you not much more than a Happy Meal – maybe three to ten dollars.'

He paused, before he added, 'We couldn't allow anybody to interfere in such a highly cost-effective way of causing chaos as *that,* now could we? Especially somebody with such a high public profile as *her*.'

Twenty-Seven

E arly the following afternoon, Hong Gildong pushed open the door that led to the subterranean parking garage and walked towards his SUV, jingling his keys in his hand.

The far end of the garage was open to the backyard of his apartment block, and Hong Gildong could see several of the residents sitting around the small rectangular pool, sunning themselves. As he approached his SUV, however, he could also make out the silhouettes of two men standing on either side of it, one of them leaning back against the hood as if he owned it.

'Help you?' he said, cautiously, as he came nearer.

One of the men came towards him, holding up an unlit cigarette. He was short and spidery-looking, with an unusually small head. He was wearing a light grey suit with wide lapels, and his left arm was supported by a triangular cream-colored sling.

The other man was blond, with a bulky torso, although he had narrow hips and shapely calf muscles, like a professional dancer. There were yellow and purple bruises around his eyes, as if somebody had hit him very hard on the bridge of the nose.

'Got a light?' asked the spidery man, with a phlegmy-sounding catch in his throat.

'Sorry. Don't smoke.'

'Well, that's no problem at all, because I have one.' The spidery man tucked the cigarette between his lips, took out a cheap pink butane lighter, and lit it. 'You and us, we have some business to discuss.'

'What business? I don't even know you.'

'That's no problem, either, because we know you. You are Mr Hong Gildong, who works as a security officer for DOVE. We need to talk to you about the kidnapping of Ms Adeola

Davis. Or at least our employer feels the need to talk to you about it.'

'Who are you? I talked to the police already, *and* the FBI.'

'Let's say we're very interested parties.'

'I have nothing to say to you. Sorry. You want to get off my vehicle?'

The blond man eased himself away from the hood of Hong Gildong's SUV and came towards him. He walked with an eerie shimmy, as if he were stepping out on to a dance floor. He stood over Hong Gildong and said, 'You *will* have something to say to us. But not here. You and us, we're all going for a ride.'

Hong Gildong hesitated for only a fraction of a second, but it was a fraction of a second too long. His hand plunged into his nylon windbreaker, but the spidery man had already yanked a nickel-plated Beretta out of his pocket, cocked it, and pointed it directly at his head. '*Whoa,*' he said, grinning.

The blond man lifted Hong Gildong's automatic out of its holster. Then he knelt down on one knee in front of him and patted his ankles, to make sure he wasn't wearing a back-up.

'This way,' said the spidery man. 'The grey sedan, by the pillar.'

'So where are we going?' asked Hong Gildong.

'What do you want to know that for? We're going there whatever.'

The blond man handcuffed him and tugged a soft black cotton hood over his head. Then the two men manhandled him into the back of their sedan and forced him down on the floor.

'You try to get up, I have a blackjack here, and I'll fucking brain you.'

Hong Gildong said nothing. The inside of the hood reeked of dried sweat and he could hardly breathe.

The car doors slammed and they squealed out of the garage. Hong Gildong felt them climb up the ramp and on to the street. They turned right on to Fountain Avenue, but then they turned left, and right, and left again, and he quickly began to lose any sense of direction.

The two men spoke sporadically, but their conversation was made up almost entirely of swearing and non-sequiturs, and it gave Hong Gildong no clue as to who they might be, or where they were taking him.

'That Hamulack. Guy can't pitch for shit.'

'And Tomoro can?'

'Tomoro? Tomoro's a goddamned cripple.'

Silence for nearly ten minutes. Then, 'Tomoro's *grandmother* can pitch better than Tomoro.'

They drove for well over two hours. The run was comparatively straight and smooth, and Hong Gildong could hear traffic on either side of them, so they must have been driving along a freeway. Eventually, they turned off the main highway and began to negotiate a winding road that felt as if it was taking them into the hills – although *which* hills, and in what direction, Hong Gildong couldn't even begin to guess.

After another forty minutes, they slowed down, turned sharply left, and stopped. Hong Gildong heard a metal gate open, and they drove through it. They turned left, and left again, and stopped again.

The car door was opened, and the spidery man said, 'OK, Mr Hong Gildong. We've arrived.'

He was so stiff that he could hardly move, but the blond man reached into the car and roughly heaved him out. He managed to stand up, coughing. It was past 3 p.m. now, but still very hot. He could hear the clanking of machinery and hoists, and the whining of forklift trucks. Some kind of factory, or maybe a warehouse.

'OK, let's go.'

The blond man half-pushed and half-steered him across a concrete yard. They went through a door into a chilly, fiercely air-conditioned interior. Hong Gildong could hear phones ringing and the soft rattling of computer keyboards. He was pushed along a corridor with a squeaky vinyl floor, and then down two flights of metal stairs.

Another door was pulled open, and from the squelching noise it made, it was well sealed. Inside, there was a musty, cement-like smell, and another smell, too, sweet and pungent, like stale urine. Hong Gildong was guided a few paces into the room and then his hood was pulled off.

He blinked. He was standing in a brightly-lit basement. One side of the basement was stacked with plywood packing cases and wooden pallets. The opposite side was lined with six wire-mesh cages, and although all of them were empty, Hong Gildong could immediately understand where the smell of urine came from. Each cage contained a dog bowl, a water basin, and a black padded dog bed.

The blond man dragged an orange metal chair in to the centre of the room, and unfolded it.

'Sit,' said the spidery man.

'I prefer to stand.'

'I said *sit*, asshole.'

Hong Gildong sat down. There was no point in inviting them to hit him.

'You're still not going to tell me who you are?' he asked them.

'You don't need to know. Besides, it wouldn't do you any good, even if you did.'

'So what happens now?'

'We're waiting.'

'Waiting for what?'

The spidery man didn't answer him. Nearly fifteen minutes went past, and none of them spoke. Now and again the spidery man checked his wristwatch, and cleared his throat, but the blond man simply stood still, with his arms folded.

Hong Gildong heard footsteps on the metal staircase outside, and then the sealed door squelched open. Two men appeared, a dark handsome man in an off-white designer suit and two-tone brown-and-white loafers; and another man in a light grey suit with a shaven head and a grey walrus moustache.

The man in the designer suit nodded to the spidery man and said, 'Well done. Nobody saw you?'

The spidery man shook his head. The man in the off-white designer suit came up to Hong Gildong and smiled at him. He smelled strongly of D&G aftershave. 'Well, now. If it isn't the ingenious Mr Hong Gildong. Do you know who I am?'

A long pause. 'I'm supposed to recognize you?'

'You don't read *Newsweek*? My name is Hubert Tocsin and I am the owner of Tocsin Weapons and Rocketry Systems, which happens to be the third most profitable arms manufacturer on the planet.'

Hong Gildong shrugged, as if to say, *So?*

Hubert Tocsin kept on smiling. 'I'm sorry if you've been

inconvenienced, Mr Hong Gildong, but it really is very important that I discuss something with you. I need to talk to you
about the kidnapping of Adeola Davis.'

'I told these two guys. I talked to the police already. I talked
to the FBI.'

'I know. But you didn't tell them the whole truth, did you?'

'I told them what happened. This guy came running up and
snatched Ms Davis, right in front of everybody. He was going
to cut her throat. We had to let him take her. What else could
anybody do?'

'Let me correct you, Mr Hong Gildong. You told the police
some of what happened, but not *all* of it. You didn't exactly
tell an untruth, but you lied by omission.'

'What do you mean? I told them everything.'

Hubert Tocsin said, 'No, you didn't. That demonstration
against the development of nuclear weapons by the North
Koreans, that was organized by the Korean Cycling Club of
Los Angeles. A legitimate demonstration, in itself. Quite under-
standably, many people feel very threatened by North Korea's
nuclear missile programme, especially those with relatives in
South Korea.

'But one of my detective friends in the LAPD discovered
yesterday afternoon that the demonstration was mainly organized by one of the cycling club's coaches, a fellow called Kim
Tong Sun, and would you believe it? Kim Tong Sun is married
to a young lady who happens to be your younger sister, Cho.

'My friend in the LAPD had a very fruitful discussion with
this Kim Tong Sun. And Kim Tong Sun admitted that he had
been asked to organize the demonstration by his brother-in-
law. Who is you.'

'So – what does that prove?' asked Hong Gildong.

'I'm not entirely sure,' said Hubert Tocsin. 'But it does seem
strange that since you were Adeola Davis' own bodyguard,
you should have set up a diversionary tactic which enabled a
terrorist splinter group to abduct her in front of hundreds of
people – well, what with the TV coverage – *millions*.'

'I am against nuclear weapons in North Korea,' said Hong
Gildong.

'And that's all? You're just a ban-the-bomber? A peacenik?
The timing of your little demonstration had nothing whatever
to do with Adeola Davis' abduction?'

'Coincidence.'

Hubert Tocsin circled around Hong Gildong's chair. 'You know, Mr Hong Gildong, I have *never* believed in coincidence. Or the occult, for that matter. I believe that you were deeply involved in the abduction of Adeola Davis – although what your involvement with the Armed Front for the Freedom of Palestine could possibly be, I have no idea.

'However, I need to find out. And the reason I need to find out is because the man who abducted Adeola Davis, and who subsequently murdered her – this man has approached an organization in which I have a very substantial financial commitment, and has asked whether he can join it.'

Tocsin took a small, leather-bound notebook out of his pocket, opened it, and peered at it. 'Abdel Al-Hadi. That name mean anything to you?'

Hong Gildong gave an involuntary jerk. He was beginning to realize that he was never going to walk out of this basement alive.

'No,' he said. 'Why should it?'

'You know which organization I'm talking about?' asked Hubert Tocsin.

'No idea. How could I?'

'Don't try to kid a kidder, Mr Hong Gildong. There's a link between you and Abdel Al-Hadi and I want to know what it is. You arranged that kidnapping, fella, didn't you? You arranged that kidnapping and I want to know why.'

Hong Gildong said nothing. But Hubert Tocsin bent over his chair and said, in a very soft voice, 'Tell me, Mr Hong Gildong – what *is* your connection to Abdel Al-Hadi?'

'I don't have any connection! OK, yes, I saw him on TV. That was all.'

'You're not telling me the truth, are you?'

'You want me to make up some story of cocks and bulls?'

'I don't have limitless patience. In fact, my patience has almost run out already. If you don't tell me voluntarily, I shall be obliged to *make* you tell me.'

Hubert Tocsin snapped his fingers. Immediately, the man with the walrus moustache left the basement, leaving the door slightly ajar behind him.

'Where did you first meet Abdel Al-Hadi?' asked Hubert

Tocsin. 'Did he offer you money, to organize that demonstration?'

'I told you. I am against nuclear proliferation.'

'Crap – not to put too fine a point on it. How much did he
pay you, Mr Hong Gildong? Presumably Ms Davis' other
bodyguards couldn't be bribed, or else you could have spir-
ited her away much less publicly. Or did you have another
agenda?'

Still Hong Gildong said nothing. But now he heard lurching
footsteps coming back down the metal staircase, and the frantic
scrabbling of claws. A brindled pit bull terrier came barging
through the half-open door, its eyes bulging, its claws skid-
ding sideways on the concrete floor. It was almost strangling
on its studded leash, and it was whining in the back of its
throat like an asthmatic.

The man with the walrus moustache had twisted the other
end of the leash three or four times around his forearm, but
it still took all of his strength to keep the dog from dragging
him across the basement.

Hubert Tocsin stood back. 'If *I* can't persuade you to be
cooperative, Mr Hong Gildong, maybe Bill can.'

'I *told* you,' insisted Hong Gildong. 'The timing of that
demonstration, that was just coincidence. All I said to Kim
Tong Sun was that the closing of the Peace Convention would
be the best time for him to make maximum impact.'

'Sorry. Your brother-in-law told my friend in the LAPD that
the whole set-up was your idea. And I don't believe that your
brother-in-law was lying. After their little chat together, my
friend in the LAPD is concerned that your brother-in-law might
not walk again. Not straight, anyways.'

The man with the walrus moustache pulled the pit bull into
one of the wire-mesh cages, released its leash, and closed the
door behind it. The dog barked and barked and crashed itself
repeatedly against the wire. At one point, it managed to climb
almost halfway up the mesh, clinging on by its pointed yellow
teeth. Its eyes bulged out at them, and it snarled as if it were
possessed by demons.

'Why don't you get acquainted?' said Hubert Tocsin. 'Bill's
a very sociable dog, once you get to know him.'

The blond man and the man with the walrus moustache
came around to the sides of Hong Gildong's chair and between

them they lifted him out of it. The spidery man pulled the chair across the basement until it was right up against the wire-mesh cage. The blond man unlocked Hong Gildong's handcuffs, but kept a clamp-like grip on his upper arm.

'Come on over,' said Hubert Tocsin. 'I always thought that Koreans loved dogs. Hey – they love them so much they even eat them, don't they?'

The man with the walrus moustache pushed Hong Gildong backwards, forcing him to sit back down on the chair. Immediately, the blond man looped a plastic-metal packing strap around his chest, pulled it very tight, and fastened it. Inside the cage, only inches away, the pit bull was barking and slavering and hurling itself against the wire in an ever-increasing frenzy. Hong Gildong felt its saliva spray against his cheek.

Hubert Tocsin bent down and spoke very quietly in his ear. 'I'm giving you one last opportunity to tell me the full story of Ms Davis' abduction. Believe me, you could save yourself a great deal of pain.'

Hong Gildong said nothing. He was very afraid; but his instinct told him that as long as he had information that Hubert Tocsin wanted, he wouldn't be killed. It was a straightforward choice between pain and death.

'OK,' said Hubert Tocsin. 'If that's the way you want to play it.'

The man with the walrus moustache poked a stick into the cage to keep the pit bull at bay. While he did so, the blond man unlatched a small hinged flap which must usually have been used for throwing in bones or dog biscuits. He took hold of Hong Gildong's right hand and forced it through the opening. Then he pulled out a pair of nylon wrist-restraints, and fastened one of them to Hong Gildong's wrist and the other to the wire-mesh.

'Like I say, Koreans love dogs so much that they eat them,' said Hubert Tocsin. 'Let's see if that affection is mutual.'

The man with the walrus moustache drew his stick out of the cage, and instantly the pit bull jumped up at Hong Gildong's hand, biting at his knuckles. Hong Gildong let out a shout of pain, and tried to wave his hand up and down so that the dog couldn't sink its teeth into it. But the pit bull had tasted blood now, and Hong Gildong's shouting only seem to excite it more.

With a sharp crunch, the pit bull buried its teeth deep into the heel of his hand, at its fleshiest part, and started to throw its head wildly from side to side, so that the muscle was torn away, a little more with every tug of its jaws.

Hong Gildong might have been screaming, but if he was he couldn't hear himself. All he could hear was a roaring in his brain, like the roaring of an open furnace.

The roaring abruptly stopped, and everything went silent, and black.

He became aware of the pain, first of all. His hand felt as if it were actually on fire, even though he no longer had a hand. This time he screamed out loud and he could hear it. He opened his eyes and Hubert Tocsin was standing very close to him, smiling.

'Well, Mr Hong Gildong, one thing we can say for sure: Bill really, really likes you.'

Hong Gildong let out two or three shuddery breaths, but couldn't speak.

Hubert Tocsin walked around him, still smiling. 'In fact, Bill likes you so much that he wouldn't mind seconds.'

'No more,' croaked Hong Gildong. 'Please, no more.'

'That's very ungenerous of you, Mr Hong Gildong. You still have another hand.'

'No more. Please. Why don't you just shoot me?'

'Because that would be homicide. And apart from that, it would be stupid. If I shot you, how could you tell me what I want to know?'

Twenty-Eight

Adeola was sitting on the veranda painting her nails a deep shade of bronze. She had twisted her hair up in an elaborate spiral, and fastened it with copper and silver pins. Rick was lying back on one of the basketwork sunloungers, reading a dog-eared copy of *How To Save The Human Race From Itself*, which he had found under the bed.

'Do you know what it says here? It says that by the year 2750, there will be no distinct races left. We'll all be the same colour and we'll all eat the same food and we'll all speak the same language. A khaki-collared world of tofu-eaters speaking Esperanto.'

'Do you believe that?'

'I don't believe anything I read in books. Or newspapers. I don't believe anything I see on TV, either, even the wildlife programmes.'

'In any case,' Adeola said, 'I wouldn't want you to be the same colour as me. I like white skin.'

'And I like mocha skin.'

'*Mocha?*'

Rick tossed the book into the yard, so that it vanished into the rose bushes. Then he climbed off the sunlounger, came across the veranda and kissed Adeola on the forehead. She looked up at him with those dark, slanted eyes of hers, and then kissed him back, on the lips.

'We have a saying in Nigeria,' she told him. '"The thirsty fig waits patiently for the rains."'

'And we have a saying in the United States. "Abstinence makes the heart grow fonder."'

At that moment, Noah and Silja and Leon came out.

'God, I'd kill for a beer,' said Noah.

'Sorry,' said Rick. 'You're supposed to be a Muslim. If Halflight smells alcohol on your breath . . .'

'What time are you going to see him?' asked Adeola.

'He said any time after eight. Mitch will be here by six thirty, so I'll go as soon as he's finished my make-up.'

'You really think they're going to let you join Nakasu?'

'Yes, I do. Come on – they're always on the lookout for nutjobs like Abdel Al-Hadi. Look at John Wilkes Booth. Or Sirhan Sirhan.'

'I still don't know how they've managed to keep Nakasu quiet for so many hundreds of years.'

'Because they always make sure they clean up after themselves, that's how. Meticulously. And if that means whacking anybody who even gets an inkling that they exist, then that's what they do.'

'Do you think they're going to ask you to assassinate some-body?'

'That's what they want me for, yes. But I don't know who. Maybe they haven't decided yet.'

Leon said, 'I've been surfing the Net . . . drawing up a list of probable targets. Like, people who have been actively nego-tiating peace agreements, all around the world. I think the favourite so far is the UN Secretary General, Mahfoud Ould N'Diayane. But the British Foreign Secretary John Williams runs him a pretty close second, and I'd say that Alvin Metzler is third, because he's trying to tie up that deal you started with the Ethiopians.'

'OK,' said Rick. 'But whoever it is, we'll have to try to hit Nakasu before Nakasu hits them.'

'We still need to find out much more about them,' put in Adeola. 'It's no good taking out just one or two of them. They're worldwide, so we need to know how they operate, how they communicate, how many people they have working for them. I'd like to know how they're financed, too. It can't be cheap, running a worldwide network of assassins. Think of the money they need for bribes and pay-offs. How does a seedy old college professor like Julius Halflight pay for an organization like that?'

Silja put her arm around Noah's neck, and kissed him on the ear. 'I am just looking forward to all of this being finished. I am tired of Abdel already, with his beard and his smelly breath.'

'That reminds me,' said Noah. 'I'd better go chew some garlic.'

It was dark by the time he arrived at Professor Halflight's house, but the only light showing was a single lantern by the front door. He paid off the taxi, climbed the steps, and rang the bell. As he waited, a cloud of bats flew overhead, softly whirring their wings. He disliked bats. When he was at Eagle Scout camp, a bat had got caught in his hair, and he had never forgotten the terror of it, or the humiliation of screaming in front of all his fellow scouts.

Berta, the maid, answered the door. She said nothing, but stood back so that Abdel Al-Hadi could step into the hallway. As he passed her, he looked down at her, and she looked up at him, and he was convinced that she knew he was wearing a disguise.

She led him into the living room. Professor Halflight was standing on the opposite side of the room, with Fariah sitting in her wheelchair beside him, and they were talking to two men. One of them was a black man in a yellow-and-orange shirt with zigzag patterns on it. The other was the blond man in the grey suit who had cut Jenna's throat right in front of him.

Abdel Al-Hadi nearly turned around and walked back out again. He could barely breathe, as if his chest cavity had been stuffed with kapok, like a quilt. He had never felt such a surge of anger and hatred in his life. It took so much self-control for him not to rush across the room and smash the blond man's head against the wall that he was trembling.

'Ah!' said Professor Halflight, turning around to greet him. 'The redoubtable Abdel Al-Hadi!'

The blond man turned around, too, and he was grinning.

'So pleased to see you,' said Professor Halflight. 'Can I ask Berta to bring you something to drink?'

'Thank you, sir. No thank you.'

'Are you all right, Mr Al-Hadi? You look a little shivery. Not pining for the grippe, are you?'

'I am well, thank you. A little tired, that is all.'

'Are you not sleeping well? Where are you staying at the moment?'

'My mind is turning over, Professor. There has been much for me to think about.'

'Of course. And if your accommodation isn't comfortable, that doesn't help, does it?'

'My accommodation is very comfortable, thank you.'

Professor Halflight gave a slanting smile, but didn't pursue the subject. When Abdel Al-Hadi had left here yesterday, Professor Halflight had called a taxi for him. Abdel Al-Hadi had told the driver to take him to the lower end of Alta Loma Road, and then he had climbed out and run down the alleyways between Holloway and Santa Monica, where Steve had been waiting for him in his car.

Steve had been taught evasive driving in the Secret Service, and he had taken them back to Scholl Canyon by a maze-like route which had involved driving through the Hollywood

Cemetery, followed by a circuit of Paramount Studios, and backing up, at speed, along two one-way streets.

Professor Halflight said, 'This is Captain Madoowbe, of the Ethiopian security services. Captain Madoowbe, this is Mr Abdel Al-Hadi. I expect you recognize him from the television news.'

Captain Madoowbe didn't stand up, but looked up at Abdel Al-Hadi with eyes as yellow as poison. 'You are a dangerous fellow, Mr Al-Hadi. I like a dangerous fellow.'

Abdel Al-Hadi nodded to Fariah, but he couldn't tell from Fariah's celluloid mask if she had acknowledged him or not. Professor Halflight didn't introduce him to the blond man, who took one or two paces back, but kept on smiling.

'The reason Captain Madoowbe is here is because of our next target,' said Professor Halflight. He limped over to a side table crowded with decanters and bottles and poured himself a generous glass of Maker's Mark whisky.

'The day after tomorrow, before he is scheduled to return to Ethiopia, the Ethiopian Foreign Minister His Excellency Ato Ketona Aklilu will be meeting with Mr Alvin Metzler, the political director of mission of the DOVE organization. They expect to be signing an agreement whereby the Ethiopian government will be making certain assurances about the Anuak people in Gambella, in particular that government forces will stop persecuting them and that they will be allowed to return to their farms without harassment.

Captain Madoowbe grinned. His teeth were almost as yellow as his eyes. 'The Anuak people. They are all rebels and malcontents. But His Excellency is *very* humane.'

'The meeting will be very short,' said Professor Halflight. 'It will take place in the presidential suite at the Century Plaza Hotel. The agreement is more of a gesture of mutual goodwill than a binding political commitment.'

'A gesture of mutual futility, more like,' said Fariah, in a thick, vitriolic croak. 'Only tired men seek to make peace with each other.'

Professor Halflight gave her an indulgent pat on the shoulder. 'Well, yes. It will be the usual farce. Handshakes, exchanging of pens, overfed men in badly-fitting suits talking about a dazzling new dawn for democracy. But it will have one unusual feature.'

'What is this?' asked Abdel Al-Hadi, cautiously.

'The President is arriving in Los Angeles the day after tomorrow, for the Pan-Pacific Economic Conference. And I have been reliably informed that he will be making a surprise appearance.'

'A surprise appearance?' asked Abdel Al-Hadi 'Then how do *you* know about it?'

'Because Nakasu has some very good friends in law enforcement, Mr Al-Hadi. And wherever the President goes, the law enforcement agencies have to know about it in advance.'

'What are you saying? You are saying that you are going to assassinate this foreign secretary from Ethiopia, and also this man from DOVE, and the President, too?'

Captain Madoowbe shook his head. 'His Excellency Ato Ketona Aklilu will survive the attack, because of the quick-thinking and courage of his head of security, Captain Madoowbe. Unfortunately Mr Alvin Metzler and the President will both be killed.'

'But the security – if the President is there—'

'Of course. Security will be very tight indeed. But you can rest assured that Nakasu can get you close enough to do what you have to do.'

'You want *me* to do this?'

'You wanted to join Nakasu, Mr Al-Hadi. You wanted to show the world that the Armed Front for the Freedom of Palestine is a force to be reckoned with.'

'Of course. But to assassinate the President!'

Fariah said, 'The President, unlike his predecessor, is a peacemaker. If you kill him, Mr Al-Hadi, then the struggle for Palestine can go on, and one day the fiercest and the strongest and the most determined will come out on top, as they rightly should.'

'But look at me! I am Palestinian! Always it takes me many hours, just to pass through airport security! How can I get close to the President?'

'Oh, I think you'll manage it,' said Fariah. She started to cough, and they all waited patiently until she had finished. She spat noisily behind her mask, and Professor Halflight reached underneath her celluloid chin with a Kleenex and wiped her mouth.

'Her lungs,' he explained. Abdel Al-Hadi nodded, trying to

look sympathetic, but Captain Madoowbe had an expression on his face of utter disgust.

Fariah fumbled inside her brown shawl with her three-fingered hand. Professor Halflight hovered, as if he wanted to help her, but she tutted at him to stop interfering. Eventually, she produced from the folds of her shawl a shining silver medallion, highly polished, with cuneiform characters on it.

She held it up, and as it spun around, the light was reflected in Abdel Al-Hadi's eyes, like a heliograph message. *Flash, flash, flash.* For a moment, he was mesmerized.

'This is mine?' he asked.

'Yes,' said Professor Halflight. 'And it has a very distinguished history. It was last carried by Paul Gorguloff, a Russian émigré who shot the President of France, Paul Doumer, in 1932, at a bookfair in Paris.'

'Gorguloff was sentenced to death and beheaded,' put in Fariah. 'But before he went to the guillotine, the medallion was taken from his neck by Marc Bailly, the executioner, who was also associated with Nakasu, and eventually it was returned to the United States.'

Professor Halflight took the medallion from Fariah and handed it to Abdel Al-Hadi. 'Like every other medallion, Gorguloff's name was polished off, so that it was ready to be re-engraved with the name of the next assassin who would wear it.'

'Feel it,' croaked Fariah. 'Feel how smooth and worn it is. It is over two thousand years old, and it has hung around the necks of dozens of assassins. Think of what it must have absorbed, from those men. The righteous madness! The exhilaration of killing another human being! The fear of being caught, and executed!'

Abdel Al-Hadi said, 'It has great power, this medallion. Great history.'

'And you, too, can be part of that history,' said Professor Halflight. 'Turn it over, look on the back. We've had your name engraved on it.'

'You are so sure of me that you have already done this?'

'Oh, we're sure of you.'

Abdel Al-Hadi turned the medallion over. On the reverse were the letters F L Y N N.

Twenty-Nine

Leon was playing *Samurai Warriors in Space* on Adeola's laptop when Rick knocked, loose-knuckled, on his open door.

'I'm going out for some beer, dude. Do you want to come?'

'Sure. Anything to get out of this place.'

'Don't be too long,' Silja called from the kitchen. 'I am making *frikadeller* this evening. And cabbage salad, with oranges.'

'Twenty minutes, Silja, that's all. Do you need anything?'

'Maybe some cigarettes, that's all.'

Rick and Leon climbed into the metallic red Grand Prix that Steve had rented for them. As they turned out of the parking space in front of the house, Rick said, 'You called your uncle Saul about the funeral?'

Leon nodded. 'It's tomorrow afternoon, at the Mount Sinai Memorial Park.'

'If you want to go, maybe we could ask Mitch to give you a false beard or something.'

Leon shook his head. 'I don't want to go to my father's funeral in disguise. I'd rather wait, you know? I want to stand in front of his headstone the way I am now, and tell him that I've gotten my revenge on the bastards who murdered him.'

'You'll get your revenge, Leon, one way or another, believe me. And so will the rest of us.'

'You really think so?' said Leon. 'It seems like there's so many of them. They're like those flying ants, you know, that come out of the cracks in the sidewalk. You squish about a hundred of them but there's always more pouring out.'

'I know. But if Noah has understood it right, Professor Halflight is like the king ant. He's the one who chooses who these Nakasu guys assassinate – well, him and that crippled partner of his – and it seems like he's the one who connects everybody with everybody else. If we can take *him* out—'

Leon looked at Rick and it wasn't only his dark, silky moustache that made him look less like a boy. 'I want to kill him, you know, Halflight. Personally, I want to kill him – *me*. I've been thinking about it a whole lot, and I know I could. Noah's been teaching me how to use your gun.'

Rick looked back at him for so long and so intently that Leon began to worry that he was going to stray on to the wrong side of the boulevard.

'I believe you,' said Rick, at last. He steered the Grand Prix towards a brightly-lit 7–11 on the corner of Cypress Avenue, and parked.

Leon said, 'I don't want you to think – well, feeling so angry like this – I never felt like this before.'

Rick laid his hand on top of Leon's, to reassure him. 'Listen, Leon, none of us have.'

Silja was blending her salad dressing when Adeola came into the kitchen, dressed in a black kimono-style bathrobe with a red dragon embroidered on the back.

'Where did you find *that*?' asked Silja.

'In the closet, next to the red satin pyjamas and the turquoise jogging suit.'

'You have to admit that Noah's friend has *such* good taste.'

'Talking of taste, what's that you're making?'

Silja offered her a spoonful. 'Orange and rosemary vinaigrette, for the salad.'

'It's wonderful. Is that paprika in it?'

'And cayenne. And Dijon mustard. And garlic. And of course orange juice.'

Adeola looked up at the clock. 'Nine thirty. Don't you think that Noah should be back by now?'

'He didn't know how long it was going to take. I'm trying not to worry about it, but I'm so frightened for him. Supposing they realize that he's not an Arab terrorist after all? They'll kill him, the same way they killed all those other people.'

Adeola put her arm around Silja's shoulders. 'I was in Damascus once, in the American Embassy, and a car bomb went off, right up against the embassy wall. The attaché I was talking to said we should go down to the shelter, but do you know something? I was so terrified that I couldn't move. I just sat there, and in the end they almost had to carry me out of that conference room.

'But this is why we are trying to stop these people. We can't live our lives, being afraid all the time. What kind of a life is it, if we are always afraid?'

Silja tore off a paper towel and dabbed at her eyes. 'You're right, of course. But with all of this – Noah and me, we are very close now. It used to be only professional, but now it is something much more. If anything happened to him—'

Adeola smiled at her. 'I know.'

She was turning towards the fridge when the kitchen door was kicked open, with a bang.

'My God! *What*—?'

A bulky, bald-headed black man in a light grey suit barged his way into the kitchen, holding up a machine pistol. His fist was so big that the gun looked like a toy, but Adeola recognized an MP9A1 when she saw one. It could blow a hole through a bullet-proof vest.

The black man was followed by another bald man with a walrus moustache, and then a spidery-looking man with his right arm in a sling.

'What's this?' Adeola demanded, wrapping her bathrobe more tightly around her, and tugging at the sash. 'Who the hell are you? What do you want?'

Silja backed away. 'I know this man,' she said to Adeola, pointing to the spidery-looking man. 'He came to Noah's house and tried to kill us.'

The spidery man came around the kitchen table, flexing the fingers of his free hand as if he were preparing to shoot craps. 'Be ye not afraid, ladies,' he said. 'This time, I haven't come to do you no physical injury. Times have changed. Events have moved on.'

'What do you want?' Adeola demanded.

The spidery man approached her and leaned forward a little, only a few inches away from her, and sniffed. 'Giorgio Wings shower gel. I would have thought that was a little flowery for a woman like you.'

He paused, and then he said, 'Mind you, it's something of an achievement, don't you think, that a dead woman can take a shower at all?'

'I asked you what you were doing here,' said Adeola.

'I think I'm entitled to ask you the same question, Ms Adeola Davis, since you were publicly plugged through the nut on network TV. But that philosophical stuff, that's my employers' concern, not mine. I'm in charge of transportation, that's all. Sometimes I transport people from this world into the next, but in your case I'm simply going to transport you to meet a gentleman who would very much like to talk to you about your recent demise.'

While they were talking, the man with the walrus moustache had been looking through the other rooms, and out on the veranda. He came back to say, 'Nobody else around.'

'I see. So where are your friends, Ms Davis?'

'They left. They're not coming back.'

'Didn't take their clothes?' snorted the man with the walrus moustache. 'Didn't take even take their toothbrushes?'

'They were in a hurry.'

'Oh, you don't have to lie to me, Ms Davis,' said the spidery man. 'In any case, it don't matter too much to me, except that I was instructed to use deadly force in the event of them trying to be obstructive, and I was looking forward to that. I don't like leaving loose ends that might require tying up later.'

He drew back his sling and checked his wristwatch. 'OK, time we were getting the hell out of here. Let's go.'

'I need to get dressed,' Adeola protested.

'You don't need to do nothing except what I tell you to do. Now let's go. You too, blondie.'

'You can't do this,' said Adeola. 'Don't you know who I am?'

'I know who you *was*,' the spidery man leered at her. 'But who are you now? The *late* Ms Adeola Davis, RIP. And dead people, they don't have a whole lot of clout, not with the living, anyhow.'

Rick and Leon were turning off Glenoaks Boulevard into Scholl Canyon Drive when a grey sedan came speeding around the corner, so fast that its tyres were squittering in protest. Rick was momentarily blinded by its headlights, but Leon looked around and said, '*Shit!*'

'What?' said Rick.

'It was Adeola, and Silja!'

'What?'

'Adeola and Silja! They were sitting in the back seat!'
'*What?*'
Rick stamped on the brakes, and the Grand Prix slewed in
a semicircle. Then he jammed his foot on the gas and they
snaked back along Glenoaks Boulevard, leaving a cloud of
rubber smoke behind them.
'You're sure it was them?'
'Totally! And there were two guys sitting in the front!'
Rick was driving at nearly eighty miles an hour now, with
the car bouncing and leaping over the bumps in the road.
'Nobody's supposed to know that we're up here!' he said,
angrily.
'Maybe one of the neighbours saw us, and tipped off the
cops.'
'Well, Mitch wouldn't have told anyone, and Steve and Ted
sure wouldn't, they're both ex-Secret Service.'
'Hong Gildong?'
'He knew, but look how much help he gave us, setting
this up.'
They sped round a long right-hand curve, with the lights
of the Ventura Freeway glittering off to their left. As they did
so, the grey sedan came into view. Rick could even see Silja's
white-blonde hair shining in the large rear window. He could
also see that there was a third man in the back seat, sitting
on Silja's right.
The sedan was a Buick Lucerne, the same type of vehicle
driven by the men who murdered Jenna.
'Bastards,' said Rick, under his breath. 'If they even *breathe*
on Adeola, I swear to God, I'm going to kill them all.'
He started to speed up, until they were less than fifty yards
away from the Buick's rear lights.
But Leon said, 'Slow up a little. You should give them some
space.'
'What the hell for? I'm going to ram the bastards.'
'But they haven't killed them, have they? They haven't cut
their throats?'
'*What?* What are you talking about?'
'They tried to kill Adeola, didn't they? They tried at least
twice.'
'They tried, yes, but they failed. Well – they managed to
kill plenty of other people, but not her.'

'They tried to kill Silja, too, when they came to Noah's place.'

The Buick was heading for the freeway, and travelling fast, but Rick was gradually gaining on them. He was trying to work out what he was going to do now: rear-end them, probably, force them into a crash barrier and then pull open the doors of their car while they were still (hopefully) dazed.

But Leon said, 'They could have killed them back at the house. But they didn't. And now they're taking them someplace. Why do you think they're doing that?'

Rick slowed up a little. 'I don't know.'

'And, like, *where* are they taking them?'

'For Christ's sake, Leon, I don't know that either!'

'Don't you think – instead of ramming them – we should follow them? Then we'll find out.'

There was a long pause, while Rick thought about it. Then he eased off the gas.

'You're right,' Rick finally admitted. 'You're absolutely right.'

He slowed up a little more, allowing the grey sedan to pull further ahead. It sped on, joining the Glendale Freeway and heading south. Traffic was light, but most of the time Rick was able to keep several vehicles in between them. He lit a cigarette to calm himself down.

'OK if I have one?' asked Leon.

'You want a cigarette? What's the matter with you – you want to die?'

The Buick turned south-east on Route 5 and kept on going, and although it was touching seventy most of the time, Rick and Leon kept on following it. A half-mile apart, the two cars sped past Anaheim and Santa Ana and Mission Viejo, and then due south to San Clemente, and along the coast towards San Diego.

The moon came out, and its flat white light turned the scenery into cardboard, as if they were driving through a child's dream.

They had bought a giant bag of cheesy Doritos at the 7–11, and Leon sat back and tore it open. Rick wasn't hungry at all, but he could have used a drink.

Eventually, just past the little strung-out community of

Oceanside, the Buick turned off Route 5 without making a signal, and headed inland. It was nearly midnight now, and there were scarcely any other cars around, so Rick made sure that he varied the distance between them as much as possible. Once or twice he indicated that he was turning off to the right, and pulled into a side road for a count of ten, before rejoining the main highway, and putting his foot down to catch up with the Buick before he lost it.

They climbed through the mountains, around one twisting bend after another, with the reservoir gleaming in the moonlight below them. It seemed wild and remote out here, but after twenty minutes they suddenly found themselves driving through the small town of Escondido, between neat white-washed houses and red-tiled roofs and orange groves.

Rick kept his speed down to twenty. He knew about these small towns and their over-zealous traffic cops. 'We haven't lost him, have we?' he asked Leon, as they left the lights of Escondido behind them.

'No, he's there, I can still see his tail lights. Look out – he's pulling over. Slow up.'

On their left, they were passing a wide scrubby area, fenced off from the road by a high grey-painted security fence. Rick slowed right down to a crawl. On the other side of the fence, he could see what looked like factory buildings: two older ones, squarish, constructed of concrete and painted grey; and three or four newer ones, almost the size of aircraft hangars, made of silvery aluminium.

The whole complex was lit by floodlights and covered by CCTV cameras. One first-floor window was lit, and Rick could see a man in a grey shirt sitting at a desk, but that was the only sign of life.

'Look,' said Leon. 'They're going inside.'

The Buick had driven along the entire length of the security fence, about three quarters of a mile, and now it was turning into the factory entrance. Rick pulled over to the side of the road. At the gate, a grey-and-white-striped barrier went up, and the Buick drove inside. Immediately, the barrier went down again.

'So,' said Rick, 'it looks like your question has been answered. They were taking Silja and Adeola *here* – wherever *here* is.'

He waited until the Buick had disappeared from sight around the side of the factory buildings. Then he drove past the front gate, as slowly as he could without attracting suspicion. A large grey sign stood outside, with a painting of a bell on it, and the words *Tocsin Weapons and Rocketry Systems, Escondido, California. Strictly No Admittance To Unauthorized Personnel.*

'Tocsin!' said Leon. 'That figures. Now we know for sure that he's connected to Professor Halflight . . .'

Rick kept on driving for another hundred yards and then stopped.

'It's all beginning to make some grisly kind of sense, isn't it? Professor Halflight needs finance to keep Nakasu active; Hubert Tocsin needs chaos in the world so that he can sell more bombs. That's what you call *symbiosis*, isn't it?'

Thirty

'How did you find out who I was?' asked Noah.

Professor Halflight eased himself into a worn velvet-covered armchair, and sniffed. 'I don't think we ever would, if a certain Korean gentleman hadn't succumbed to some friendly persuasion.'

'Hong Gildong?'

'You shouldn't blame him, Noah – you don't mind if I call you Noah? Hong Gildong was under considerable duress when he told us all about you and your video. I must admit your killing of Adeola Davis was very well done. Totally convincing. And of course your psychology was spot on. You knew how much we wanted Ms Davis eliminated, and how grateful we would be to anyone who did the job for us.'

'You should have an Oscar!' grinned Captain Madoowbe.

'And so should your make-up artist,' said Professor Halflight. 'Your disguise is absolutely brilliant. Your accent slipped now and again, but I have to confess that didn't ring any alarm bells. I just thought that Abdel Al-Hadi had picked up some Americanisms since he had arrived here. From his brothers in Orange, New Jersey, maybe.'

He let out a loud, harsh laugh, and he was still laughing when his cellphone played *Satisfaction*. He took it out of his shirt pocket and said, 'Yes?'

He listened for a moment, and then he said, 'Only those two? Where were the others?'

Another pause, then, 'Damn. All right, then. But, good.'

He closed the cell and dropped it back into his pocket.

'Bad news, I hope?' said Noah.

'Not quite as good as expected. But good enough.'

'So what happens now?' Noah fixed his eyes on the blond man standing in the corner. 'You're going to cut my throat, just like you cut my girlfriend's throat, and Mo Speller's throat, and Trina's, and all those other people?'

'My dear Noah, of course not! We admitted you to Nakasu, even if you tricked us into doing so, and now you are a Nakasu assassin.'

'You don't still expect me to shoot the President, do you?'

'Why ever not? In fact, when I was told who you really were, and what you had done to join us, I was delighted! Every assassination presents us with knotty logistical problems – the main problem always being, how to escape afterwards.

'This particular assassination was always going to be very tricky: confined space, very high security. But *you*, Noah – you showed me how to solve that problem.'

'Oh, really?'

'Yes, really! You see – our original plan was to wait for the photocall after the peace agreement was signed. As soon as the cameras started to flash, one of Captain Madoowbe's security men would take out his gun, shout out some rabid political slogan, and shoot the President and Alvin Metzler at point-blank range. Three other security men would immediately surround him and disarm him, but at the same time, of course, they would be shielding him from the President's Secret Service detail.

'The security men would then rush the assassin out of the hotel and drive him at high speed to the Ethiopian Consulate on Wilshire Boulevard. Once inside, he would be protected from arrest by diplomatic immunity. The Ethiopian Consul

General would insist that he should be deported to Ethiopia to stand trial in Addis Ababa, because he could never be given a fair hearing in the US.'

'Are you kidding me?' said Noah. 'You don't seriously think that you could get away with a plan like that? They'd have a SWAT team abseiling through the windows in ten minutes flat.'

'If this were a Bruce Willis movie, maybe they would. But this is real life, Noah, and in real life diplomatic immunity is taken very seriously. In 1984, for instance, a female police officer was shot and killed outside the Libyan Embassy in London, and the police laid siege to the embassy for eleven days. In the end, they had to let all the diplomats leave the country, including the man who had shot her.

'However, we're not faced with that difficulty any more, because we have you.'

Noah shook his head, and in the mirror he could see Abdel Al-Hadi shaking his head, too. 'If you think that I'm going to shoot the President for you – if you think that I was *ever* going to shoot anybody for you – then you're pissing up the wrong post, Professor. The only person I was ever intending to shoot was you – and smiler over there.'

'I'm sure you were. But that was before. And this is now.'

'So what's changed?'

'First of all, we know who you are. Second of all, we know that Adeola Davis isn't dead at all. And most important, we now have Adeola Davis in what you might call our protective custody. That cellphone call confirmed that Ms Davis is safely on her way to a secure destination, where she will be taken care of until you have successfully carried out your task.'

'You've *kidnapped* her?'

'"Kidnapped", Noah? That's a little strong. Let's say "relocated".'

'So what happens to Adeola if I refuse to shoot the President?'

'Ms Davis is dead already, as far as the police are concerned. She was shot by a Palestinian terrorist called Abdel Al-Hadi. But we don't mind shooting her again, just to make absolutely sure. After all, they won't be looking for *us*, will they?'

'How much of a cold-hearted bastard are you, Professor?'

Professor Halflight sniffed, and took out a large grey handkerchief and blew his nose. 'More than you think, Noah. More than you think. You see, we have also relocated Ms Silja Fonselius, and if you fail to do what we have asked you to do, she will be suffering the same fate.'

Noah stalked across the room and wrenched Professor Halflight's cane out of his hand. He lifted it up, but the blond man said, '*No.*'

Noah looked across at him. He was pointing a gun directly at Noah's head, one hand supporting his wrist.

'You're going to shoot me?' said Noah. 'I thought I was the answer to your prayers.'

'Let's put it this way,' said Professor Halflight, 'if we have to shoot you, then we won't have any further use for Adeola Davis or Silja Fonselius, will we? But if you behave yourself, there is at least a chance that all three of you might survive. Where there's life, Noah, there's hope.'

Noah dropped Professor Halflight's cane on the floor. Captain Madoowbe got up from his seat and picked it up, and returned it to its owner. The blond man holstered his gun.

'So what's your plan now?' asked Noah. 'How can *I* get close enough to the President to shoot him? The Secret Service wouldn't let me get within two states of him, looking like this.'

'But you won't look like that,' said Captain Madoowbe. 'You will look like *this.*'

He took a security tag out of his shirt pocket and handed it to Noah. The photograph showed an Ethiopian, about thirty-five years old, with a shaven head. His skin was so black it was almost dark blue. His nose was narrower than many Ethiopians', more Arabic than African, and his lips were thinner.

'Kebede Gebeyehu,' said Captain Madoowbe. 'One of my security team. Licensed to carry a concealed weapon, and authorized to enter all restricted areas. If your make-up man can make you look like a Palestinian, I'm sure that he can make you look like an Ethiopian.'

'You can't be serious!'

'Never more so,' said Professor Halflight. 'The Secret Service may check your security tag, but you'll be wearing dark glasses, and Captain Madoowbe will be treating you as if you're the real Kebede Gebeyehu. And, let's be honest, who can tell one jet-black Ethiopian from another jet-black Ethiopian, except another jet-black Ethiopian?' He paused, and then he turned to Captain Madoowbe and added, 'If you'll forgive me, Captain Madoowbe.'

Captain Madoowbe waved his hand dismissively.

Noah was breathing deeply, as if he had been running. It was partly anger and partly his reaction to the enormity of what Professor Halflight was proposing.

'So what happens once I've shot the President and Alvin Metzler?'

'Our plan remains the same. You will be whisked away to the Ethiopian Consulate. But of course we won't have to keep you there, as we would have been obliged to do with the real Kebede Gebeyehu. You will simply remove your black make-up, and we will spirit you out through the service entrance.

'The real Kebede Gebeyehu will be flying back to Addis Ababa tonight. So when the FBI come calling at the consulate, the Consul General will be only too happy to cooperate with them, and allow them to search the building from top to bottom.'

'So after I've assassinated the President, you're really going to let me go? Knowing what I know? You couldn't afford to.'

'Why not? You came after us, didn't you, Noah, because you wanted us to leave you alone? That was why you set up that little terrorist video. Well, we *will* leave you alone, provided you have amnesia about this for the rest of your life.'

'And Silja? And Adeola Davis?'

'The same applies to them. Trust me.'

Noah steadied his breathing. He believed that Professor Halflight would arrange for him to be smuggled out of the Ethiopian Consulate, but he doubted if he would survive for very much longer after that – just about long enough to be driven out to the desert and shot in the back of the head. And he didn't believe for a second that Adeola and Silja would be freed – even if they were still alive now.

Professor Halflight said, 'Why don't you go back to Scholl Canyon, and call up your friend the make-up artist? Tell him what you need, so that he can get hold of all the necessary skin colorants. Then arrange for him to visit you the day after tomorrow, early, and transform you into Kebede Gebeyehu.

Tell Captain Madoowbe what your measurements are, and he'll fix you up with a suit. And sunglasses, too.'

'Supposing I go back to Scholl Canyon and you never see me again?'

'Oh, I don't think that's likely to happen, Noah. You wouldn't want anything unpleasant to happen to Ms Fonselius and Ms Davis. But in case you do think of pulling a disappearing act –' he turned in his chair and pointed his cane at the blond man in the corner '– our friend here is going to accompany you – and stay with you, until the day after tomorrow.'

'That bastard killed my girlfriend. I don't want him anywhere near me.'

'I'm sorry, Noah. That's the way it has to be.'

Noah closed his eyes for a moment. *Survive, Noah. Play along with this, until you get your chance to get away.*

He opened his eyes again and said, 'OK. Doesn't seem like I have much choice, does it? But before I agree to any of this, I want to talk to Silja, and Adeola.'

'Of course,' said Professor Halflight. 'Quite understandable.'

He took out his cellphone and punched out a speed-dial number. The phone rang for a long time before anybody answered.

'Hallo?' said Professor Halflight. 'Hallo, yes, it's me. As expected, our friend would like to have a word with your two travelling companions . . . That's right.'

He passed the phone to Noah. 'Ms Davis for you. But don't be so rash as to ask her where she's headed.'

'Adeola?' Noah could hear the swooshing sound of traffic in the background.

'Noah? They've discovered who you are?'

'Never mind about that. Are you OK?'

'We're fine, both of us, for now. They haven't hurt us.'

'OK. Can I talk to Silja?'

Silja came on. She sounded almost too calm. 'Noah? Don't worry, please. Adeola and I, we will manage.'

'Silja?'

'What is it?'

'Take good care of yourself. I love you.'

The phone went dead. Noah handed it back to Professor Halflight.

'You're happy now?' asked Professor Halflight.

Noah tightened his lips. He couldn't speak.

'What men will do for love!' Fariah croaked, from behind her mask. She laughed, and then she started coughing again, until she retched.

Thirty-One

'The Century Plaza it ain't,' said the spidery man, opening the door for them, 'but the management sincerely hopes that you'll enjoy your stay here.'

He ushered them into a sparsely-furnished room with white-painted walls and a dirty, royal-blue carpet. There were two mismatched couches, one mustard-yellow and the other crimson, a brown Formica table and two kitchen chairs with plastic seats. On the end wall there was a large framed print of Thai temple dancers.

'You want any refreshments?' asked the spidery man. 'Soda, maybe? Coffee? I have instructions to take good care of you.'

'Nothing,' said Adeola. She walked across to the window. The Venetian blinds were open, but all she could see outside was the floodlit factory yard, with a row of yellow forklift trucks parked against a wall, and the black hills beyond.

'I would like a cigarette,' said Silja.

'Sorry, this is a non-smoking facility.'

'What are we supposed to do now?' Adeola asked.

'Make yourselves comfortable. My employer will be here in a minute.'

'Hubert Tocsin?'

'Just make yourselves comfortable, OK?'

The spidery man left the room but left the door slightly ajar. Adeola didn't bother to open it and look outside. She knew that the black man with the MP9A1 would inevitably be standing guard.

Silja sat down on the yellow couch. 'Why do you think they have brought us here?'

'I'm not sure, exactly. But they must be using us to put pressure on Noah.'

'He sounded very worried.'

'You're surprised? *I'm* very worried.'

They waited for almost a half-hour. Silja was growing increasingly fretful, and eventually she opened the door. Adeola was right. The black man *was* standing outside.

'Can you please find me a cigarette?' Silja asked him.

'Nobody ain't allowed to smoke here. But here.' He reached into his breast pocket and pulled out a pack of Winstons.

Silja came back into the room, blowing out smoke. 'I always promised myself that I would quit on my twenty-fifth birthday.'

'When's that?'

'Week after next. Doesn't look like I'm going to make it, though, does it?'

'I don't know, Silja. I don't know what these maniacs want. I don't know why they didn't cut our throats immediately.'

Silja had only half-finished her cigarette when the door opened and Hubert Tocsin walked in, wearing a white silk shirt with HT embroidered on the pocket, and navy-blue pants.

'Adeola!' he said, opening his arms to her. 'It's so good to see you again! Do you know – I thought you were dead!'

'I'm beginning to wish that I were.'

'Don't say that! You can't imagine how distressed I was, when I thought that you had been killed! I was *devastated*.'

'Of course you were. But I'll bet you were even more devastated when you found out that I was still alive.'

Hubert Tocsin walked around the back of the yellow couch. 'And this is Ms Silja Fonselius. It's a pleasure to make your acquaintance, Ms Fonselius. I don't know if anybody has told you, but we have a strict non-smoking rule here at Tocsin.'

Silja took a deep draw on her cigarette. Hubert Tocsin reached over, took it away from her, and crushed it on the carpet. 'We couldn't risk a fire here, Ms Fonselius. We wouldn't want to flatten half of San Diego County. Besides, it's so bad for your health.'

'I don't think that Nakasu is particularly good for our health, either,' said Adeola.

'Nakasu! Yes, I gathered that you and your friends had discovered all about Nakasu. One of the best-kept secrets of the past two and a half thousand years.'

'It's only a best-kept secret because you've murdered anybody who suspects Nakasu exists.'

'Oh, come on. It's like a company protecting its patents, that's all. Like KFC, protecting its secret recipe for eleven herbs and spices.'

'By cutting people's throats?'

'Ms Davis – Adeola – without Nakasu we would still be living in the Middle Ages. Without Nakasu there would be no airplanes, no cars, no plastics, no nuclear energy, no antibiotics . . . the list of benefits that have come out of human conflict is endless. Wars always bring progress. Great wars bring great progress. If a few reactionary people have to be sacrificed to keep mankind moving forward . . . well, so be it.'

Adeola stared at him for a long time. Hubert Tocsin smiled at her and kept on smiling.

'What are you going to do to us?' she asked, at last.

'That really depends on your friend Noah. By noon, the day after tomorrow, we'll know if he's been cooperative or not.'

'Cooperative, in what way?'

Hubert Tocsin approached her and took hold of the lapels of her Chinese bathrobe between finger and thumb, stroking them.

'You really are a stunning woman, Ms Davis, but you have such inner tension. You always remind me of an animal, about to pounce.'

'Cooperative, how?' Adeola repeated.

'You'll soon find out. Ha! One way or another.'

Rick and Leon had been sitting in the dark for over an hour and a half before headlights swivelled across the ceiling, and a vehicle drew up outside the house.

Rick went across to the window and parted the blinds. 'Buick sedan. Hard to tell in this light, but it looks like grey.'

He lifted his SIG-Sauer automatic out of its holster and cocked it. Leon came up and stood close behind him. 'You said they'd come back for us.'

'They know we know all about Nakasu, that's why. They're not going to let us get away that easily.'

They waited. After almost a minute, the Buick's doors opened and two men climbed out. One was blond and wide-shouldered. The other, to Rick's surprise, was Abdel Al-Hadi.

'It's Noah,' said Rick.

'But that fair-haired dude who's with him,' said Leon, 'he's one of the dudes who tried to kill us.'

'You're sure?'

'Sure I'm sure. He's the one who was going to cut my throat, until Silja kicked him.'

'So what the hell is going on? What are they doing here?'

They watched as Abdel Al-Hadi came up the steps towards the front door. The blond man was close behind him, although it didn't look as if he were holding a gun.

'Quick,' Rick hissed, 'out the back – into the yard.'

Crouching low, the two of them hurried through the darkened kitchen and out through the back door. They crossed the veranda and knelt down beside the veranda steps. The moon was up again, bone-white and bright, but the bougainvillea that hung down over the veranda roof gave them a deep, inky shadow in which to conceal themselves.

They heard voices, and then the kitchen light was switched on.

'First thing you gotta do, call your make-up guy.'

'It's late. He's probably in bed asleep by now.'

'I don't care if he's in bed pronging his old lady. You heard what the professor said. Call him. Tell him it's a matter of life and death.'

They couldn't hear the answer to that. It sounded as if Noah had gone back through to the living room, and the blond man had followed him. They stayed in the shadow for another ten minutes, listening, and then the blond man came back into the kitchen.

'You won't mind if I help myself to a beer?'

Indistinct answer.

'You want one, too? Shit, man, it's your beer.'

Another indistinct answer, then the snap of a beer can being opened.

Another five minutes passed. Inside the house, somebody switched on the television, very loud. Then they heard the

kitchen door swing. Footsteps crossed the veranda, and somebody leaned on the railing right above them, and lit a cigarette.

Rick looked up. '*Noah?*'

'Rick? Leon?' Noah had pulled off his beard, and peeled
the latex bump from the bridge of his nose, but his hair was
still black and curly and his face was still spattered with moles.

'What's happening, man?' Rick whispered. 'They took
Adeola and Silja. We saw them do it.'

'I know. They're holding them hostage. They got Hong
Gildong. They tortured him, I think. Anyhow, he told them
all about the video and where we were hiding out and everything.'

'Shit! What's that blond dirtbag doing here?'

'Keeping an eye on me. They want me to shoot the President,
day after tomorrow.'

'*What?* The President? You're putting me on!'

'He's coming to LA for some economic summit. But he's
going to make an appearance when they sign that Ethiopian
peace agreement that Adeola was working on. I'm supposed
to black-up to look like one of the Ethiopian security guys –
shoot the President, and Adeola's boss, too.'

'That's, like, *lunacy.*'

'Maybe it is, but so was killing JFK, and they pulled that
off. They've got it all worked out.'

'So they're holding Adeola and Silja why? To make sure
you do it?'

'That's right. As if they're not going to kill us all anyhow.'

'We know where they are,' said Rick.

'You're kidding me!'

'We followed them. They took them down to Escondido,
to the Tocsin missile plant. It's our guess that Tocsin's been
bankrolling Nakasu.'

There was a roar of laughter from the television. The blond
man was laughing, too.

Noah said, 'What the hell are we going to do? I can't shoot
the President.'

'Wait a minute,' said Rick. 'We're a hit squad, remember?
You and me and Leon and Silja and Adeola. We decided we
were going to go after Nakasu and whack the bastards before
they whacked us.'

'How the hell can we, when they're holding Silja and Adeola hostage? If I put one foot wrong, if I don't shoot the President, they'll kill *them*. They won't even hesitate.'

'Just helping myself to another beer here,' came the the blond man's voice from the kitchen.

Noah didn't turn around but lifted one hand as if to say that he could take whatever he wanted.

Rick whispered, 'Listen, knowledge is power.'

'What are you talking about?'

'We know where Adeola and Silja are being held hostage, don't we? But Nakasu don't know that we know. That may be the only edge we've got, but it's still an edge.'

'Hey, you should watch this,' the blond man called out. 'It's fucking hilarious.'

Thirty-Two

At 7.17 a.m. on Thursday morning, Mitchell DeLorean arrived by taxi. He was wearing a peacock-blue satin shirt and tight white jeans, and he was in a seriously irritable mood.

Noah opened the door for him before he had a chance to ring the bell.

'If I didn't owe you so many favours, Noah, I swear . . .'

'This is the last time, Mitch, I promise you.'

'You're not pulling another one of those snuff video stunts, are you?'

Noah led him into the living room. The blond man was slouched in front of the television, cleaning out his ear with his finger. Mitchell said, 'Hi!' but the blond man simply looked him up and down and said nothing.

'Come through,' said Noah, and took Mitchell into the bedroom. Mitchell opened up his case and started taking out pots and tubes of make-up.

'Who's your surly friend?'

'He's no friend of mine, believe me.'

'What's going on here, Noah? First of all you want to be a Palestinian and now you want to be – *what?*'

Noah picked up the identity card from the dressing table. 'Ethiopian. *This* Ethiopian. Kebede Gebeyehu.'

Mitchell peered at the photograph and wrinkled up his nose. 'Hmm. He's a very *noir* young man, isn't he? But it shouldn't be too difficult. The main problem areas with a black face are always the eyes and the lips. And the hands, of course. The hands are always a challenge.'

'Well, the eyes should be OK. I'll be wearing shades most of the time.'

'That'll help. And I use my own blackberry-based dye to colour the lips. What about the hair?'

'He doesn't have any hair.'

'*Exactamundo.* You'll have to wear a latex bald cap. Either that, or – no, you wouldn't want to do that, would you?'

'Shave my head?'

'It does give a much, much better effect. Even the best bald caps look like bald caps, especially close up.'

'Actually, it's not going to be me. I'm swapping places with somebody else.'

'Not Mr Congeniality in there?'

'No. Wait here a second.'

Noah looked out of the bedroom and made sure that the blond man was still sitting in front of the television. All he could see through the living-room door was the blond man's elbow, twisting methodically from side to side as he cleaned out his ears, and the lower part of his right leg, and his foot, in a shiny black loafer. He went quietly through the kitchen and out on to the veranda.

'*Rick!*' he called, leaning over the railing. '*Mitch is here! Come on in!*'

Rick emerged from the bushes. Noah led him back to the bedroom and closed the door. 'I've explained to Mitch what you have to look like. He says you'll look more convincing if you shave your head.'

'Whatever it takes,' said Rick. 'Listen, I can take this from here. You get out of here and hightail it down to San Diego.'

'I'm getting confused here,' said Mitchell. 'You want me to make *Rick* look like this Ethiopian character – not you?'

'That's right. Only blondie isn't to know.'

'Listen – by the time I've finished, Rick's own mother isn't going to recognize him.'

'OK,' said Noah. 'There's your suit, laid out on the bed. There's your shades. Good luck, man. Try to stay safe.'

'You too.'

Noah opened the bedroom door and looked cautiously towards the living room. The blond man hadn't moved, so he went through the kitchen and into the backyard, and out through the side gate.

The morning was already hot, and there were only the faintest streaks of mares' tails high in the sky. The Grand Prix was parked around the corner, in Canyon Crescent, and Leon was waiting for him in the front seat. He was wearing Rick's brown leather jacket and his hair was tousled.

'How's it going?' Noah asked him, sitting down behind the wheel and starting the engine.

'I'm OK,' said Leon.

'You're sure? You look kind of frazzled.'

'I'm OK. I know what to do. Rick and me, we went over it twenty thousand times at least.'

'Good. Because we're really relying on you, you know that.'

'I know. But I always remember what my dad used to say: ninety per cent of being reliable is showing up.'

Noah dropped Leon off at Stars Diner on Sunset. They synchronized their watches, and then Noah took hold of Leon's hand and gave it a hard squeeze.

'When this is over, we'll take a vacation together. How about that? Do some guy stuff. Fishing, or hunting.'

'Sure,' said Leon. 'See you later.'

Noah felt as if he ought to say something momentous and meaningful, considering what they were expecting Leon to do, but he couldn't think of any words that would effectively sum up their fear, and their tension, and the isolation they felt. There was nobody they could trust, except each other.

Leon climbed out of the car and gave Noah an offhand wave, as casual as if he were going off to nothing more momentous than baseball practise.

'Later,' said Noah, under his breath.

* * *

Noah drove south to San Diego as fast as he could. By 10.25 a.m. he had reached Balboa Park, and was driving along El Prado, between the palms and the Spanish Revival houses. He turned into the entrance of the Reuben H. Fleet Science Centre and parked.

George Burdaky was waiting for him, sitting in a bronze Explorer. He climbed out and walked across to Noah, grinning. George was a short, stocky man with a grey buzz cut and a bulbous nose, and his eyes were always narrowed as if he couldn't believe what he was looking at. He was wearing a red short-sleeved boiler suit that showed off his tattoos, including a hula-dancing girl in a grass skirt, and the Seabees bee.

'Well, well. In like Flynn. Didn't think I'd see you till the next reunion, you miserable bastard. How's the stuntman business?'

Noah embraced him. 'How are you doing, George? How's Molly?'

'Me and Molly, we're kind of having a vacation from each other. But I guess we'll get back together again. You know what we're like – Tom and freaking Jerry.'

'You managed to get the stuff?'

'When he called me, that friend of yours wasn't too sure exactly what you wanted. What was his name, Dick? So I got you a variety. We're doing a big demolition job down at Imperial Beach, all the old administration buildings, so it wasn't difficult to divert a few kilos of RDX. I got you some Thermite-TH3, too.'

'That's great. Thanks, George.'

'Hey, don't even mention it. I owe you one. In fact, I owe you several. There's a Colt .45 in there, too, and half a dozen clips.'

They looked around, but apart from a bus-load of chattering children arriving for a tour of the science centre, the parking area was empty, and they couldn't see anybody who looked as if they might be watching them. George brought over a large milled-aluminium suitcase and stowed it into the trunk of Noah's car.

'I don't know what you're intending to do with this stuff, and I don't want you to tell me, but whatever it is, you miserable bastard, I hope it all works out.'

Noah embraced him again. 'See you at the next reunion, OK? Remind me to buy you more than one beer.'

George went back to his Explorer and drove off. Noah checked the time. It was 10.43 a.m. He climbed back into the Grand Prix, turned around, and headed out of San Diego on Route 15, towards Escondido.

Rick straightened his necktie and put on his sunglasses, and the bald Ethiopian in the mirror did the same.

'Mitch,' he said, 'you're a genius. Even *I* don't recognize me.'

Mitchell was washing his hands in the basin. 'I think Noah and me, we're quits now. Tell him if he wants me to turn him into a Chinaman, forget it.'

Rick looked down at his hands, turning them this way and that. Mitchell had even managed to give him the pale, sandy-collared palms of an Ethiopian.

The bedroom door suddenly opened, and the blond man looked in. 'You ready yet? We should be making a move.'

'I'm ready,' said Rick, in a mock-Ethiopian accent. 'What do you think?'

'I'm not paid to think nothing,' the blond man told him. 'Come on, let's get going.'

Mitchell fastened the clips of his make-up case. 'Can you give me a ride? I have to be over at Fox by eleven thirty.'

'Sorry,' said the blond man.

'OK, I'll just have to call myself a taxi.'

He took out his cellphone and started to look for the number, but as he did so the blond man approached him and grabbed his wrist.

'What the hell are you doing?' Mitchell demanded. 'Let go of me, will you.'

'Listen,' said the blond man, 'I want you to understand that this isn't personal, OK? It's just the way we have to do things.'

Mitchell tried to tug his arm free, but the blond man bent it round behind his back and forced it up between his shoulder blades.

'Hey, let go of me – that hurts!' Mitchell shrilled at him.

Rick shouted, 'Leave the guy alone!' He took one step across the bedroom floor, but he was too late. He didn't even see the knife before the blond man sliced it across Mitchell's throat, left to right, and blood sprayed all across the cream-coloured bedcover.

Mitchell made a gargling noise and his knees collapsed under him. He dropped on to the carpet, quaking and quivering like a fallen horse, one leg kicking at the closet doors.

Rick approached the blond man, both hands raised, but the blond man pointed the bloody knife at his face and said, 'Don't even think about it. You know what you got to do, and if you don't do it, those women are going to get the same.'

A large bubble of blood came out of the slit in Mitchell's throat, and then burst. He stopped kicking and lay still, staring at the end of the bed as if he was mesmerized by it.

The blond man pushed him with his foot to make sure that he was dead.

'You son of a bitch,' said Rick. 'I swear to God you're going to pay for this.'

The blond man looked at him and frowned. After all, Rick didn't smoke, and his voice wasn't as throaty as Noah's. But all he said was, 'You think so?'

It obviously hadn't occurred to him that the white man who had gone into the bedroom and the Ethiopian who had emerged from it were two different people. He wiped the knife on the bedcover and pushed it back into the sheath on the side of his belt.

'Let's get out of here,' he told Rick. 'The professor ain't going to be happy if we're late.'

Rick looked down at Mitchell, lying on the blood-spattered carpet. But there was nothing he could do, and nothing he could say. The blond man raised his hand to push Rick into the living room, but Rick raised his hand, too, and said, 'Don't you touch me, you son of a bitch. Don't you ever touch me.'

Thirty-Three

When they arrived at the Century Plaza, the lobby was already crowded with police and Secret Service agents and television cameras. The blond man drew the grey sedan up to the main entrance, and a Secret Service man opened the door for him.

Rick got out of the car and showed his security pass.

'OK, sir. Go in by the side door, please.'

As he pushed his way through the throng of reporters and cameramen and TV technicians on the steps, Captain Madoowbe came out of the lobby to meet him.

'Sergeant Gebeyehu! I have to say that you are looking *very* well this morning!'

'You murdering bastards,' said Rick, in his Ethiopian accent, smiling as he did so.

'Now, now,' said Captain Madoowbe. 'You have to understand that nobody who knows about Nakasu can be allowed to live.'

'I suppose that includes me, and Adeola Davis, and Silja.'

Captain Madoowbe led him through the glass doors. 'Of course not. Professor Halflight has made a deal with you, hasn't he? And why should we silence you, when you will keep your own silence? What you are doing today, that is not something you are going to shout out to the world, is it?'

He turned and grinned at Rick with his orange teeth. Rick said nothing. As they crossed the lobby, he caught sight of himself and Captain Madoowbe in a mirrored pillar. Two intensely black men in black suits and white shirts and sunglasses. He felt as if he were walking through a nightmare, and that he would soon wake up.

Captain Madoowbe took him up in the elevator to the presidential floor. His Excellency Ato Ketona Aklilu had a suite there, and in a large red-carpeted side room his security detail was gathered, five of them, all wearing black suits and white shirts and sunglasses, talking to each other in Amharic.

Captain Madoowbe led Rick over to the table. He opened a folder and took out a diagram.

'This is the room where they will be signing the peace agreement. His Excellency Ato Ketona Aklilu will be sitting here, on the right. Alvin Metzler from DOVE will be sitting here, on the left. When they have signed, the President will come in through these double doors behind them, and greet them both.

'I will be standing closest to the table, here. You will be standing on my right, and slightly behind me. As soon as the President takes hold of Alvin Metzler's hand, and the press cameras start to flash, you will take out your gun and shout out, "Death to all appeasers!" and shoot the President first and then Alvin Metzler.

'We will surround you at once and take away your gun, and rush you out of the building.'

'And you seriously think the Secret Service are going to let you?'

'We will be taking His Excellency with us. You don't think that they will risk harming the Ethiopian Foreign Secretary, do you?'

Rick looked over at the rest of the security detail. They were all staring at him in silence. After all, he looked exactly like one of them, and yet they knew that he was a white man.

Captain Madoowbe went over to one of the security men and came back with a big automatic pistol with a brown plastic handle, a Russian-made Stechkin APS.

'Here . . . it is already fully loaded. I don't know if you have used one before, Mr Flynn, but it is very similar to a Colt .45.'

Rick took the gun and hefted it in his hand. He had actually fired an APS during his Secret Service training, as well as other Russian guns, but he shook his head, and said, 'Never seen one of these babies before. Looks like a man-stopper, though.'

'Oh, yes,' grinned Captain Madoowbe. 'Today, men will be stopped, believe me.'

It was 11.28 a.m. when Noah arrived outside the Tocsin Weapons and Rocketry plant outside Escondido. He parked beside the perimeter fence, well away from the main gate, and hidden from view by bushes.

There was no traffic on the road, and the plant itself was almost deserted, except for one man in a forklift truck moving packing cases from one side of the main factory building to the other. The morning was even hotter now, and the cicadas were deafening.

Noah opened the aluminium case that George had given him, and took out a small charge of plasticized RDX. It was yellow, like a half-melted church candle. He pushed his way through the bushes until he reached the fence. Then he shaped the RDX into a ball and pressed it up against one of the concrete uprights. He inserted an electronic detonator, and then pushed his way back out on to the road again.

He drove all the way along the perimeter fence, passing the main gate, but then he stopped, and steered the Grand Prix off the road, parking it on a dusty patch of ground overlooking the reservoir.

He lifted out the aluminium case and walked back until he was only fifty feet away from the main gate, but hidden by bushes from the security guard who was sitting in his sentry box by the barrier. The security guard had his feet up and he was reading a newspaper.

Noah checked the time again. 11.36 a.m. Right now, the President and his entourage should be arriving at the Century Plaza. Right now, the room where His Excellency Ato Ketona Aklilu and Alvin Metzler would be signing their agreement would be filling up with invited dignitaries and media.

Noah waited until 11.40 a.m. Then he took out his cell-phone and punched 7. Instantly, there was a loud, flat thump, which echoed and re-echoed from the surrounding hills. A cloud of dark grey smoke rolled up into the sky, and fragments of concrete and pieces of wire mesh began to clatter on to the roadway.

The security guard threw down his newspaper and hurried out of his sentry box. He hesitated for a few seconds, but then he went back into his sentry box and activated a klaxon alarm. After he had done that, he put on his cap and went running along the perimeter fence to the place where Noah had set his explosive.

Noah waited until more men came running out of the factory. Then, crouching low, he dodged in through the main gate, underneath the grey-and-white barrier pole, and headed for the nearest building. There were twenty or thirty men swarming across the factory yard now, all of them shouting, and the regurgitating noise of the klaxon was adding to the general confusion. Noah had done this several times before, in Kuwait, setting off a decoy explosive and then taking advantage of the panic to set more devices.

He had no idea where Silja and Adeola were being held, but he guessed that the likeliest location was the office block, rather than the factory. He reached one of the aluminium buildings and ran the whole length of it, until he reached the door. Three men in pale blue coveralls came hurrying out, and one of them even held the door open for him.

'Thanks, man,' he said, and stepped inside.

The interior of the building seemed even larger than the outside. It was brightly lit, with rows and rows of production lines, belts and pulleys and moving tracks. For the moment, production had been stopped, because the building was silent, except for a few echoing clanks and bangs, and only four or five men were standing around, obviously waiting to find out what the explosion had been, and whether they ought to carry on working or not.

Considering what they were putting together, they were probably wise to wait. As Noah made his way between the production lines, he realized that he was surrounded on all sides by missile warheads, painted red and white.

He knew from his experience in the Gulf what these were, and what they could do. Sunburst pyrophoric missiles, which were designed to penetrate a tank's armour and then ignite inside the hull, starting a fire so intense that the crew would be virtually vaporized.

He worked quickly and expertly, attaching devices to three parallel production lines, right underneath, where they would be difficult to detect. Each device was a large block of RDX, a smaller block of Thermite-TH3, and four 4 July sparklers. There were several different ways of igniting thermite, such as magnesium strips and blowtorches, but Noah had always preferred sparklers because they were safer and more effective, and they gave him plenty of time to get away before the thermite reaction started, and everything started to melt.

He used less than half the explosive that George had given

him, but he left the aluminium case underneath one of the production lines, with its lid open.

Noah left the factory building and walked quickly across to the office block next to it. A few men were still standing around the breach that he had blown in the perimeter fence, but most of them were walking back across the yard.

He pushed open the office doors and found himself in a large reception area, with potted palms and white leather couches. On the rear wall was a stainless steel bell shape with the stainless steel letters 'Tocsin Weapons and Rocketry Systems'. A girl with a blonde French pleat and a pale blue suit was sitting at a curved, stainless-steel desk.

She raised her thinly-plucked eyebrows. 'May I help you, sir?'

'I think so. Mr Hubert Tocsin here, by any chance?'

'You do have an appointment, sir?'

'Not exactly. But I have to see him pretty urgently.'

'I'm sorry, sir. Mr Tocsin doesn't see anybody, except by appointment.'

'Oh, I think he'll want to see me.'

'Excuse me, sir, but if you don't have an appointment, may I ask how you passed through security?'

Noah looked at the clock on her desk. It was 11.54 a.m. He was running out of time. He took out the Colt .45 that George had given him, cocked it, and pointed it at her.

'Will you please tell Mr Tocsin that I need to see him, right now.'

The girl stared at the gun, wide eyed.

'*Tell him,*' Noah repeated.

The girl clicked a switch and said, 'Mr Tocsin? I'm sorry to interrupt your meeting, sir, but there's a gentleman in reception who insists on seeing you.'

She listened to her earpiece for a moment, and then she said, 'Yes, sir. I know, sir. But he has a gun.'

She listened again, staring at Noah all the time she was doing so. 'A gun, sir. A real one, I think. Yes.'

Eventually she said, 'He's coming right down.'

The presidential suite was crowded now. A large table had been covered with a purple cloth, and decorated with the Stars and Stripes, the national flag of Ethiopia, and the DOVE flag, which depicted a white dove with an olive branch in its beak. In front of the table, over a hundred gilt chairs had been arranged in a semicircle, and these were now filled with diplomats and specially-invited guests.

Alvin Metzler came in first, smiling broadly. There was a smattering of applause and he raised his hand to acknowledge it. Then His Excellency Ato Ketona Aklilu came in, wearing a traditional green silk robe and a gold-embroidered hat. He bowed, and there was more applause.

Captain Madoowbe stood close to the left-hand end of the table, and Rick stood only inches behind him. He felt breath on the back of his neck, and when he turned around he saw that another Ethiopian security guard was almost on top of him. The other four weren't far behind. Rick had always been sensitive about personal space, and these five made him feel almost unbearably claustrophobic, particularly since the nearest security guard smelled as if he had been eating some kind of dried fish.

It was 12.03 p.m. and the signing ceremony was running a few minutes late. But eventually Josephine Blascoe appeared, the Under Secretary for Democracy and Global Affairs at the State Department – a terrifyingly smart woman in her late thirties with a shining chestnut bob and a bright 'can-do' look in her eyes, wearing a pale jonquil suit.

There was more applause as she took her seat between the Ethiopian Foreign Secretary and Alvin Metzler.

'Today –' she said, speaking in a clear South Carolina accent that was a little too high for comfort '– today, we are reaffirming our hope that the peoples of Africa can at last find peace.'

Captain Madoowbe turned to Rick and said, 'Only a few minutes now. You are ready?'

'Ready as I'll ever be.'

Hubert Tocsin pushed open the door into the reception area. Close behind him came the spidery man with his arm in a sling, and the bald man with the walrus moustache.

He walked directly towards Noah as if he intended to snatch his gun right out of his hand. But when Noah swung his arm around and pointed the gun directly at his head, he stopped.

'You think I'm afraid of you?' he demanded.

'I sure hope so,' said Noah.

'I'm not afraid of you, and whatever it is you want from me, you can't have it.'

'Well, you've got stones,' said Noah. 'I have to grant you that.'

'So what is it you want?'

'Adeola Davis and Silja Fonselius. That's all. And I want them now.'

Hubert Tocsin's left eyelid twitched. 'What makes you think that I've even got them?'

'I know you have. And you have ten seconds to produce them. I just hope for your sake that they're safe and well.'

'And supposing I say no?'

'You won't. Because if you do, I'll blow your head off. And then I'll find out where you're keeping them, and I'll take them anyhow.'

Hubert Tocsin glanced at the clock on his receptionist's desk. It was 12.06 p.m.

'They're not here,' he said. 'It may take some time to find them.'

'I don't have time,' Noah told him. 'I want them now. Don't try to stall me, Mr Tocsin. I know why you took them. I know about Nakasu and I know what Nakasu is planning to do today.'

'Could be you're too late already,' said Hubert Tocsin, with a sloping smile.

'Too bad for you if I am. You have *five* seconds now.'

'And if I refuse? What are you going to do? Shoot me in cold blood?'

'I can do better than that.' Noah took out his cellphone and held it up. 'You see this cellphone? All I have to do is press one number and your missile plant next door is history.'

'I suppose that was your doing, then? That firework display outside?'

'You got it.'

Hubert Tocsin glanced at the clock again. 12.08 p.m.

'All right, then,' he said. 'I expect it's all over by now, in any event. You can have your two lady friends back. But don't think that we won't be coming after you.'

He clicked his fingers at the receptionist. 'Tell Michael to bring our two guests downstairs. He'll know what you mean.'

They waited uneasily for two or three minutes. Then the door opened again and Adeola and Silja appeared, accompanied by the black man who had been guarding them. Both of them looked tired, and Adeola's hair was a mass of untidy curls.

'My God!' said Silja. 'I don't believe it!'

'It turns out that you have a knight in shining armour,' said Hubert Tocsin.

Adeola went right up to him and said, 'You are going to pay for this, Mr Tocsin. I am going to make sure that you rot in jail for the rest of your life.'

'We'll have to see about that,' said Hubert Tocsin. 'But first you need to think how *your* story is going to sound.'

'What do you mean?'

'What do I mean? You actively participated in a little charade in which you deceived the world into thinking you had been shot dead, didn't you? And why? So that an associate of yours could be accepted by Nakasu and become an assassin.

'He *was* accepted, thanks to you, and his very first assignment was to shoot not only Mr Alvin Metzler, of DOVE, and the Foreign Secretary of Ethiopia, but the President, too.'

'*What?*' said Adeola.

'Oh, yes. The President was due to make an appearance at DOVE's little demonstration of international huggy-kissy.'

He nodded towards the clock. 'I haven't heard the news yet, but it should all be over by now.'

Adeola was shaking. 'You're insane,' she said. 'You're absolutely stark staring mad.'

'Who are you calling insane, Ms Davis? You want to know what insanity is? Trying to make peace is insanity, Ms Davis. It flies in the face of human nature. Men have always been at war. Men always will be. The enemy is people who try to suppress struggle, and the progress that always comes out of it. The enemy is *you*.'

'My God, Mr Tocsin,' said Adeola, 'you're a murderer! Hasn't that ever occurred to you? Any man who makes a weapon that kills innocent people, and makes a profit out of it, he's a murderer, and he deserves to burn in hell.'

'Come on, Adeola,' said Noah. 'Come on, Silja. Let's get the hell out of here.'

Hubert Tocsin said, 'It's a long way back to Los Angeles.

Don't count on making it in one piece. And even if you do – just remember that there are plenty of men in grey suits who will be happy to welcome you.'

Thirty-Four

A lvin Metzler signed the peace agreement and passed it across to His Excellency Ato Ketona Aklilu. His Excellency signed it, too, in a blizzard of flashlights.

At that moment, the double doors behind them opened, and four Secret Service men came through, followed by the President. Everybody in the room stood up and applauded.

The President lifted both hands in acknowledgement. He was very tall, with an eagle's wing of grey hair, and a well-weathered face that looked as if it had already been sculpted on the side of Mount Rushmore. He stepped up to the centre of the table, smiling and giving that special twinkle of his eyes to those members of the media whom he personally favoured.

'Friends,' he said, as the applause died down. 'And let me say this: it is more than just a pleasure to call you "friends", because this is a day on which the word "friends" has taken on a new political significance. A day when the people of Ethiopia have decided at last that they can *all* be friends, no matter what their tribes, or their religions, or their different ways of life.'

Rick reached inside his coat for the plastic-clad butt of his Stechkin APS. Flashlights were flickering like summer lightning, and five or six photographers had pushed their way forward to hunker down right in front of the table, so that they could get more intimate shots.

The President took hold of His Excellency Ato Ketona Aklilu's hand and shook it, turning towards the assembled dignitaries as he did so. Then he grasped Alvin Metzler's hand, and leaned forward to say something in his ear.

Captain Madoowbe hissed '*Now!*' in Rick's ear.

Rick lifted out the APS, cocked it, and pointed it at Captain Madoowbe's right ear. There was an ear-splitting report, and half of Captain Madoowbe's head was blown across the room, splattering up against the pink fleur-de-lis wallpaper. He fell sideways, with the left side of his face missing, and only a curved piece of skull at the back.

There was instant pandemonium. The President's bodyguards immediately clustered around him, pulling out their guns, and hurried him out of the room, slamming the double doors behind him. The Ethiopian security men grabbed hold of His Excellency Ato Ketona Aklilu's robes and dragged him out of the side door so roughly that he lost one of his golden slippers.

Rick ducked down and rolled across the carpet twice, out of the door and into the corridor. A hotel security guard came towards him, shouting, 'Hey! *Hey!*' The man tried to snatch at his suit, but Rick barged him out of the way with his shoulder and sprinted along the corridor towards the stairs.

He crashed through the door to the stairwell and began to leap down the stairs five and six at a time. He knew from his own Secret Service experience that the hotel elevators would all be stopped, to prevent anybody from escaping.

He ran down all sixteen flights to the ground floor, his footsteps rattling and echoing on the concrete stairs. When he reached the lobby level, however, he stopped for a moment, and took several deep breaths, and calmed himself down.

He opened the door to the lobby. It was pandemonium here, too. The reception area was crowded with police and media and guests, and everybody was shouting and pushing. He started to walk across to the front doors. The police were preventing anybody from leaving, but they might let him out if he showed them his Ethiopian security pass, and gave them some story about going to find His Excellency's car.

He was halfway across the lobby, however, when he saw the blond man in the grey suit pushing his way through the crowd. The blond man was grinning at him, and walking towards him almost as if he were going to ask him to dance.

'Going somewhere?' the blond man asked him, as he approached.

'I needed some air,' said Rick.

'Oh, yes? Things didn't go too well, from what I hear. Seems like your aim was a little off.'

'I don't think so,' Rick told him.

'Well, nobody's very happy with you, Mr Flynn, let's put it that way. I think you and I should go to the restroom and have a discussion about this.'

He took hold of Rick's left elbow and tried to steer him away from the hotel's front doors. As he looked around, Rick took out his APS and shot him in the back of the head.

The blond man spun around on one heel and fell heavily on to the carpet. All around them, people were shouting and screaming and trying to get away. Rick backed two or three steps away from the blond man's body. He tossed the APS on to the floor and held up both hands high.

'Ex-Secret Service!' he shouted. 'My name is Rick Kavanagh and I'm ex-Secret Service!'

He was surrounded by police and FBI and Secret Service agents, all with their guns drawn.

'I'm ex-Secret Service!' he repeated. 'Ex-Secret Service undercover!'

'Down on the floor!' ordered one of the Secret Service agents, a grey-haired man with a face like an angry bulldog. 'Down on the floor and don't move a muscle!'

Rick lay face down on the carpet. The grey-haired men knelt down beside him, and stared at him.

'Kevin?' said Rick. 'Kevin Pritchard? Look at me. You know me. We spent two weeks in Philly together. Remember that night at McGillin's Old Ale House?'

'The Rick Kavanagh I knew was white,' the agent retorted, in a rasping voice.

'Go get a cloth,' Rick told him. 'A napkin, a bar towel – anything.'

The Secret Service agent took a handkerchief out of his breast pocket. 'This do?'

'Sure. Now wipe my forehead with it.'

The agent rubbed Rick's forehead and then looked at the smears of black make-up on his handkerchief.

'You are,' he said. 'You *are* Rick Kavanagh. What the hell are you doing, all blacked up like Morgan Freeman?'

Leon walked up the steps of Professor Halflight's house and rang the doorbell. It was past midday now, and very hot, and he wiped his forehead with the back of his hand.

After almost a minute, Berta opened the door.

'Yes?'

'I want to talk to Professor Halflight.'

'Is he expect you?'

'Kind of.'

'What shall I say name?'

'Leon – Leon Speller. I'm one of his students.'

Berta said, 'Wait here please.' But as she turned to go back inside, Professor Halflight appeared, wearing a pink polo shirt and crumpled khaki pants.

'Who is it, Berta? Oh – *Leon*. This is quite a surprise!'

'That's funny, Professor. I thought you would have been expecting me.'

'Now, why should I have been doing that?'

'You killed my dad. You killed my stepmother. What did you think – I was just going to forget about it?'

'I killed your dad?' said Professor Halflight. He shook his head and kept on shaking it. 'I think you're labouring under some kind of misapprehension here, Leon. I'm a professor of ancient history, not a professional killer.'

'I know what you are,' said Leon. He pulled Rick's SIG-Sauer from out of his windbreaker.

'Now, Leon,' said Professor Halflight, 'let's be reasonable, shall we? Violence never solved anybody's problems.'

'You don't believe that,' Leon retorted. 'You believe the exact opposite. You believe that violence solves everybody's problems, and you don't care who gets killed or who gets hurt.'

'Leon –' said Professor Halflight '– Leon, I'm very sorry about your father and your stepmother. But you really have to understand—'

Leon shot him in the chest, and Professor Halflight staggered backwards into the hallway. Leon shot him again, somewhere in the abdomen, and he pitched over sideways, his cane clattering on the polished mahogany floor.

'You don't know what you've done,' gasped Professor Halflight. 'You stupid little shit, you don't know what you've done!'

Leon stepped into the hallway and pointed the automatic right between the professor's eyes. The professor looked up at him and licked his lips, as if he were thirsty.

'Go on, then,' he said. 'Go on, if you're going to.'

Leon pulled the trigger and Professor Halflight's brain, with all of its ancient languages and all of its philosophical knowledge, not to mention all of his personal memories, was splattered in lumps across the floor.

Leon stood up straight. Somebody was wailing – a hoarse, unearthly wail. He hesitated for a moment, and then he walked through to the living room.

Fariah was sitting there, in her wheelchair. The wailing was coming from out of her celluloid mask. Leon stood and stared at her for a long time. Then he approached her, and levelled the automatic at her head.

She kept on wailing, her single three-fingered hand tugging at her brown blanket. She didn't try to beg him for mercy. She didn't even try to curse him.

He shot her, once, in the face. The celluloid mask instantly turned red.

Berta was watching him, fearfully, from the door on the opposite side of the living room. He ignored her and walked out of the house, stepping over Professor Halflight's body as went.

They walked away, across the factory yard. Hubert Tocsin stood outside the office door, his arms folded, watching them, with the spidery man standing beside him.

They had nearly reached the main gate when the security guard came out of his sentry box, and he was carrying a pump-action rifle. He lifted it up and pointed it at them.

'I told you!' Hubert Tocsin called out, in a mocking voice. 'You're not going anywhere!'

Adeola stopped and looked back at him. 'He's not going to let us go, is he? He can't.'

'You think so?' said Noah. 'We'll see about that.'

The security guard came closer, aiming his rifle at Noah's chest. 'Take out your weapon, fella, and toss it!'

Noah lifted out the Colt between finger and thumb and held it up so that the security guard could see it. Then he threw it on to the ground.

'OK – now turn around and walk back towards the office!'

Noah turned around. As he did so, he lifted his cellphone out of his pocket, and pressed 5.

There was a pause. He thought, *Please Lord, don't tell me that it's not going to work.* But then there was a bellowing explosion from inside the factory building, and a thirty-foot section of the aluminium roof was blown upward, like a skeletal hand.

'Stop him!' shrieked Hubert Tocsin. He sounded like a hysterical woman. 'Stop him!'

Noah pressed 6 and 7, and there were two more explosions. The aluminium sides of the factory building were dented outwards, as if the Incredible Hulk were inside, punching at the walls.

The security guard came running up to them, still pointing his rifle at Noah's chest. He didn't understand what was happening, or how Noah could be causing all these explosions, and all he could do was shout, 'Stop it! Whatever the fuck you're doing, stop it!'

The black smoke that was pouring from the factory building's roof was suddenly interlaced with orange flames. The thermite had ignited, and soon the inside of the factory building would reach 2,500 degrees Kelvin, and everything that was made of metal would become molten.

The spidery man was running across to the factory door. He tugged at it, but it must have been distorted by the blast, because he couldn't get it open. Hubert Tocsin hurried across and joined him, and they pulled at the door together.

There was another explosion from the inside of the factory, and then another, and another. The sunburst warheads were starting to blow up.

'Oh, Christ,' said the security guard. He took his eyes away from Noah and stared at the factory building in mounting horror. 'If that all goes up—'

He was still staring at the smoke and the flames when Silja swung around in a circle, with one leg extended, and kicked him in the back of the head. He dropped his rifle and fell to the ground, stunned.

'Time to get out of here,' said Noah. 'Come on, this is going to be one hell of a bang.'

They ran towards the main gate. Behind them, they heard a rippling series of half a dozen explosions, like a giant fire-cracker.

Hubert Tocsin and the spidery man were still pulling at the

door. Suddenly, it opened. A white-hot river of molten steel and aluminium poured out of it, like lava, and engulfed them both.

The spidery man vanished instantly. They heard him scream and saw one arm raised, but then he was gone. Hubert Tocsin tried to run, but the flood of incandescent metal was too fast for him, and in seconds it was up to his knees.

He let out a noise that didn't even sound human. He was still trying to run, but his lower legs had been vaporized, and he was stumping along on his knees.

'Help me!' he cried out. 'Oh God in heaven, help me!'

But then he fell forward. His hands and his forearms disappeared into the shimmering metal with a crackle of incinerated flesh. His white suit caught fire. For a split second his head remained, his face blackened, his mouth stretched open in a silent scream. Then he was swallowed up, and he was gone, with nothing more than a hiss and a faint sizzling of steam.

Noah and Silja and Adeola hurried away through the main entrance and along the road. They had only just reached the Grand Prix when the factory blew up. There was an explosion like a huge iron door slamming and a massive fireball rolled up into the sky, a monstrous fiery jellyfish, trailing tentacles of white smoke. Leaves flew off the trees and shrubs all around them in a rattling storm, and the bushes closest to the factory caught fire.

They climbed into the car and Noah swerved away from the factory as fast as he could. There was another explosion, and another, and then dozens of smaller explosions. In his rear-view mirror, Noah could see that a column of dark smoke was billowing into the air, blotting out the sun.

He passed his cellphone to Adeola. 'Call Rick for me. Call Leon. I'm just praying that they're safe.'

He turned on the car radio, too, to hear if there was any news about the President. The first station he turned to was playing *Satisfaction*.

Somebody whispered, '*Chaos and Old Night.*'

Noah sat up. He was lying on the couch at Dave McCray's house, with Silja sleeping next to him. There was nobody else in the room.

He watched Silja sleeping for a while. Her breathing was so quiet and so shallow that she could have been dead. The waning moonlight cast a sharp shadow on her cheekbone, and her blonde hair glistened. He couldn't decide if he loved her or not, or even if he ought to. There was no future in it, was there? But after everything that had happened in the past few days, who could tell if any of them had any future at all?

The one thing he was sure of was that he would do everything he could to look after her and keep her safe, and maybe that was a kind of love.

He reached across to the nightstand and picked up the medallion that Professor Halflight had given him. He held it up, and the moon caught it. Cuneiform characters on one side, F L Y N N on the other.

He eased himself off the couch and went to the bathroom. When he came out, he went out on to the veranda, taking his cigarettes with him. He was surprised to find Adeola out there, sitting in the basketwork chair.

'Couldn't sleep?' he asked her.

'I'm worried about Rick.'

'Oh, Rick's going to be OK. You heard what they said on the news. He's a hero.'

'Actually, I'm worried about all of us.'

Noah lit his cigarette and blew out smoke. 'You think they'll still come after us? I guess they probably will. They've been murdering people for two and a half thousand years, to keep themselves secret. I doubt if they're going to stop now.'

He smoked for a while in silence. Then he said, 'Leon sounded OK, all things considered. A little tired, you know. A little mumbly. He's going to stay with his uncle Saul in Pasadena for a while, and then he's probably going to go up to Monterey. He has cousins there.'

'How about you?'

'Me? First thing I'm going to do is rescue my parrot from Ted. Then – I don't know. There's an audition coming up next week for a new *Mission Impossible*. How about you?'

'I don't know, either,' said Adeola. 'I'm not so sure that I believe in peace any more.'